PICTURE OF THE Y...

Seven Moslem peasants know too much. They are
executed before news of their endeavours can
trickle through to the outside world, victims of a
sham trial held in camera. Jackie Paine knows too
much. Her naked body is found at the family
home, brutally murdered by a cool, ruthless
assassin. And Harry Paine, who perhaps knows
more than most, has gone missing from his post.

As the death toll mounts, Michael Radford, an
officer with the Department of Subversive
Warfare, starts to make the crucial connections
. . . connections which will send some
high-ranking KGB members running scared, and
make possible the intelligence coup of the
decade.

A DIFFERENT DRUMMER

'here's an author who understands violence, its
surface and inner workings'

The Observer

'Generates Grade A tension'

The Guardian

TROIKA

'An engrossing study of gradual disenchantment'
The Observer

'A labyrinthine head-whirler'

The Guardian

**Also by the same author,
and available from Coronet:**

A DIFFERENT DRUMMER
TROIKA

About the author

Clive Egleton is widely regarded as one of
Britain's leading thriller writers. He began
writing in 1969 after a distinguished army career
and a life spent travelling abroad. He is the
author of fifteen highly acclaimed novels,
including THE RUSSIAN ENIGMA,
A CONFLICT OF INTERESTS, TROIKA and
A DIFFERENT DRUMMER.

Picture of the Year

Clive Egleton

CORONET BOOKS
Hodder and Stoughton

Printed and bound in Great Britain for Hodder and Stoughton Paperbacks, a division of Hodder and Stoughton Limited, Mill Road, Dunton Green, Sevenoaks, Kent TN13 2YA (Editorial Office: 47 Bedford Square, London WC1B 3DP) by Richard Clay Limited, Bungay, Suffolk. Photoset by Rowland Phototypesetting Limited, Bury St Edmunds, Suffolk.

British Library C.I.P.

Egleton, Clive
    Picture of the year.
    I. Title
823'.914[F]   PR6055.G55

ISBN 0-340-42151-7

For Dickie and John
with best love

The Negative

The trial had been held 'in camera' on the twenty-fourth and twenty-fifth of October, a mere ten days after they'd been arrested. The seven accused were the menfolk of a family of Azerbaijani Shiite Moslems from the Kirova Depression near the border with Iran. Although citizens of the Soviet Union, they could not understand a word of Russian and the lawyer who had been appointed to defend them had been an Armenian who couldn't speak their language.

In keeping with the Soviet Criminal Code, they had been served with a copy of the indictment. Despite the fact that it had been set out in both languages, the charges had completely baffled them. They had planted the seeds as before and their labours had been supervised by the same agricultural expert; to be accused and convicted of acts of sabotage was therefore a nonsense.

A horn blared somewhere off in the darkness and two warders emerged from the guardroom to open the heavy wooden gates, then a Zil truck escorted by a Gaz Jeep drove into the courtyard and halted opposite the prisoners. The cotton uniforms they'd been issued with afforded little protection against the cold and they stood there in the prison courtyard shivering in the chill wind blowing in from the Caspian Sea. Reacting to a harsh word of command from the officer sitting in the jeep, the four soldiers in the back of the truck lowered the tailboard and jumped out. Despite the alien tongue, the prisoners knew what was expected of them and they shuffled forward, their leg irons hobbling them to such an extent that they found it difficult to place one foot in front of the other. A foothold had been cut out of the tailboard but they were physically incapable of raising their legs high enough to take advantage of it and had to suffer the indignity of being picked up and tossed inside the vehicle as though they were so many sacks of potatoes. A few moments later, the truck started up and moved off.

The canopy was not a perfect fit and in the gusting wind which billowed the canvas like a sail, it was possible to catch an occasional glimpse of the outside world illuminated by the headlights of the jeep some thirty yards or so behind them. The landmarks however meant nothing to the Azerbaijanis; they had been conveyed to and from the court in a closed prison van and had had no idea where they were being held.

The truck rolled on, snaked through the hills on the outskirts of Baku and descended to the coastal plain around the industrial area of Chernyi Gorod, commonly known as The Black City. Bypassing the marshalling yards of the railway district, they went on through the business centre and residential suburb of Armenikend, then started climbing again. Beyond the Wolf's Gap, they crossed and re-crossed the main line to Batum several times as the road descended to sea level once more. The sun began to appear over the horizon shortly after the driver swung on to the coastal highway below Aliat.

Three hours and one hundred and twelve miles after leaving the prison, their vehicle halted above the shallow valley they had been farming for the past four years under the supervision of the Moscow-trained agricultural expert.

Everything happened fast. While the escort party from the jeep unfastened the flap and threw it back, the guards inside the Zil truck withdrew the cotter pins and dropped the tailboard. Then, hauling the prisoners to their feet, they shoved them out of the vehicle and made them stand in line above a small gully. Even as the officer in charge of the detail began to read the sentence aloud in a bastardised, phonetic version of their language, they heard the guards cocking their assault rifles.

The firing squad was drawn from the ranks of the 11th Security Brigade, a KGB outfit charged with guarding the frontier with Iran who were answerable only to their own Chief Directorate in Moscow. They were the sword and shield of their country and knew the peasants for what they were – disciples of the Ayatollah Khomeini and proven terrorists. With the selector switch on automatic, each man emptied a magazine of thirty rounds into his assigned target.

Their bodies virtually cut in half by the hail of fire, the Azerbaijanis toppled into the gully ten feet below, the first victims of a minor purge that would never make world headlines, their anonymous epitaph a seemingly unrelated photograph that was destined to become the picture of the year.

1

The house was on the outskirts of Riccall hidden from the rest of the village by a sharp bend in the road and an overgrown spinney. Although Dollmann had never met the present owners, he fancied he knew the Paines better than many of their closest friends. He was damned certain he was the only person in Riccall who knew that Paine had called his wife, Jackie, from Zürich airport soon after his Swissair flight had landed at 13.15 hours and that in a little over twenty minutes time his connecting train would pull into Arosa. He could visualise Jackie now stretched out on the couch in front of the TV, a Dubonnet and lemonade within reach, the door ajar so she could hear the phone in the hall.

Dollmann glanced at the illuminated odometer in the dashboard, saw that he had driven nine miles since leaving York, and immediately eased his foot on the accelerator. Up ahead, the road curved gently to the right to run arrow straight towards the dangerous left-hand bend and the house belonging to the Paines. Moments later, the main beams picked out the hazard warning sign and, drifting across the centre line, Dollmann shifted down into third gear. He put the wheel hard over, swung into the open driveway and quickly doused the headlights before he stopped the car and switched off the engine.

The house lay some distance back from the main road and was screened from passing traffic by a thick hawthorn hedge interlaced with brambles so that there was very little danger of anyone noticing his Ford Escort. Opening the

13

glove compartment, Dollmann took out a khaki-coloured balaclava and slipped it on over his head, then he reached up, switched off the courtesy light and got out of the car to cross what passed for a strip of lawn. Despite the light burning in the porch, he nonchalantly went through his bunch of skeleton keys until he found one which unlocked the front door.

The lounge-diner was at the back of the house directly opposite the kitchen. When he walked into the room, Jackie Paine was curled up at one end of the settee, both legs tucked under her, a Siamese cat perched on her right hip. Totally engrossed in a video recording of *Kramer versus Kramer*, she wasn't aware that she had company. The cat however was completely indifferent to Hoffman and Streep; it stopped cleaning itself and turned its head round to glare spitefully at him through narrowed blue eyes, then yowled loudly. Jackie glanced over her shoulder and suddenly reared back as though she had inadvertently touched a faulty switch. The colour drained from her face and he could see the scream welling up in her throat.

"Shut it." Dollmann whipped out a flick knife and pressed the stud in the hilt to release a needle-sharp five-inch blade. "I get very nervous when anyone starts screaming. You understand?"

She nodded dumbly. The Siamese cat jumped down on to the carpet, dug its claws into the pile and stretched luxuriously.

"What do you want?" There was a tremor in her voice but she had finally managed to find it. "There's only a few pounds in the house."

"What makes you think I'm after your money?" Dollmann let his eyes wander over her body. Jackie Paine was about five foot seven and not bad looking, with short and dark curly hair, brown eyes and a pert nose and mouth. Most men, however, didn't pay too much attention to her face. They usually zeroed in on her thirty-six bust and travelled downwards to linger on a pair of long, shapely legs and a tight little ass that was begging to be fondled.

"If it's not money then what do you want?"

"Oh come on now, isn't it obvious? Everyone says you've been putting it around so I figured I might as well get my share."

"You've picked the wrong time of the month."

"So what? I hear you know more tricks than a whore." Dollmann moved a pace nearer.

"You're sick." She clenched her hands and made a determined effort to keep her voice steady. "My husband will be back any minute; he only nipped down to the village to get some fish and chips."

"Are you trying to frighten me?"

"No," Jackie shook her head. "No, of course not."

"I don't scare easy."

"I'm sure you don't. I just don't want you to do anything foolish." The tip of a very pink tongue made a brief appearance and explored her bottom lip while she got her act together. "Look, if you leave now, I won't say a word to anyone. That's a promise."

"What about your husband?"

"He'll do anything for me," Jackie said breathlessly. "He won't report you to the police."

Dollmann smiled at the girl, then shot out a hand, grabbed a fistful of her hair and tugged it hard enough to make her cry out. Slowly, inexorably, he drew Jackie towards him until her face was pressed into his crotch. "Don't give me that shit," he said softly. "I've been watching this house all day and I know you're alone."

Dollmann hauled Jackie to her feet and steered her out into the hall; then, releasing his grip on her hair, he grabbed hold of an arm and twisted it round and up behind her back. He took the staircase at a rush and hustled her across the landing into the double bedroom above the lounge-diner. Still holding the girl in a painful wrist lock, he made her switch on the light and draw the curtains.

"We don't want any Peeping Tom getting a cheap thrill, do we?" Dollmann said.

The last spark of resistance had been extinguished and

15

he knew there was nothing she wouldn't do to please him. Physically there wasn't all that much difference between them. At a hundred and forty-three pounds, Dollmann was just over half a stone heavier but even in her stockinged feet, Jackie was only a fraction of an inch shorter. Had she gone for him, he would have found it difficult to restrain her without using a considerable amount of force. But the fact that he was armed with a flick knife had terrorised her.

"Should I lie down?" Jackie asked, close to tears.

Dollmann couldn't remember the last time he'd seen a woman looking so pathetic but he felt no pity for her, only contempt. "Take your clothes off," he said harshly.

She raised her skirt and rolled the tights down to her knees, then sat down on the bed to pull them off. The rest of her clothing was shed in haphazard order – panties, sweater, bra and skirt. When she had finished undressing, Dollmann unhooked a velvet dressing-gown that was hanging up behind the door and tossed it on to the bed.

"Put this on," he told her. "You're going to have a bath; I like my women to be squeaky clean."

The bathroom was across the landing to the left of the stairwell and next to the smallest bedroom at the front of the house. The suite consisted of a matching bidet, toilet, pedestal washbasin and triangular-shaped fibreglass bath, all in black. The fittings, including the shower attachment, were gold-plated.

"What are you waiting for?" Dollmann asked her. "You know what to do."

Jackie leaned over the bath, pushed the gold-topped plug into the waste outlet and ran both the hot and cold taps. Then, moving past him, she opened the medicine cabinet, took out a bottle of bath foam and poured a generous measure into the water.

"Is that supposed to make you smell nice?"

"No." She brushed a lock of hair out of her eyes. "No, it just makes you feel relaxed and takes the stiffness out of your body."

16

"I'm all for that," Dollmann said and laughed.

Jackie exchanged the bath essence for a couple of tissues from the box of Kleenex on top of the cabinet and blew her nose loudly, a subterfuge to disguise the fact that she was busy wiping the tears from her eyes. He watched her shove the crumpled tissue into the pocket of the dressing-gown and lean forward over the bath again to test the water. The general effect was provocative enough to make him reach out and fondle her buttocks. She flinched at his touch and caught her breath as though he'd physically hurt her.

"I thought you were going to enjoy it," Dollmann said menacingly.

"I'll be all right in a minute." Jackie closed both taps, slipped out of the dressing-gown and stepped into the bath.

"Don't sit down."

"What?"

"Turn round and face me. I want to look at you."

Dollmann transferred the knife to his left hand and pointed the blade at her throat; then reaching out with his other hand, he caressed the dark pubic hair between her legs with his fingertips. He moved on up across the gentle curve of her belly and teased each nipple in turn. She moaned and swayed, her eyelids drooping, her head bowed forward until the rounded chin was touching her chest.

Dollmann carefully placed the knife on the floor, slipped his left arm around her thighs and bent down as if to kiss her belly. The gold-plated taps on the shower attachment were directly behind Jackie in line with the small of her back and he had to get it absolutely right. In one co-ordinated movement, he reached up, grabbed a fistful of hair and simultaneously yanking both legs from under her, smashed her skull against the taps. She grunted just the once and went down like a log, creating a tidal wave which spilled over the bath and drenched his tight-fitting jeans below the knees. Although obviously unconscious, Dollmann continued to hold her head under the water long after the last air bubble had floated to the surface. When

17

finally satisfied that Jackie Paine was dead, he dropped a bar of soap into the water, then dried his hands on the velvet dressing-gown, picked up the flick knife and went downstairs.

Kramer was on the witness stand being cross-examined by his ex-wife's attorney when Dollmann entered the lounge. Stopping the film, he rewound it to the beginning, then switched off the video and TV. No one saw him leave when he walked out of the house two minutes later, nor did he pass another vehicle on the road until he reached Fulford on the outskirts of York.

Kalin came down the hill into Arosa, turned left at the bottom opposite the post office and followed the Obersee promenade round to the Bahnhof. Reversing into the parking area near the ticket hall, he shifted the gear lever into neutral and deliberately kept the engine running while he waited for the 18.50 from Chur. The temperature was registering minus ten degrees centigrade, it was snowing heavily and he saw no point in economising on fuel because the trains were always on time in Switzerland. At exactly ten minutes to eight, the six-car unit would emerge from the tunnel to his left and draw into the platform. In one hour, it would have travelled nineteen miles and climbed five thousand nine hundred feet on a single track that snaked up the mountainside on an average gradient of one in six. With exclusive use of the track and a schedule that called for a maximum speed of twenty, Kalin didn't see how the train could ever be late unless there was a major power failure.

Three minutes to go: Kalin unzipped his anorak and reached into the inside pocket for the snapshots. Both exposures were grainy and had been taken at long range. Despite the poor definition, however, Kalin was sure he would recognise Harry Paine. It was also a fact that most of the weekend skiers tended to arrive by car and there were never many tourists on the 18.50 from Chur, especially in March when the season was drawing to a close.

Furthermore, Kalin was willing to bet the Englishman would be the only person on the train who wouldn't be dressed for the occasion in either unisex salopettes or ski pants.

Both suppositions were proved correct a few minutes later when the Up train slowly emerged from the tunnel and drew into the Bahnhof. Of the twenty or so passengers who alighted, Paine was the only one who was travelling alone and, though smart, the leather coat he was wearing clearly offered little protection against the cold. As he got out of the Datsun and went forward to meet him, Kalin noticed that the Englishman was shivering.

"Good evening, Mr Paine," he said cheerfully. "Permit me to introduce myself – I am Andrei Kalin. I believe you were told to expect me?"

Paine nodded. "That's the message I got in Zürich when I called at the flat."

"Good. My car is just over there."

"I'd like to call my wife and let her know that I've arrived safely."

"You can phone from the house. Mr Bartowski won't mind." Kalin placed a large hand on the Englishman's shoulder and steered him towards the Datsun. "I trust you had a comfortable journey."

"It was okay." Paine sniffed and brushed a dewdrop from his nose. "I just don't see why we couldn't have settled our business in Zürich rather than coming all the way up here."

"Mr Bartowski felt he needed a change of scenery."

Kalin opened the nearside door for the Englishman, then walked round the car and got in behind the wheel. Shifting into gear, he pulled out of the parking area and headed back to the Obersee Platz.

"Have you been to Arosa before, Mr Paine?" he asked politely.

"No."

"It's a very nice place. You should bring your wife here for a winter holiday. You don't have to be a good skier to

19

enjoy it, there's something for everyone." Kalin pointed to the lake on their left that had frozen solid. "For instance, we have horse racing on alternate Saturdays and there's curling and a big, open air skating rink . . ."

"You got a part-time job with the local tourist board by any chance?"

Kalin ignored the barbed comment and drove on past the post office to circle round the lake. "We also have a very fine ice hockey team," he continued unabashed. "You can see the stadium up ahead on the right."

"You mind telling me where we're going?"

"This road leads to Maran, the centre for langlaufing. In summer, the piste reverts to being a golf course."

"I don't want a travelogue," Paine told him, "just a straight answer to a straight question."

"Mr Bartowski has rented a chalet in Waldstrasse, half-way between Arosa and Maran."

Kalin made another left turn by the Valdana Hotel and started climbing out of the valley, the snow chains enabling the tyres to find a grip on the treacherous surface. The street lights became fewer and farther between as the road snaked up the mountainside. Three quarters of a mile beyond the outskirts of Arosa, he turned off the road into a dark lane that had been bulldozed through the pine forest to reach a natural shelf. The headlights played on virgin snow and the absence of any tyre tracks ahead of them began to worry Paine.

"We're about five hundred feet above the village," Kalin told him. "The Bahnhof is on your left. You may be able to catch a glimpse of the lights through the fir trees."

Around the next bend, the lane terminated abruptly in a clearing the shape of a half moon. On a natural shelf slightly above them and facing due south were four chalets in varying stages of completion. Stopping opposite the end one, Kalin switched off the headlights and cut the engine.

"What the hell's going on?" Paine demanded angrily. "I thought we were going to see Bartowski?"

"We are."

"Yeah? What's he doing living rough in a dump like this?"

"This is a check point."

"A CP?" Paine shook his head in disbelief.

"Mr Bartowski has a lot of enemies and you could be one of them. We have to satisfy ourselves that you're clean and I could hardly carry out a body search back there at the Bahnhof."

Kalin removed the ignition key and got out of the Datsun. He wasn't at all sure the Englishman would follow him and he almost sighed aloud when, a few moments later, he heard the car door slam and the crunch of his footsteps in the deep snow.

"Who's we?" Paine asked.

"The guide who will take you on to see Mr Bartowski."

Kalin trudged up the short slip road that led to the chalet and made for the adjoining garage which, unlike the house, had been completed except for the up-and-over door. Raising one corner of the tarpaulin that had been draped across the entrance, he invited Paine to go first, then followed him inside.

The Englishman froze. He was still standing there pointing like a gun dog when the guide, lurking at the back of the garage, switched on his flashlight. The beam zeroed in on Paine's feet and travelled slowly up. As it did so, Kalin heard the Englishman gasp and knew that he had seen the freshly dug grave in the concrete floor and the small pile of ready mixed cement that would conceal his final resting place.

"You guessed it," Kalin told him softly. Then, drawing the .22 calibre automatic from his shoulder holster, he put four rounds into his head at point blank range.

2

Radford left the Underground station at Charing Cross and made his way to Carfax House, a narrow building on the south side of Trafalgar Square near Admiralty Arch. A brass nameplate inside the entrance indicated that, in addition to a hotchpotch of government-sponsored quangos, it was also occupied by Natural Resources, a sub section of the Board of Trade. But like the friendly, uniformed commissionaire on duty in the hallway, the brass nameplate was bogus. Natural Resources was the cover name for the Department of Subversive Warfare and access to that particularly sensitive area was controlled by the commissionaire. The permanent staff, whose faces were known to him, were allowed to pass unhindered. Casual visitors, including temporary desk officers like Radford, were always intercepted at the desk.

This morning things were different; this morning he was not required to produce his identity card before proceeding to the lift at the far end of the passageway. Basic security was not however affected by the apparent laxity; the TV cameras ensured his image was displayed on the monitor screen upstairs and when he stepped out of the lift on the sixth floor, a security guard met him at the gate, alerted by the buzzer the commissionaire had discreetly pushed once Radford's back was turned.

The office Radford had been allocated was next door to the central registry and was small enough to persuade him it had been a storeroom in the not too dim and distant past. Moreover, the spartan way it had been furnished also suggested it would revert to its former usage should he fail to make the grade.

Although he was now halfway into his second week with the department, Radford still didn't know what was really expected of him. Cedric Harper, the Director of Subversive Warfare, had interviewed him the day he'd arrived but apart from inferring that the skills he'd acquired in the Royal Signals and the Special Air Service would undoubtedly be an asset, he'd not said how he proposed to employ him. Drew, who was the senior desk officer, was supposed to be his guide and mentor and had been detailed to show him the ropes. So far, this had consisted of a brief lecture on the role and organisation of the department and a list of approved reading material which he was required to wade through.

Radford shucked off his raincoat, hung it up on the brand new hook behind the door and sat down at the desk. Moments later, one of the clerical assistants breezed into the office, wished him a cheerful good morning and deftly filled his in-tray to overflowing with three box files.

"Compliments of the Chief Archivist," she told him.

"More standing orders?" Radford asked warily.

"Except for the signal from the army's Directorate of Personnel Services inside the brown folder. The Chief Archivist showed it to Mr Drew and he said you might care to see it first before it was circulated."

The signal was addressed to all interested branches in the Ministry of Defence with a copy to the Department of Subversive Warfare. It read: EVENTS OF POTENTIAL INTEREST TO THE PUBLIC (.) 32895310 STAFF SERGEANT H PAINE INTELLIGENCE CORPS REPORTED ABSENT WITHOUT LEAVE WITH EFFECT FROM FIRST PARADE MONDAY 11 MARCH 85 (.) SECOND (.) W/ 370992 CORPORAL J PAINE WRAF, WIFE OF FIRST NAMED FOUND DEAD 1200 HOURS SAME DATE AT HOME ADDRESS FOUR WINDS, RICCALL, SOUTH YORKSHIRE (.) CIVIL POLICE STILL INVESTIGATING BUT NO EVIDENCE OR SUSPICION OF FOUL PLAY AS YET (.) The flimsy had been stamped with a signature block for circulation purposes. Initialling the signal where the Chief

Archivist had indicated, Radford transferred it to the out-tray, then had second thoughts.

Senior NCOs didn't go on the trot for the hell of it. If Paine had murdered his wife, he'd have every reason to cut and run, but the signal implied there had either been some kind of fatal domestic accident or that she'd died from natural causes. Borrowing the Ministry of Defence directory from the central registry, he looked up the listing for the Directorate of Security and then made the first of several telephone calls. When Drew walked into his office an hour later, he'd already gathered a considerable amount of background information on Paine and was busy talking to a Warrant Officer who'd known him in Berlin.

"You mind telling me why you're hogging the MOD directory?" Drew asked as soon as he put the phone down.

"I wanted some information and didn't know who to approach. I figured the Green Book would set me in the right direction."

"And did it?"

"Up to a point." Radford showed him the signal, saw the way his eyes narrowed when he looked at the distribution list and hastily tried to set the record straight. "I know we're only an information addressee . . ."

"But the officer who drafted the signal is an educated idiot who can't be trusted to do his job properly?"

Drew was everything the Chief Archivist had intimated he was – abrasive, hard-nosed, arrogant. Turned forty, he was the longest serving desk officer in the department and did not suffer fools gladly.

"Paine has been positively vetted," Radford said, un-ruffled. "NCOs of his seniority with that kind of security clearance are the backbone of the army and they just don't go around absenting themselves without leave."

"Who says so?"

"I asked one of the staff officers in Personnel Services when was the last time a man like Paine had taken off and he couldn't remember. Fact is, he had to go through their

24

records all the way back to 1979 before he was able to answer my question."

"You got any other earth-shattering news?" Drew asked bitingly.

"Paine is one of the best photomen in the Intelligence Corps, which is why he was posted to the Air Reconnaissance Interpretation Centre at RAF Church Fenton. Mondays to Fridays, month in month out, he spends his whole time studying aerial photographs of the Soviet Union taken by satellite. The raw material arrives twice weekly by special delivery, courtesy of the US Air Force."

"Has any of his stuff gone missing?" Drew still sounded sceptical but it was no longer a pose. He was the professional Intelligence officer intent on eliminating as many of the imponderables as possible before he offered an opinion.

"Not according to the unit security officer." Radford frowned. "But that's hardly convincing proof, is it? I mean, Paine didn't need to steal any negatives or prints; it's all up there in his head. He could tell the KGB what ARIC has been looking at and what they've discovered. The Russian Intelligence Service would be willing to pay a lot of money for that kind of information, assuming Paine was prepared to sell it to them."

Drew wrinkled his nose in a way that suggested he was singularly unimpressed.

"I contacted the Intelligence Corps Depot," Radford continued, "and they put me in touch with a Warrant Officer who'd served with him in Berlin from '79 to '81. Paine was with the Intelligence and Security company in those days and his wife worked as a radar operator at RAF Gatow. The Warrant Officer went to their wedding and according to him, Jackie Paine was a nice enough girl but a bit of a social climber, very ambitious for her husband and reckoned he ought to be an officer. Anyway, Paine applied for a commission shortly after their first anniversary."

"So what happened?"

25

"He failed the board. It appears Paine was pretty upset about it at the time but apparently he eventually got over his disappointment. When the WO ran into him again at the Depot in Ashford a few weeks back, he said Paine was as happy as Larry." Radford paused, then said, "The board didn't think he was good enough for a regular commission but, as a Photo Interpreter, he can bank on being offered a Short Service one in a few years' time. There's a shortage of officers in that trade."

"Is that it?"

"There could be more."

"Then get it," Drew said tersely.

"I'll need some help. The RAF at Church Fenton won't talk to me unless the ground has been prepared beforehand. I'd also like to have a word with the local police."

"I daresay something can be arranged."

"Good. While you're at it, how about putting Special Branch on to Paine? Maybe they can run him to ground."

"No." Drew's tone was categorical. "Tracing an absentee is a job for the military police and this department isn't about to provoke an inter-service row over a staff sergeant."

"There doesn't have to be one," Radford said calmly. "We phone the Provost Marshal's office and in all innocence ask them to confirm they've no reason to suppose that Paine has left the country. If that doesn't produce a request for Special Branch to check out the departure points, nothing will."

"You know something?" Drew said thoughtfully. "I think you might just make the grade with us. You've got the kind of devious mind that Harper approves of."

Krystyna Bartowski had ash blonde hair, blue eyes and was five foot seven and a half. Born in Chicago, Illinois, she was twenty-five years old and described herself as a schoolteacher. She was also one of the best looking girls Warrant Officer Iremonger had seen in a very long time; unquestionably the most attractive visitor the unit had had since he'd joined 261 Intelligence and Security Company at Dempsey Barracks in Berlin. Returning her passport, Iremonger dismissed the regimental policeman who'd escorted her from the guardroom near the main gate, then apologised for the fact that the only spare chair in his office was pretty uncomfortable. "We can provide a reasonable cup of coffee though," he added hastily.

"That would be nice," she said and smiled.

"How would you like it?"

"Black, no sugar, please."

"You've got it." Iremonger poked his head out into the corridor and repeated the order in a loud voice to the company clerk in the adjoining office and returned to his desk. "Would you mind answering a personal question, Miss Bartowski?" he asked. "Exactly how do you pronounce your first name?"

"Christina, but everyone calls me Krysia – that's spelt K-R-Y-S-I-A." The smile appeared again, brilliant as a summer's day. "In case you haven't already guessed, my family originally came from Poland."

"Well, now," he said cheerfully, "what can we do for you, Miss Bartowski?"

"Are you in charge here, Mr Iremonger?"

The company commander was attending a conference at Brigade Headquarters, and the second-in-command had an appointment at the dental centre. Although one of the desk officers was somewhere in the building, Iremonger was not predisposed to refer her to a junior officer. "I certainly am," he said, stretching a point.

"Well then, hopefully you can put me in touch with one of your noncoms – a Staff Sergeant Harry Paine. He and my brother, Stefan, were good friends when they were stationed in Berlin." Krysia produced an envelope from her handbag and gave it to Iremonger. "As a matter of fact, Harry wrote to him towards the end of last month."

The envelope was addressed to Master Sergeant S. Bartowski, care of Miss K. Bartowski, 2980 Riverside Drive, Chicago and had been posted in York on the twenty-first of February. Turning it over, Iremonger saw that Paine had printed his army number, rank, name and initials on the back flap and had given the Combined Manning and Record Office at Exeter as a forwarding address.

"Are you on friendly terms with Staff Paine too?" he asked.

"I met him in the July of '81 when I was spending part of my summer vacation here in Berlin. Actually, the four of us had dinner one night at Kempinski's – Harry, Stefan, Jackie and me." Her eyes sparkled with amusement. "It's all right, Mr Iremonger," she said, "I'm not planning to steal Jackie's husband."

"I didn't think you were."

"It's just that I believe Harry's the only person who can tell me where my brother is."

"Doesn't the Pentagon know?"

"No, but they'd like to. Stefan went AWOL on the eighteenth of February."

If the US Army had no idea where he was, Iremonger was intrigued to know why Krystyna Bartowski was thinking that Paine did. The untimely arrival of the company clerk with a mug of coffee prevented him from asking her straight out. When finally he did put the question to her after the clerk had left, Krystyna had had plenty of time in which to decide exactly how much she was prepared to tell him.

"I only moved to the Riverside address in the middle of January. Harry must have heard from him since then to know where I'm living."

"Oh yes?" Iremonger raised his eyebrows. "What did Paine have to say in his letter?" he asked.

"Not a lot. There was nothing in his letter to suggest why Stefan had taken off and your staff sergeant certainly didn't point me in any particular direction. If he had, you can bet the army would have picked up my brother long before now. They intercepted and opened Harry's letter and then sent it on to me. You don't have to be an ace detective to tell when an envelope has been resealed."

Iremonger eyed her thoughtfully. He had a gut feeling that she was holding something back.

"Where was your brother stationed when he went absent?" Iremonger asked casually.

"Wurtemberg."

"And how long are you staying in Berlin?"

"I haven't really given it much thought but I'm not due to take up my new teaching post until after Easter. Why do you want to know?"

"The British Army won't disclose a soldier's address until they're satisfied there's no ulterior motive behind the request and that means I'll have to tell our people about your brother. Is that all right with you?"

"Sure."

"I'll just make a note of his service number."

"You can keep the envelope, Mr Iremonger," she said brightly. "There's nothing in it."

"Right. How do I get in touch with you again?"

"You can reach me at the Hotel Berlin Ambassador on Bayreuther Strasse." Krystyna Bartowski finished the rest of her coffee and stood up. "You've been more than kind," she said.

"It's been my pleasure, Miss Bartowski."

Iremonger accompanied her to the guardroom, told the regimental policeman on gate duty to phone for a cab, then walked back to his office. Whether the army should give her Paine's address was something the Major could take up with the Manning and Record Office when he returned from Brigade Headquarters, but in the meantime he thought it would do no harm to fire off a signal to the Intelligence Corps depot in England. Like every other member of the corps, Paine had been PV'd and as a senior NCO he was likely to have access to highly classified information. In the circumstances, it was therefore only prudent to advise the top brass that he had been a close friend of an American serviceman in the same line of business who'd recently gone AWOL.

*

In his more impish moods when mingling with people who scarcely knew him, Cedric Harper, the Director of Subversive Warfare, liked to describe himself as Mr Average. So far as his height and weight were concerned, this was not wholly inaccurate but there were a considerable number of very senior civil servants in Whitehall who bitterly regretted the day they'd taken him at his word. Harper possessed a quick decisive brain, knew what he wanted and was ruthless enough to ensure he always got it.

Harper ran a lean, highly efficient department on a tight budget. Despite being under constant attack from the Treasury, the morale of his subordinates remained extraordinarily high and the fact that not a single officer had ever been tempted to write an exposé after leaving the Department had earned him the gratitude of successive administrations. It was this factor perhaps more than any other that had enabled him to obtain a year's extension in post on reaching the compulsory retirement age of sixty, much to the dismay of those who disliked him and his unorthodox methods.

The Department of Subversive Warfare was the bastard child of the wartime Strategic Operations Executive. It was effective because Harper was singularly adept at persuading other government agencies to carry out various tasks on behalf of his organisation. Requests for assistance were never made through the proper channels; they were entirely unofficial and were looked upon by both parties as a sort of favour that would eventually be repaid with interest. In furtherance of this modus operandi, it was not Harper's policy to deal with the top man; instead, he deliberately cultivated the up-and-coming subordinate with an eye to the main chance. One such neophyte was Detective Chief Superintendent Derek Marsh of Special Branch.

Marsh was thirty-eight. A thickset man, he had the wide shoulders, barrel chest and heavy thighs of a second row forward and could make a Savile Row suit look like an off-the-peg job within a few weeks of buying it. Although in his own mind he was reasonably confident that he would make Commander, his eyes were fixed on the dizzier heights of Assistant Commissioner and to obtain that rank he needed the powerful backing of influential friends. Friends such as Cedric Harper.

Occasionally he felt the arrangement was a bit of a one-way street, that Harper demanded a lot more from him than he gave in return, but on the whole, Marsh had no real complaints. If nothing else, he could always be sure of a convivial lunch in an expensive restaurant whenever Harper wanted something from Special Branch. Today, however, they were lunching in the Director's office, a turret-shaped room at the end of a long corridor with a peep view of the National Gallery. Although Marsh could have wished for a pleasanter venue, there was nothing austere about the buffet lunch – smoked salmon, game pie, profiteroles.

"When do I start to earn my lunch, Cedric?" he asked jokingly.

"Very shortly." Harper showed him the signal they'd received from the army's Directorate of Personnel Services. "Harry Paine," he said. "A high grade photo interpreter in the Intelligence Corps with constant access to top secret material. If he hasn't already done so, the Provost Marshal will be contacting your Commander to ask Special Branch to run the usual checks with Customs, Immigration, the airlines and so on. If you come up with a trace, I'd like to know about it before anyone else."

"That shouldn't present any problems, Cedric."

"Paine was reported absent with effect from Monday the eleventh of March. That means he was last seen on Friday the eighth."

"Then we'll take that as the starting date when we talk to the airlines."

"Good." Harper smiled warmly. "The only other point I wanted to discuss with you is the little matter of the legend my people have cobbled together for Michael Radford."

31

"Who's he?"

"A temporary desk officer on loan from the army. An interesting young man – left school at the age of fifteen and joined the Army Apprentices College at Harrogate where he trained as a Special Telegraphist. From Harrogate he was posted to Cyprus for a three year tour of duty with 9 Signal Regiment and was then moved to Germany, by which time he was twenty-three years old and a paid acting sergeant. The Royal Signals were grooming Radford for stardom and they saw him as a potential regular officer, but apparently he was tired of monitoring Soviet radio frequencies and wanted a more active life. So he applied to transfer to the SAS and reverted to the rank of trooper after passing the selection test."

Harper plucked a buff-coloured folder from his pending tray and laid it open on the desk for Marsh to see. Mounted on the inside cover was a candid camera shot taken as Radford entered Carfax House. The physical description at the top of the opposing page was superfluous; Marsh could see for himself that he was a typical Celt – dark hair, blue eyes, features that looked as though they'd been carved with a chisel. He was a quarter of an inch over six foot and weighed a hundred and eighty-five pounds.

"It took Radford six years to get his former rank back," Harper continued. "Then in 1983 he was commissioned into the Parachute Regiment. Prior to that he'd been on active service in Northern Ireland, Oman and the Falklands where he was awarded a bar to the Military Medal he'd won for some undisclosed operation."

"The Royal Signals, SAS, the Paras and now the DSW." Marsh clucked his tongue. "He gets around a bit."

"You're right there. As of now, he's a detective sergeant in the Special Branch."

"Don't tell me, Cedric, let me guess. He works for me – right?"

"Let's say he's doing a job for MI5. The Security Service approached you and intimated that they were concerned about Mrs Jackie Paine and asked if someone could have

32

a word with the local police. Specifically, they wanted to be absolutely sure that her death was due to a domestic accident."

"And you'd like me to smooth the way for Radford?"

"That's the general idea." Harper smiled fleetingly. "I don't think there'll be any comebacks. After all, we both know how secretive MI5 is and they'll neither deny nor confirm your story should anyone up in Yorkshire decide to verify it."

"I think you just talked me into it." Marsh eyed the smoked salmon hungrily and almost smacked his lips. "Are we going to have lunch now?" he asked.

"Better have a word with your people first," Harper said blandly. "Radford left for York an hour ago and we don't want any embarrassing hiccups, do we?"

3

A reputation for being highly efficient and totally discreet was the only attribute the Neu Standard Gesellschaft of Zürich had in common with the major banking corporations. That apart, their service charges were steeper and they offered a lower rate of interest on deposit accounts than did their competitors, but their customers regarded this as a small price to pay for the special kind of expertise the Neu Standard provided in the personage of Wolfgang Thierack.

A tax lawyer, chartered accountant and economist, Thierack had more than quadrupled the bank's profits in the six years he'd been the Director of Finance. His success was founded on a simple philosophy: business was business, and it didn't matter to him where the money had come from or how it had been come by. No transaction was too questionable provided he was satisfied that the reputation of the Neu Standard would remain unsullied in the unlikely event that any irregularities came to the notice of the Federal Banking Authorities. In short, Thierack was the complete technician, a human calculating machine untroubled by moral scruples. Losing a valued client to a rival concern was the only thing that ever distressed him and while the Bartowski account was by no means the biggest in the bank's portfolio, it would still represent a considerable loss. Even more galling to Thierack was the knowledge that Bartowski was doing this to him on the advice of his shyster lawyer now seated opposite him, and there was nothing, absolutely nothing, he could do about it.

"Is something wrong?"

Thierack looked up from reading the letter he'd been given and stared disdainfully at the burly man. "No, Herr Kalin," he said quietly, "these instructions are perfectly clear."

"Perhaps you doubt their authenticity?"

Thierack shook his head; the signature was genuine and Bartowski had called him from Arosa to explain why he couldn't be there in person to complete the transaction and had then put Kalin on the phone.

"Then maybe you think he has been badly advised?"

"It's not for me to say, though personally I can't see what pecuniary advantages there are in transferring the account to the Volksbank in Dresden. The East German Mark is practically worthless."

"It's worth a lot more than the Zloty." Kalin smiled wryly. "At least I managed to convince Herr Bartowski of that. I told him that if he had this compulsion to settle in Warsaw, he should take steps to ensure he could lead a reasonably comfortable life."

"He's going to live in Poland?" Thierack asked incredulously.

"Yes. He may have been born in Chicago but he has this great emotional feeling for the homeland of his ancestors — like most Jews entertain about Israel."

"Incredible."

"I must confess I don't understand him either." Kalin rubbed his heavy jowls. "However, that's neither here nor there. Herr Bartowski has made up his mind and his one concern is that you should not suffer as a result."

"It's not unknown for a bank to lose an account." Thierack managed a faint smile. "Even one that's worth two million and eighty-five thousand Francs."

"Two million. I've warned Herr Bartowski that the bank charges on this particular commission will amount to twenty-five thousand and the rest of course will be his going-away present to you."

"I'm to receive sixty thousand Francs?"

"In cash and in whatever denominations suit you." Kalin reached for the executive briefcase by his chair and placed it on the desk. "The only condition is that I've been instructed to retain the money until such time as you are able to prove to me that the account has been transferred to the Volksbank. Do I make myself clear, Herr Thierack?"

"Perfectly."

"Good." Kalin rubbed his hands. "I knew it would be a pleasure to do business with you," he said.

The bathroom was smaller than the photographs had led Radford to expect. With the bidet, toilet, pedestal wash-basin and triangular-shaped bath taking up most of the available floor space, there was hardly enough room for him to move around and he could have done without Inspector Jolliffe breathing down his neck. In the short time they had known one another, the Yorkshireman had made it evident that he had precious little regard for Southerners and none at all for Special Branch officers from Scotland Yard who appeared to be finding fault with the way the Paine investigation had been conducted.

"It was an accident," Jolliffe said belligerently. "She slipped on a piece of soap, struck her head against the shower attachment, was knocked unconscious and drowned in eight inches of bath water. All the evidence we found points to that conclusion."

"Yes." Radford sorted through the photographs he'd been given and found the one that showed Jackie Paine lying on her back under the water, her head over to one side facing towards the bidet.

"You don't sound convinced, Sergeant."

"I was just wondering what the deceased was doing when she dropped the bar of soap. I mean, was she standing up or sitting down?"

"How the hell would I know?" Jolliffe demanded. "Perhaps she heard the phone ringing or perhaps the cat was scratching at the door; she got up in a hurry and in

36

the process the soap slipped through her fingers and she inadvertently stepped on it."

"She didn't react; that's what puzzles me." Radford went through the photographs again and looked out one that had been taken in the morgue prior to the pathologist carrying out a post mortem. "There's extensive bruising around the right temple but no other marks on her body. Most people instinctively try to grab hold of something when they lose their balance but she didn't even fling out an arm."

"Because it happened too fast. Her feet shot from under her and she went down like a log, creating a small tidal wave that overflowed on to the floor and stained the ceiling in the hall below. Read the autopsy again; it's all there in the report."

"Some tidal wave."

Jolliffe snorted. "Jesus Christ, Sergeant, I know you people in Special Branch have got a complex about Reds under beds, but what we have here is a fatal accident, pure and simple."

"Try convincing the Security Service."

"The occasional 'sir' wouldn't come amiss now and again."

"No, I don't suppose it would," Radford said tersely. "But the fact is, sir, it's no use going on at me. I'm only the messenger boy for MI5. Paine has been cleared for Top Secret with every caveat known to man, and now he's absent. The desk officers at Leconfield House don't like the look of that and when they think there's a bad smell in the wind, it's us they send for because we're their sniffer dogs."

Like any good legend, there was more than a grain of truth in it. Radford had used the same explanation earlier that afternoon on the Detective Chief Superintendent in charge of the Regional Crime Squad and it had been convincing enough to open all the right doors for him once the DCS had checked his story with Marsh. The more often he repeated it, the more polished it became and for all his surly attitude, he knew Jolliffe would swallow the story. So far as the Yorkshireman was concerned, the high-priced help had given Radford the seal of approval and that was all that interested him.

"Have you seen all you want to upstairs, Sergeant?" Jolliffe asked.

"Not quite. Which was their bedroom?"

"The one across the landing."

The master bedroom was above the lounge diner and the kitchen at the back of the house and overlooked an unsightly copse choked with secondary growth. The whole of one wall was taken up by a large fitted wardrobe which the Paines shared between them, his suits and uniforms on the right, hers to the left. The centre drawers dividing the wardrobe in two contained an assortment of underclothes, nightdresses, scarves and sweaters mostly purchased from Marks and Spencer.

"You mind telling me what you're looking for, Sergeant?"

"Something out of the ordinary." Radford checked a few suits at random, paying particular attention to the makers' labels. "Like this Jaeger jacket for example."

"What about it?"

"It didn't come cheap," Radford said. "Neither did this Burberry outfit."

"She was a corporal in the WRAF, he's a staff sergeant in the army; the services are pretty well paid these days."

They were also buying a £32,000 house on a mortgage and with interest rates running at thirteen per cent, that item alone would cost them a fair old penny and make a tidy dent in their budget. "When's the inquest being held?" Radford asked, changing the subject abruptly.

"Tomorrow morning at eleven o'clock. As soon as the Coroner announces the verdict, the family will be able to make all the necessary arrangements for her funeral."

Radford nodded. They could expect precious little co-operation from the banks once the police declared the

38

case closed and clearly, there wasn't enough time now to go through the official channels. If the Paines had been living above their joint incomes, he would have to find some sort of evidence to support that contention before he left the house. Looking round the room, his eyes zeroed in on the handbag lying on the seat of the Cintique chair by the dressing table.

"Is that the one she was using at the time of her death?" he asked.

"We think so. It certainly contains her personal knick-knacks – key ring, lipstick, comb, eye shadow, face powder."

It also contained her cheque book. According to the stubs, it looked as though Jackie Paine had been in the habit of spending forty-five pounds a week on housekeeping, a sum she drew every Thursday, regular as clockwork.

"You won't find a credit card, if that's what you're looking for," Jolliffe told him.

"How about jewellery?"

"None, apart from the engagement ring she was wearing – a tiny solitaire set in platinum. Shouldn't think it cost Paine more than a hundred and fifty."

"Did you find any food in the fridge?" Radford asked.

"We didn't bother to look."

"There's no time like the present."

"And there's nothing like wasting your time and mine." Still grumbling, Jolliffe followed him downstairs and into the kitchen. "I don't know what you're trying to prove, Sergeant, but the pathologist put the time of death at between seven and midnight on Saturday the ninth of March. She had been drinking Dubonnet and lemonade prior to that and he also found traces of biscuits and cheese in her stomach. Cream crackers and Wensleydale cheese – we found the remains of her last meal on a plate in the washing up bowl."

"Did your officers impound any loose cash, sir?" Radford asked.

39

"What the hell are you getting at, Sergeant?"

"Mrs Paine drew forty-five pounds on Thursday the seventh; I saw only six pounds and some loose change in her purse. Doesn't look to me as though the difference went on food. Look, there's hardly anything in the fridge."

"There's a deep freeze in the garage," Jolliffe said.

It was a large chest type and the bottom was empty. Examining the top layer, Radford came to the conclusion that the Paines hadn't bothered to re-stock the freezer since the end of January.

"Maybe they went out to dinner one night."

Radford smiled. "Or maybe Harry Paine borrowed the housekeeping money."

"Let's hope she knew about it, Sergeant." Jolliffe had a nice open-and-shut case with all the evidence slanted towards a verdict of accidental death and he wanted to keep it that way. "At least he didn't take the car."

A basic '79 model Ford Escort. Radford opened the nearside door and checked the interior. Sixty-five thousand on the clock, faded cloth seats, worn carpeting and no extra trimmings. Except for a few of her clothes in the wardrobe upstairs, it seemed the Paines didn't believe in spoiling themselves.

"It's just an ordinary runabout," Jolliffe said, stating the obvious.

Radford ignored the exasperation in his voice and going back into the house, wandered through to the living room. The three-piece suite, sideboard, dining table and chairs were 'G' Plan and the quality of the fitted carpet was equally good. The TV and video recorder were two more expensive items but he supposed they could be on hire from a rental firm. The desk tucked away in the alcove by the stone chimney breast was not as expensive as it appeared on first sight. By a process of trial and error, Radford discovered that only the centre drawer above the kneehole was locked. Digging into his jacket pocket, he took out a bunch of old keys and selected one that looked as though it might be the right size and shape.

Behind him, Jolliffe cleared his throat noisily. "What do you think you're playing at, Sergeant?" he asked.

"Look the other way if it worries you," Radford told him.

He turned the key to the right, felt the lug disengage and forced the drawer open. The bank statements were in a green plastic wallet and covered the previous eighteen months. Leafing quickly through them, Radford saw that although the Paines had never been overdrawn, they were rarely more than a few pounds in credit at the end of the month. Right at the back of the wallet, he came across a slim pocket-size notebook which he deftly palmed when Jolliffe wasn't looking.

"How much longer are you going to be, Sergeant?"

"About two shakes of a lamb's tail." Radford re-locked the drawer and turned about to face the older man. "I'm ready when you are, sir," he said earnestly.

It had been his intention to call in at RAF Church Fenton and talk to the officer in charge of the Air Recce Interpretation Centre but it was getting on for five o'clock and he didn't know if Harper had been in touch with the RAF yet to prepare the way for him.

"Fancy stopping off for a drink on the way back?" he said.

"No, thank you, Sergeant." Jolliffe's tone of voice implied that he didn't think Radford should drink and drive either.

There were no messages waiting for him when he got back to the Post House in York. Collecting his key from the desk, Radford went up to his room on the second floor, helped himself to a whisky and soda from the mini bar and then sat down to study the pocket book he'd lifted. The entries were in two different hands and the first few pages consisted of various measurements which he assumed were the sizes of the carpets and curtains the Paines had bought for the house. Thereafter, there were just four lots of neatly printed eight-figure numbers, each prefixed with the letters 'ZNS'. Radford wondered if they referred to life

41

endowment policies but, on reflection, he couldn't recall seeing any entries in the bank statements which would indicate that the Paines had a number of standing orders payable to an insurance company.

Drew cleared his desk of everything except his scratchpad and stowed the In, Pending and Out-trays in the security cabinet. Then he closed the doors, threw the locking bar and spun the combination dial. Office hours were officially nine to five-thirty but this really only applied to the clerical staff, and any Intelligence officer who managed to get away by six was very lucky indeed. Drew had no thoughts of leaving early; he had merely carried out the usual security procedures ahead of time because he knew Harper would keep him talking long after everyone else had left the building. Collecting the scratchpad, he left the office and made his way along the corridor to the turret-shaped room at the far end. When he walked inside after tapping on the door, Harper waved him to a chair, said he wouldn't be a minute, and carried on reading.

Drew looked round the office. He had joined the department in 1965 at the age of twenty-one and it seemed to him that nothing very much had changed since then. The original carpet had been replaced some time back when the Property Services Agency had suddenly discovered that the RAF were holding a large stock of pale blue Wilton which was surplus to their requirements, but the furniture was still the old heavy Victorian pieces that looked as if they belonged in the smoking room of a London Club. Although he vaguely recalled that the walls had once been a lavatorial green, the woodwork had always been a sort of creamy yellow. And for all that the department had promised to do something about it donkey's years ago, the only source of natural light was still the porthole window which was continually being fouled by the pigeons roosting on the ledge outside.

"Well now," Harper said and dumped the file he'd been reading into the out-tray. "What have you got for me?"

"It seems we're not the only people who are interested in Staff Sergeant Paine. 261 Intelligence and Security Company in Berlin had an unexpected visitor this morning, a Miss Krystyna Bartowski from Chicago, who's anxious to get in touch with him. He and her brother, a master sergeant in the US Counter Intelligence Corps, are supposed to have been close friends and she thinks Paine may know his present whereabouts."

"Do I gather this Master Sergeant Bartowski has also gone absent?"

Drew nodded. "He disappeared on the eighteenth of February, some three weeks before Paine did."

The Change of Circumstance report had reached the Department via the Intelligence Corps Depot and the Directorate of Personnel Services at the Ministry of Defence where one of the staff officers, recalling that Radford was interested in the case, had finally got in touch with Drew and passed the message on. 261 Company in Berlin hadn't said when Bartowski had gone absent; that particular item of information, together with a character profile, had been supplied by the American Military Attaché in London who, as a favour to Drew, had contacted the Judge Advocate General at Headquarters 7th US Army in Frankfurt.

"What else can you tell me about Bartowski?" Harper asked.

"He's a lifer – enlisted at seventeen and is now pushing thirty-one. Married at nineteen, divorced three years later, eight months after returning from Vietnam where he was awarded a Bronze Medal." Drew glanced at the notes on his scratchpad and continued, "He had a whole string of Outstanding reports until 1980 when he collected an Excellent before dropping to Very Good the following year, which is roughly equivalent to the kiss of death. It could be just a coincidence but that was round about the time he met Paine."

"Is that what the Americans think?"

"They don't appear to know about Paine. Anyway, it

seems Bartowski is slipping in other ways; he's a good stone overweight, has difficulty in passing the annual battle fitness test, and his commanding officer had him on the mat for drinking too much before he went absent. Bartowski also enjoys the bright lights, especially in Frankfurt where he spent most weekends shacked up with his German girlfriend."

"Did your friend in Grosvenor Square give you a name?"

"Monika Starnberg; she's an air hostess with Lufthansa." Drew frowned. "Or rather, she used to be until she disappeared with her lover boy."

"What route was Monika Starnberg flying before she ran off?"

Drew felt his jaw drop; he had been caught out. "I didn't think to ask," he said lamely.

"It might be useful to know. Better get her home address while you're at it."

"Right."

"What did you learn about the sister?"

Drew relaxed, confident he was on much firmer ground. While waiting for his friendly ally in Grosvenor Square to prise the information he needed out of 7th Army, he'd spoken to Warrant Officer Iremonger in Berlin and questioned him at length about Krystyna Bartowski.

"She's a schoolteacher . . ." Drew began, then the phone rang and he broke off while Harper took the call.

One minute later, his face completely impassive, Harper murmured a thank you and slowly replaced the receive. "That was Marsh," he said. "Special Branch have got a lead on Paine from Swissair. According to their records, he was on their Flight 803 departing Heathrow for Zürich on Saturday the ninth of March at 10.15 hours. What's even more interesting is the fact that he was planning to catch a return flight from Zürich the following evening at 18.50 local time."

"He must have changed his mind."

"Or someone changed it for him." Harper pursed his

lips as if considering the validity of his own observation, then said, "I assume 261 Int and Sy company know where to find Miss Bartowski?"

"Yes, she's staying at the Hotel Berlin Ambassador."

"Good. Ask them to keep an eye on her until early tomorrow afternoon when we expect to have our own people on the ground, then get in touch with Radford and tell him that unless he's on to something really hot, he's to drop everything and get back here."

"Because we're going after the Bartowski girl," Drew said flatly.

"I wouldn't put it quite like that. Five people have come to our notice – the two Paines, the Bartowski brother and sister and Monika Starnberg. Of these, one is dead and three are missing." Harper smiled fleetingly. "I wouldn't be best pleased if Krystyna Bartowski disappeared."

The heath was one of the few remaining tracts of land in the Münster area that hadn't been engulfed by the ever-expanding city. During daylight hours from Monday to Friday, it was used as a local training area by the British troops stationed in the suburb of Loddenheide. At weekends, it was the favourite playground for children, model aircraft enthusiasts and the Wolbeck angling club who had to be the most optimistic bunch of fishermen in all Westphalia considering the polluted state of the river. At night, the heath was also a popular haunt for a third group known as the carriage trade – the freelance amateurs on wheels who cruised the streets looking for clients who'd part with a hundred Marks for a quick tumble on the back seat.

Not surprisingly, a lot of people found the activities of the carriage trade deeply offensive and from time to time pressure was brought to bear on the authorities to do something about it. Translated into practical terms, this meant that the hookers were periodically subjected to a certain amount of harassment. As part of their clean-up campaign, the police would descend on the training area and invite the occupants of any car they found there to accompany them to the police station.

Right from the moment he got out of the patrol car and moved towards the Audi saloon parked amongst the bushes near the river, the police officer knew there was something very different about this particular vehicle. For one thing, it looked almost brand new and all the prostitutes he'd encountered preferred to drive around in something far more utilitarian; for another, the licence plates indicated that the Audi had been registered in Frankfurt. That he could see no one up front didn't surprise him but instead of the usual mating couple entwined on the back seat, he found only the girl and she was lying on the floor wedged between the seats. She was on her left side, her wrists lashed together behind her back, a gag stuffed into her mouth and naked from the waist down. When he opened the offside rear door and took a closer look at her, he could see that she had been strangled with a pure silk scarf which had been knotted around her neck.

From the contents of the brown leather handbag on the back seat, it appeared the deceased was one Fräulein Monika Starnberg of Bockenheimer Sophienstrasse 368, Frankfurt Am Main.

4

Radford left his suitcase with the commissionaire on duty in the hallway of Carfax House and then took the lift up to the sixth floor. The cleaners were only just beginning to leave the building and as he walked towards the Director's office at the far end of the corridor, he could hear the buzz of an electric shaver in the duty officer's room. Not everyone was at his best at seven fifteen in the morning, especially on a dull chilly day, but Harper was one of the exceptions. He looked remarkably fresh and was in a buoyant mood, as though he'd had several glasses of champagne for breakfast and was still high on it.

"I'm sorry to drag you into the office at this ungodly hour," Harper said cheerfully, "but as your flight to Berlin leaves at 08.50 hours, I really didn't have much choice." A warm smile lit up his face. "I presume Drew explained why it was necessary to recall you from York, Michael?"

"I gathered it had something to do with a Miss Krystyna Bartowski. He implied that she might be able to give us a new slant on Paine."

"Whereas you feel there's still some unfinished business up in Yorkshire we should attend to first?"

"There's no reason why we can't pursue both lines of enquiry simultaneously." Radford produced the small notebook he'd found in Paine's desk and flipped it open at the appropriate page. "It could be helpful to know what these four lots of eight-figure numbers refer to. If they're insurance policies, he's not paying the premiums with a banker's standing order, and I didn't come across any

47

dividend statements when I was going through his drawer. Of course, it might only be an aide-mémoire."

"For what?"

"Your guess is as good as mine." Radford shrugged. "I once knew an army officer who could never remember the entry code for his cashpoint card so he recorded it in his pocket diary disguised as a telephone number."

"But this is a notebook that Paine kept locked away in a drawer."

"Yes. Well, maybe he only needed to use that number occasionally."

Harper weighed the notebook in his right hand. "Do you mind if I hang on to this?" he asked.

"Not at all." Radford paused, then said, "I know the RAF are satisfied that Paine didn't remove any material from the Air Reconnaissance Interpretation Centre but they haven't said what he was working on before he went absent."

"I can get that information."

Radford didn't doubt it but he would have welcomed the opportunity to question Paine's associates. No matter how close an interest a commanding officer might take in the men under his command, he rarely saw them when they were off duty and letting their hair down. Only someone on Paine's own level could give a picture of what he was really like as a man. There was however one aspect of his behaviour they could investigate and perhaps come up with the right answer.

"I'm told Paine flew to Zürich last Saturday morning," Radford said, broaching the subject.

"What of it?"

"I'm just wondering if it was a one-off trip or part of a regular pattern that started shortly after he was posted to Church Fenton. I imagine the airlines and travel agencies can at least check their records for the current financial year."

"Anything else you'd like done while you're away?" Harper asked, a note of tetchiness in his voice.

"I don't think so."

"Good. Now let's talk about your trip to Berlin – who you'll be working to, what I expect from you, and how we propose to keep the Bartowski girl under surveillance."

Harper was concise and kept to the point. Nevertheless, by the time he had finished briefing him, Radford had less than forty-five minutes to make it out to Heathrow. Fortunately, the rush hour traffic was heading in the opposite direction.

The aerial photographs of the Kirova Depression in Azerbaijan some forty miles from the Soviet border with Iran were part of the consignment that had arrived from Brize Norton on Tuesday. Normally they would have been studied by Staff Sergeant Paine whose preliminary evaluation was then submitted to the chief analyst for the Middle East section. In his absence, the task had been farmed out to George Elder, an RAF sergeant who, though junior in rank, was several years older than Paine and had been wearing a uniform a damn sight longer. These two factors alone were sufficient to guarantee that there would be friction between the two men but what angered Sergeant Elder even more was the conviction that he was a far superior photo interpreter. Having to do Paine's work as well as his own was the final straw and in the circumstances, it was hardly surprising that he approached the task with a conspicuous lack of enthusiasm.

Elder carried the pile of photographs over to the workbench in the window and began to arrange them in sequence according to the frame number in the top left-hand corner of each print. It was a bit like doing a jigsaw puzzle except that the pieces overlapped each other and had to be topped and tailed with a guillotine after they'd been paired off. He worked swiftly, bonding the exposures together to form a mosaic with the aid of a can of sickly-smelling dope that made his eyes sore and gave him a headache.

When he'd finished, the sergeant left the office, locked

the door behind him and took a stroll round the block while he waited for the extractor fan to disperse the fumes. Strictly speaking, he was committing a breach of security regulations which required him to lock all classified material away before leaving the room unattended but, like a good many other NCOs on the station, he reckoned the rule was only applicable when the length of absence exceeded five minutes. In any event, the door was re-inforced with a steel plate on the inside and a man would have to be as strong as an elephant to push it open once the locking bar was engaged with the recesses in the floor and ceiling. Furthermore, the window was only one way; it was possible to look out but not in.

The sergeant completed three circuits of the block, killed some more time smoking a cigarette, then returned to the office to find the atmosphere relatively clean. Opening the centre drawer of the workbench, he took out a stereoscope, unfolded the thin legs and placed it on the mosaic of aerial photographs. He leaned over the instrument, peered through the 3D lenses and began to study the terrain.

The stereoscope he was using was as old as Methuselah, an item of equipment that had remained virtually un-changed from the day it had first come into service back in World War I. The techniques and means of collecting the raw material had however been revolutionised out of all recognition since then. In the '14–'18 era, aerial photos were taken with a large hand-held camera by the observer leaning over the side of his cockpit in a 90-horsepower, sixty-five-mile-an-hour Bleriot Experimental biplane flying at eight thousand feet. Twenty-five years later, the ob-server was out of business and the camera was activated by the pilot of the Mark XXII high-altitude Spitfire. More latterly the vehicle for the spy-in-the-sky had been the English Electric Canberra, then the U2, and finally the satellite orbiting the earth at seventeen thousand miles an hour.

And it was also a fact that the Air Force now had the technology to zero in on a tiny dot and keep on enlarging it until that tiny dot eventually became a petrol bowser or a T70 tank. Unfortunately, in this particular instance, the high technology was wasted; all it had revealed was a barren and hostile wilderness.

Some Intelligence officers maintained that even negative information helped to build up a picture of the enemy's strengths and weaknesses but not the chief analyst of the Middle East section. He was only interested in the hard stuff, like the number and type of surface-to-air missiles protecting the oil refineries at Baku or the positive identification of another aircraft carrier of the Moscow Class under construction in the shipyards of Sevastopol. Knowing this, the sergeant devoted the next ten minutes to listing all the reasons why the Air Reconnaissance Interpretation Centre should forget all about the Kirova Depression before he presented the latest mosaic to the great man in the sanctity of his office at the opposite end of the building.

The chief analyst was a civilian, a tall thin-faced ascetic-looking man with a greying beard who projected an image of being 'holier than thou' and who, as a result, was referred to as 'Creeping Jesus' behind his back. It was Elder who'd first called him C.J. to his face and when asked why, had blandly replied that those were the initials of his Christian names, weren't they?

"You got a few minutes to spare, C.J.?" he asked as he walked uninvited into his office.

"But of course."

The pious voice was accompanied by an earnest expression that made Elder feel he'd just been granted an audience with the Pope. Smothering a grin, he placed the mosaic on the desk.

"This is the latest view of the Kirova Depression," he said. "It was taken on the nineteenth of October last year, so the Yanks are hardly rushing the prints straight to us from the dark room, but it still makes a pig's ear of Paine's assumption that something was going on down there. The Red Army isn't massing on the Iranian border; what we have is evidence that the agricultural programme for this part of Azerbaijan suffered a major setback. I don't know what they were trying to grow but whatever it was, the crop was diseased and they decided to burn it. Take a look for yourself, C.J., if you don't believe me. All you'll see is a lot of scorched earth."

"Perhaps that is what they wanted us to see and by the same token, draw the very conclusion you have just reached."

Elder could feel himself turning brick red, the colour rising from his neck. A whole string of pungent obscenities sprang instantly to mind, but he was forced to concede that the bearded wonder had a point. The Russians knew they were being looked at by the spy-in-the-sky they couldn't knock down and when you were faced with a problem like that, you copied Merlin the Magician and concocted a few illusions.

"I don't think we should get too excited about this thing, C.J.," he said stiffly. "I mean, let's not forget how it all started. The Yanks weren't on to anything when they decided to send us a whole load of photographs of this region; they just wanted a second opinion. Hell, most of the stuff they gave us was ancient history and the task was given a low priority by the US Defence Intelligence Agency and by our own people. We even drew lots to see who should be landed with the job and Paine ended up with the short straw."

"It doesn't matter how it started. The point is Paine discovered what appeared to be a fogbank in an arid region where a fogbank had no right to be at that time of the year."

"Oh, for Christ's sake." Elder pushed a hand through his wiry black hair. "I work in the same office with Paine and I know what he thought of his great discovery. You should have heard him bitching about the job he'd been given. Shit, he was just going through the motions. I tell you, the day our section head walked into our office, Paine was just sitting there staring at a mosaic, goofing off as usual." He paused, waiting for some reaction; when none was forthcoming, he said, "Don't you understand? He made a big deal out of a few lousy wisps of smoke in order to get himself off the hook."

"Did he tell you that?"

"Not straightaway. As a matter of fact, it must have been a week or so later, towards the end of February, when the Yanks began to unload their library on to us."

"Because they believed we'd found something they hadn't," C.J. said meaningfully.

It took some time for the penny to drop but when finally it did, Elder was left in no doubt that he was required to look again and go on looking until he came up with something that would keep the Yanks happy.

The office was on the ground floor of the barrack block. From the window in Iremonger's room, Radford could see the regimental pennant of the 3rd Fusiliers hanging limply from the flagpole outside the guardroom. Apart from the sentry on the main gate, there was very little sign of life.

"The battalion's away on exercise except for the company at Spandau Prison," Iremonger said, answering his unspoken question. "It's our turn to guard Hess."

"Do you have a lot to do with the 3rd Fusiliers, Sergeant Major?"

"Not a lot; we just happen to occupy the same barracks." Iremonger fetched a chair for him, then sat down behind the desk. "Can I get you a cup of coffee, sir?" he asked, very much as an afterthought.

"No thanks." Radford tapped his throat. "I'm up to here with coffee, thanks to British Airways."

"I guess you want to know the set-up for keeping Miss Bartowski under surveillance?"

Radford shook his head. Drew had that in hand and was being briefed by the company commander in his office along the corridor from them. "I'd like to hear what you thought of Miss Bartowski. I'm going to be talking to her later this afternoon and it would be helpful to know what she's like. For instance, do you think she's truthful?"

Iremonger gave the question some thought, then said, "For the most part. At first, I was pretty suspicious when she walked into my office and asked me if I could put her in touch with Paine. I thought she was either going to stick him with a paternity suit or else he owed her some money, but then she produced this letter Paine had written to her brother and I changed my mind." Iremonger opened a side drawer, took out an envelope and passed it across the desk. "I didn't actually see the letter and Miss Bartowski didn't tell me what Paine had said either, but she was very frank about her brother. In fact, that's why I sent a change of circumstance report."

Radford glanced at the name and address of the sender on the back of the envelope, then looked up frowning. "54063060? There's no such army number."

"I noticed that. Had to look up his correct number in one of the old company nominal rolls before I could fire off a signal to our depot."

Although the eight-figure number bore no relation to the ones Radford had found in Paine's notebook, he thought there was something vaguely familiar about it. "How do I raise the exchange supervisor?" he asked.

"You want 993." Iremonger dialled the number for him and then handed over the phone.

When the supervisor answered, Radford gave her Paine's name and address in Riccall and asked her to ring back with his phone number and area code.

"She won't discover that in a hurry," Iremonger predicted confidently. "Means a call to Directory Enquiries in the UK and the line's always busy."

"About Miss Bartowski?" Radford reminded him tactfully.

"Yes, well, she didn't tell me too much about herself – claims she's a schoolteacher and is supposed to be taking up a new post after Easter. Character-wise, she comes across as a very warm and outgoing person but I had this gut feeling that she was holding something back. My guess is that Krystyna Bartowski wasn't too surprised when her brother went AWOL. I don't know whether she was having me on or not, but she reckoned the army had intercepted Paine's letter and opened it before sending it on to her."

Radford looked at the postmark on the envelope. The letter had been handled by the GPO and the US Mail and he didn't see how the army could have intercepted it. Only the FBI could have done that.

"How close is the tie-up between 261 Int and Sy Company and their American counterparts?" Radford asked, taking a different line.

"There isn't any," Iremonger told him. "We operate independently; they've got their job to do, we've got ours. Same applies to the French, but the chiefs get together twice a month to exchange information."

"Is that how Paine and Bartowski met?"

"I doubt it. That sort of gathering is much too high-powered for the likes of us Indians. We just collect the raw material on the VOPOs and the Soviet order of battle."

"What about joint operations with the Americans?"

"Such as?"

Radford shrugged. "You tell me – counter Intelligence surveillance, interrogation of defectors . . ."

"We haven't had any defectors since I've been here. Anyway, MI5 have got their own security organisation in Berlin and they deal with those kind of incidents. Chances are, Paine and Bartowski were introduced to one another at some social function."

The telephone interrupted Iremonger before he had time to finish what he wanted to say. Answering it, he told the caller to hang on a minute and then put Radford on the line.

The exchange supervisor was brisk, efficient and courteous. She said, "The subscriber's number you asked for is 54063 preceded by 075784, the area code for Riccall. The UK code is, of course, 060."

"Don't tell me," Iremonger said, after he'd thanked her

and put the phone down. "The numbers are identical. Right?"

"They're close enough."

Paine had started with his phone number and then added the UK international call sign to make it up to eight figures while the area code had been tagged on to the forwarding address. Radford was also willing to bet that it was a pre-arranged emergency code which told Bartowski how to contact him in a hurry. There was, however, one flaw to this otherwise convincing theory; Paine had sent the letter care of a third party which suggested he had lost touch with the American.

"Krystyna Bartowski told me she was introduced to Staff Sergeant Paine in July '81 when she was over here on holiday," Iremonger said thoughtfully.

"So?"

"Well, it's standard practice to weed a file before consigning it to the shredder, and anything which is thought to be of historical importance is retained indefinitely."

"And a major operation involving our allies could have considerable historical value."

"That's what I was thinking," Iremonger said.

"In that case, you'd better start looking from the sixth of April '79."

"Is that the date when Paine was posted to 261 Int and Sy Company?"

"According to my information, it is," Radford told him.

Gustav Fellgiebel had large hands, broad shoulders, a well-muscled body and a weather-beaten face; physical characteristics which indicated even to the uninformed that he was a manual worker who'd spent the greater part of his life outdoors. In fact, Fellgiebel was a builder and a much respected member of the business community in Arosa. Widely regarded as a very affable and easy-going character, he prided himself on being able to get on with the vast majority of people, whatever their background, whatever their profession. Architects were, however, the one professional group for whom he had very little regard. Fellgiebel had yet to meet one whose plans he hadn't found it necessary to modify on the grounds of cost or in order to avoid a potential disaster with the plumbing. Yet architects continued to think they were the élite and some of them even behaved as if they were. And when it came to sheer arrogance, the junior partner of Reitlinger, Meyer and Stuckhardt of Chur had more than his fair share.

Fellgiebel glanced at his wristwatch again and wondered just how much longer he was going to be kept waiting. An on-site inspection was always a pain in the arse but it was an even bigger ball-ache when the architect failed to show up on time. Somewhere on the main road, he could just hear a vehicle grinding its way uphill but there had been many such false alarms and he paid little attention to it. In all probability, the driver was making for Maran, the last of the season's skiers arriving to do some langlaufing before the snow vanished from the piste. Although there had been a moderately heavy fall on Saturday, the temperature had been climbing steadily ever since and a general thaw had set in.

He turned about and looked up at the four chalets on the shelf above him. They were nearing completion and it didn't really matter a damn what the weather conditions were like. The chalets were now in the hands of the carpenters, electricians and plasterers and a blizzard could be raging outside for all they cared. Two more weeks and the job would be done and the best thing about it was the fact that he would have no further dealings with this particular firm of architects.

The BMW came on down the track doing close on fifty, the slush spraying out from under the tyres like fountains. At the last possible moment, the driver yanked on the handbrake, put the wheel hard over and executed a 180 degree turn before skidding to a halt. Seconds later, the architect got out of the car, wearing a broad grin as Fellgiebel went forward to greet him.

"Good afternoon, Herr Baumeister."

57

Fellgiebel made it a point never to address the architect by his name. If he was in a fairly benevolent mood, it was Herr Architekt; if he was feeling particularly acid, it was Herr Baumeister, a title which implied the younger man was a superlative craftsman among architects. Fellgiebel's tone of voice was intended to make it abundantly clear that he thought nothing of the kind, but his sarcasm had no effect whatever on his youthful adversary.

"Good afternoon, Herr Fellgiebel," he said briskly. "Shall we begin our inspection?"

It was a command, not an invitation, and one the architect proceeded to execute with the speed of an Olympic class sprinter. Breathing heavily, Fellgiebel did his best to keep up with him as he inspected each chalet in turn from attic to basement. By the time they reached the end house, Fellgiebel's complexion was brick red. Making straight for the adjoining garage, the younger man raised the up-and-over door which had been fitted that morning and walked inside. He paused briefly to look around, then his eyes suddenly focused on some irregularity towards the rear of the lock-up and he almost crowed with delight.

"Look at that, Herr Fellgiebel," he said, pointing to an uneven section of the concrete floor. "It's totally unacceptable; you'll have to dig up the entire floor and re-lay it."

"Surely that's unnecessary? All we need do is pour in another load of cement and smooth it over."

"And end up with a raised step the owner will feel every time he drives his car into the garage? Oh no, Herr Fellgiebel, that would never do at all."

"The plant is no longer on site, Herr Baumeister."

"Then hire whatever you need – generator, pneumatic drill . . ."

"It'll cost us."

"You, Herr Fellgiebel. You're the one who's responsible for this example of bad workmanship, not my client."

Fellgiebel could have cheerfully strangled him but from a strictly legal standpoint, the pompous little prick was holding all the cards. Recognising that time was also money, he told the site foreman to put a couple of men on the job with picks and shovels while he drove back to Arosa to lay his hands on the necessary plant.

Three quarters of an hour after Fellgiebel had left the building site, two thoroughly disgruntled carpenters cum temporary labourers uncovered a human foot and realised they'd found a shallow grave.

5

Dollmann entered the anonymous grey building on Normannenstrasse in East Berlin, reported to the control desk in the foyer, and was escorted up to Manfred Leber's office on the second floor. At sixty-nine, Manfred Leber was the only survivor of the old guard, the bunch of ex-Nazis who'd set up the State Security Department in the German Democratic Republic under the supervision of the NKVD immediately after the war.

The years had been kind to him; physically he was in very good shape and despite the crop of white hair, still closely resembled the blond, athletic Gestapo officer who'd first caught the eye of his Soviet masters shortly after being taken prisoner north-east of Warsaw in August 1944. There was nothing wrong with his mind either; all the grey cells continued to function as God had intended. Nevertheless, in Dollmann's opinion, he should have been retired years ago to make room for younger men like himself but it seemed probable the Russians would insist he remained at his desk until he had to be carried out of the building feet first. His experience was too useful for them to do otherwise.

Manfred Leber had made his reputation in France. Between the third of August 1940 and the seventeenth of October 1943 when he had been transferred to the Eastern Front, he had done more to smash the Resistance network in Le Havre, Rouen, Paris and Chartres than any other Gestapo, SS or Abwehr Counter Intelligence officer. He had been equally successful in Poland; a master of the doublecross game, the 'V' men he'd planted inside General 'Bor' Komorowski's Home Army had discovered virtually every detail of the plan to seize control of Warsaw and had given the German High Command the precise date of the uprising. Regarded as a war criminal by both the French and Polish governments, Manfred Leber had had every reason to be thankful that he'd fallen into Soviet hands. His good fortune owed everything to the fact that among the refugee German Communists in Moscow who were being groomed for stardom by the Politburo, there was no one capable of organising a state security service. In Leber and a few of his contemporaries, the NKVD had the right men for the job, professionals whose loyalty could be bought and retained indefinitely for the price of a new identity. In Dollmann's opinion, he would make a bad enemy but an even more untrustworthy friend.

"Welcome home, Erich," Leber said warmly shaking hands with him. "I trust you had a safe journey?"

"It was uneventful."

Dollmann sat down in a chair facing his superior officer and lit a cigarette. He had left York early on Monday and caught a train to London where he'd then boarded the Alitalia flight to Rome. The following morning, he'd doubled back to Vienna and had made his way to Budapest by train. Malev Airlines had subsequently flown him to Prague and from there he'd completed the rest of the journey by car, staying overnight on the Wednesday at his parents' house in Dresden before going on to Berlin. As on previous occasions, he'd travelled on a West German passport; as on previous occasions, he'd been very careful not to set foot inside the Federal Republic.

"And may we assume your mission was successful?" Leber asked.

"The problem has been satisfactorily resolved."

Dollmann was thirty-six, well-educated, intelligent and widely read. He did not consider himself a psychopathic killer and was convinced he had been truly horrified when, along with his high school classmates, he'd been taken on

61

a conducted tour of Buchenwald. That he could refer to Jackie Paine, whom he'd murdered in cold blood, as a problem which had been satisfactorily resolved was but one example of his capacity for self deception.

"And everything went according to plan?" Leber said, pressing him for more information.

"Were there no reports of the accident in the English newspapers?"

The Political Assessment Section spent their entire time reading the Capitalist press and it was inconceivable that Leber had not insisted that he be kept fully informed.

"I prefer to hear the news from your lips, Erich."

You would, Dollmann thought, then said, "The woman believed she was going to be raped and was only too anxious not to provoke me. As you might expect, the flick knife convinced her that I wouldn't hesitate to cut her up if she tried to resist."

"I can understand that." Leber smiled grimly. "Did Centre give you all the support you needed?"

"Their surveillance team did a first-rate job; by the time they finished briefing me, I knew everything there was to know about the Paine woman. I'll make a point of mentioning it in my final report."

"The operation may not be over yet, Erich."

"Oh? How come?"

"There's been an unexpected development; Bartowski's sister flew into Frankfurt the day you left for England. She saw the Provost Marshal at 7th Army Headquarters, then tried to contact Monika Starnberg at her flat in Bockenheimer Sophienstrasse. Now she's here in the Western Sector staying at the Hotel Berlin Ambassador."

Dollmann didn't ask how the information had reached him because he really didn't want to know. He had a shrewd idea of what was in the wind and wanted no part of it. But his studied air of indifference had no effect whatever on the older man; as if bestowing a favour, Leber opened a drawer in his desk and took out a blow-up of a photograph that had obviously been taken at Berlin-Tegel.

"I'm not going into West Berlin," Dollmann said, forestalling him.

"You won't have to, Erich; we've been keeping an eye on her. Yesterday, she went out to Dempsey Barracks to see someone in 261 Intelligence and Security Company. We think she was hoping the British would put her in touch with Staff Sergeant Paine. If so, her actions would seem to indicate that Bartowski was telling the truth when he claimed he'd never confided in her."

"Then she can hardly be described as a potential threat."

"I agree with you, but our friends may see things differently. That's why I want you to make a contingency plan in case we are asked to deal with her."

"Why don't you tell the people in Moscow to do their own dirty work?"

"Because, my dear Dollmann, I'm not completely stupid."

The Berlin Ambassador on Bayreuther Strasse was part of the Etap Hotel chain. A five minute walk from the Kurfürstendamm and convenient for the Zoo Bahnhof, the eight-storey, 120-bedroom hotel provided everything a business executive could want – garage, snack bar, cocktail lounge, sauna, swimming pool and haute cuisine restaurant as well as special accommodation for banquets and conferences. When Radford walked into the lobby that afternoon, the place was crawling with dentists attending a convention. In his service dress slacks and army sweater plus a beret and stable belt provided by the Intelligence Corps, he was very conscious of being the odd man out amongst all the pinstripe suits. The uniform had been Drew's idea and was intended to lend substance to the cover story they had prepared for Krystyna Bartowski; as far as Radford was concerned, he couldn't help feeling like a third-rate actor performing a bit part in a lousy play.

Approaching the reception desk, he gave his name to a pretty brunette and told her that Miss Bartowski was expecting him. Iremonger had described her as something of a looker but her allegedly eye-catching contours were not readily apparent to Radford when she stepped out of the lift and walked towards the reception desk. A large floppy sweater and grey pants tucked into a pair of matching suede boots effectively concealed her figure. Her hair was a natural ash blonde, her eyes round and clear blue and she was wearing a minimum of make-up.

"Captain Radford?"

"Miss Bartowski?"

A faint smile twitched the corners of her mouth. "I certainly didn't expect your army to react this quickly, Captain," she said.

"Sometimes we even surprise ourselves."

"Are you and Mr Iremonger in the same unit?"

"No." He shook his head. "I work in Headquarters Berlin; we hang out in the old Olympic Stadium."

"Oh yeah, so you said when you phoned earlier this afternoon."

Despite her neutral expression, Radford couldn't make up his mind whether Krystyna was just making small talk or was hoping to catch him out.

"Is there somewhere reasonably private where we can talk?" he asked.

"We could try the snack bar across the lobby."

It turned out not to be a bad suggestion. Like most professional people attending a convention, the dentists believed in making the most of the amenities and were gravitating towards the cocktail lounge; consequently, the snack bar was two-thirds empty. Leading Krystyna to a corner booth after he'd paid the cashier for their pastries and coffee, Radford waited until she was halfway through a slice of Apfelstrudel before mentioning the Paines.

"Iremonger tells me you've met Mrs Paine," he began quietly.

"Yes, Jackie's quite a girl."

"You're using the wrong tense."

"What?" Krystyna froze, a fork in line with her mouth.

"There's no easy way to tell you this. Jackie's dead. She

was about to take a bath and it seems she slipped on a piece of soap and knocked herself out. They found her lying under the water, face up."

"My God." Krystyna lowered the fork on to the plate and pushed what was left of the pastry to one side. "My God, how is Harry taking it?"

"Paine doesn't know his wife is dead; he's AWOL like your brother." Radford unbuttoned his hip pocket, took out a slim leather wallet and produced the envelope Paine had addressed to Master Sergeant Stefan Bartowski. "You didn't need to ask Iremonger how to get in touch with Harry; the information was already in your possession. These two groups of figures give his home phone number together with the international and requisite area code. You could have dialled 060–075784–54063 from anywhere in the world – Berlin, Paris, Rome or even Chicago – and Paine would have answered."

"You seem to be implying that I should have known that?"

"Let's say Iremonger got the impression you weren't exactly surprised when your brother went AWOL."

"Your Mr Iremonger doesn't know how I feel . . ."

"He alleges you told him Paine's letter had been intercepted and opened before it was sent on to you," Radford said, talking her down.

"What is this, some kind of inquisition?"

"If you've got the letter on you, I'd like to see it."

"You've got a nerve."

"I probably have," Radford agreed, "but I'd still like to see it."

"Suppose I refuse, what could you do about it?"

"Quite a lot. This is an occupied city, Miss Bartowski, and what we say goes. If we don't like the look of you, we can put you on the next plane out of Berlin."

At first it looked as though Krystyna was going to defy him but after some hesitation she finally produced the letter from her handbag, then took out a packet of Marlboro and lit a cigarette.

"Can you really do that?" she asked presently.

"Do what?"

"Kick me out of Berlin."

"I'm not sure, but we could give it a damned good try."

The letter to Bartowski had been written on a plain sheet of notepaper and without a sender's address in the top right-hand corner. The content was about as informative as a laundry list; it gave no indication when the two men had last seen one another and Paine had been careful not to disclose where he'd been or what he'd been doing since leaving Berlin at the end of his tour of duty in November '81. Apart from the lack of news, the style and composition also suggested that Paine had written the letter knowing there was a possibility it would be intercepted in the States.

"Do you have any idea when the FBI began to take an interest in your brother?" Radford asked. "Or why?"

"What the hell have the FBI got to do with it?"

"Everything. The letter Paine wrote was posted in England and was addressed care of your apartment in Chicago. It was handled by the GPO and the US Mail, neither of whom would lightly surrender a letter in their charge. Furthermore, Paine would never have substituted his phone number for his army number if he'd thought there was a chance that someone like Iremonger would see the envelope. And if MI5 had been keeping an eye on our boy, we'd have heard about it. That only leaves the FBI."

"What an interesting theory, Captain. I bet you could prove the moon is made of green cheese if you really put your mind to it."

"You're still avoiding the question."

The dangerous glint in her eyes and the way she crushed her cigarette in the ashtray were warning signs of an imminent eruption. "Stefan isn't the brother I used to know but I can't think of a single reason why the FBI should have him on their wanted list. Okay?"

"No, it's not okay," Radford told her. "Whatever the problem was, you were worried enough to drop everything and fly over here to sort it out. And you were also sufficiently worried to come to us and ask for our help when you ran into a brick wall with the US Army."

"Stefan is the only close relative I've got and I hadn't heard from him in four months. My letters went unanswered, I couldn't raise him on the phone and the army gave me the brush-off when I wrote to the Pentagon asking if he was okay. Then Harry's letter arrived and the following day I hear from the Provost Marshal's office in Washington that Stefan has gone AWOL. I guess someone like you, Captain, would have taken all that in his stride but I just felt I had to do something about it."

"Because, apart from Stefan, you're all alone in the world?" Radford said with mock concern.

"I wouldn't put it quite like that."

The room temperature seemed to drop several degrees. "What happened to your parents?" Radford heard himself ask.

"They died within eighteen months of one another when I was seven; my father in an automobile accident, my mother from cervical cancer. Stefan and I were brought up by a maiden aunt who moved to California during my third semester at Chicago University."

A little Orphan Annie story and all the more effective for the laconic way Krystyna Bartowski told it. All the same, Radford thought the sisterly concern was overdone and there had to be more to it than she was prepared to admit.

"Have you ever met Stefan's girlfriend, Monika Starnberg?" he asked casually.

"Only the once." Krystyna frowned as though trying to recall the occasion. "Monika was stopping over in New York on slip crew duty or something. It must have been nearly eighteen months ago, one weekend around the beginning of October '83."

"You don't like the Fräulein?" Radford asked.

"She was Frau Ziegler when I met her in New York and you're right, we're not exactly bosom friends. I didn't like her then and I'm none too wild about her now that she's divorced from her first husband. The lady has expensive tastes; as far as I'm concerned, Monika is the reason why Stefan has disappeared."

"Maybe you should look for him in Zürich."

"Why there?"

"Because that's where your brother told Paine to meet him."

The letter Paine had mailed to Chicago wasn't the only one he'd written; Radford was certain it had been a sort of business circular, one of several identical notes that had been sent to every address known to have been frequented by Bartowski in the past. And then suddenly he thought he understood the significance of the numbers Paine had recorded in his notebook.

"We think something had happened which was about to upset their joint business venture," Radford continued. "It couldn't have been too serious because Paine evidently believed they could sort things out over the weekend of the ninth and tenth of March. Anyway, we know that when he left Heathrow on the Saturday, he'd already booked himself on Swissair flight 808 departing Zürich at 18.50 hours the following evening."

"Stefan and Harry in business together? Who are you trying to kid?"

Krystyna Bartowski pulled out all the stops – wrinkled forehead, raised eyebrows, quirky expression – but to Radford her performance was a shade over the top to be totally convincing.

"You tell me," he said quietly. "All I know is that they must be on to a good thing. Both Paine and your brother have several numbered accounts with a bank in Zürich."

Just remember one thing, Drew had advised him, people always lose their cool when they're angry or frightened. Rattle them enough and they'll shop their own mothers. Radford didn't know if the advice held good in her case but there was only one way to find out.

"I think I know what's bothering you, Miss Bartowski,"

68

he continued. "You're no longer getting your cut from the business; that's why you're over here."

Very slowly, very deliberately, Krystyna stood up. "I don't have to stay here and take this," she said in a furious stage whisper that everyone in the snack bar could hear. "Especially from a cretin like you."

The low background murmur of conversation ceased abruptly and several heads swung round to watch Krystyna leave. Radford hung on, stared at the remains of the pastry on her plate and the cup of coffee she'd barely touched and waited for the other customers to lose interest. Few of them did, and he was uncomfortably aware of being the centre of attention as he made a none too dignified exit a few minutes later.

Drew was waiting for him in a Mercedes parked outside the U Bahn station at the Zoological Gardens. The smirk on his face as Radford got in beside him said it all.

"You look as though you've caught the sun," he said.

"You heard every word then?"

"Clear as a bell. You're wearing a very sensitive mike." Drew pulled out from the kerb and blithely ignoring the rules of the road as well as the angry reaction from every other motorist in the area, made a U-turn on Budapester Strasse. Weaving in and out of the traffic, he went on up Hardenberg and turned left in Ernst Reuter Platz. "About those numbered accounts," he said presently. "Do you know something I don't or was it just a ranging shot in the dark?"

"Call it a flash of inspiration."

Radford slid a hand under his jersey, unbuttoned the flap pocket of the khaki shirt he was wearing and took out a retractable ballpoint. A custom-made transmitter powered by a long-life battery, it had an operating range in excess of a mile and was not affected by screening in an urban area. Holding the pen in his right hand, Radford pressed the cap which simultaneously retracted the ball-point and switched off the transmitter.

"I guess you can't be too careful," Drew said, glancing at

the fake pen. "There's no telling who might be listening."

"Maybe. Truth is, I'm not so sure the KGB have got their hooks into Paine, or the GRU for that matter. Neither Intelligence service is noted for being a generous paymaster and no one ever made a fortune selling information to the Russians. If Paine does have a numbered account in Zürich, he's got to be into something far more lucrative than plain, old-fashioned espionage."

"Well, I wouldn't beat my brains out trying to fathom that particular conundrum. Sooner or later the Bartowski girl will give us the answer."

"Provided she doesn't give us the slip."

"There's no chance of that," Drew said confidently. "Every Kraut Intelligence officer in Berlin is keeping an eye on her."

Still lane-hopping, he went on down Bismarck Strasse towards the rather seedy hotel in the Charlottenburg District where they were staying.

There had been nothing to identify the dead man that Fellgiebel's workmen had found buried under the concrete floor of the garage belonging to the end chalet, but the labels inside his clothes indicated he was English. The cause of death, however, was not a mystery; from the number of entry wounds it had been self-evident to the local police chief that someone had put four bullets into his head at close range. Although it was the first murder investigation the Polizeiwachtmeister had conducted, standing orders laid down the procedures which were to be observed. Accordingly, he had telephoned a preliminary report to Divisional Headquarters at Chur and had arranged for one of the photographers in the village to take several head and shoulder pictures of the deceased. These would help to jog people's memories when his officers began their door-to-door enquiries, but while the exposures were being developed, the investigation had necessarily come to a grinding halt except for the purely administrative tasks. Of these, the delivery of the corpse in a black plastic body bag to the Path Lab in Chur had been given over-riding priority.

The post mortem examination began with a routine description of the cadaver. Aware the deceased was English, the pathologist made due allowance for this when describing the physical characteristics. The dead man was, he noted, 1.68 metres/5 feet 8 inches tall, weighed 72 kilos/158 pounds, had light brown hair and hazel-coloured eyes. Under the heading of visible distinguishing marks, he noted that both legs were bowed which suggested the Englishman had suffered from a bone deformation as a child and that the right eye was fractionally lower than its twin. The most significant feature was a tattoo on the upper part of the left arm depicting a white rose superimposed on a larger red one, the whole surmounted by a crown and resting on a laurel wreath below which was a scroll bearing the legend 'Intelligence Corps'. A second and larger scroll displayed the Latin tag MANUI DAT COGNITIO VIRES.

The pathologist could speak English and knew Latin. Quick to appreciate the significance of the tattoo, he rang the Kommissar of Police at his home and persuaded him to contact the British Military Attaché in Berne.

6

Radford showed his ID card to the sentry on duty at the main gate at Dempsey Barracks, then drove round the one-way circuit to the accommodation block opposite the guardroom which was occupied by 261 Intelligence and Security Company. Parking the Volkswagen he'd borrowed from Drew in the slot allocated to the second-in-command of the company, he grabbed the small carrier bag on the adjoining seat, got out of the car and walked back to the entrance where Iremonger was waiting for him.

"One cap badge plus one Intelligence Corps stable belt," Radford said, handing the carrier bag to the Warrant Officer. "Now what have you got for me?"

"A bit of a non-event that ended up with the Special Investigation Branch and us at each other's throats."

"What was the dispute about?"

"The usual thing – who does what." Iremonger put his head round the orderly room door and told the company clerk to fetch two mugs of coffee, then led Radford into his office. "We said it was a security matter; the military police said one of our soldiers had been found dead in suspicious circumstances and that their Special Investigation Branch was going to look into it whether we liked it or not."

"I bet that went down well."

"Like a lead balloon. There's not a man serving in this unit who was here when this case broke in 1980 and the same goes for the Red Caps, but the feud persists to this

72

day, kept alive by a few loud-mouths who ought to know better." Iremonger lifted a thick folder from the pending tray and dropped it on to the desk. "This is the SIB report; we weren't on the distribution list and I must have sunk the best part of a bottle of whisky with their chief clerk yesterday evening before he agreed to let me take a photocopy."

Radford had realised Iremonger had had a skinful when he'd phoned him a few minutes before nine pm; one look at his hungover appearance from the night before and he could also understand why Iremonger had suggested they should meet this morning.

"This is Operation Heron, sir." Iremonger held a second and much thinner file aloft. "I recommend you read this first because it'll tell you how Paine and Bartowski came to meet one another."

Heron had been a low level operation launched in September '79 entirely on the initiative of the officer then commanding the Int and Sy Company. The information which had led him to set it up had come from a source with no previous track record whose motives, in Radford's opinion, were definitely questionable. The target had been an Irish girl employed at 'Hildegard's', one of the sleazier nightclubs off the Kurfürstendamm. Although they'd never charged her, the Kriminalpolizei had believed she was on the game. According to the source, she had strong Republican sympathies and had openly boasted to him that the only reason she chatted up the British troops who frequented the establishment was to obtain information from them.

"The source wasn't exactly unbiased, was he?" Radford said, looking up from the report. "He was sharing her bed until she kicked him out of it. Seems to me he had an axe to grind."

"It gets better the more you read."

Iremonger was right. Heron had been launched in a fit of enthusiasm, without adequate preparation, and at a time when the unit had been temporarily under strength and overstretched. The operator selected for the undercover job had been a twenty-year-old corporal recently arrived from Northern Ireland where, for a very brief period, he had been employed on similar duties. Reading between the lines, Radford came to the conclusion that he'd been selected for the task largely because he'd arrived in Berlin with hair long enough to pass himself off as a civilian.

Simplicity had been the one plus mark of the scenario they'd put together for the corporal. An Ulsterman from Newcastle, County Down, he was supposed to have left Northern Ireland for the Federal Republic in order to find employment and get away from all the aggro in the Province. To back up his story, they had provided him with a German work permit and a glowing testimonial from a Gasthof proprietor in Bielefeld who'd hired him as a temporary barman. His case officer had then turned him loose armed with the fictitious reference which eventually enabled him to get a job at 'Hildegard's'. On the twenty-sixth of June 1980, some nine months after Operation Heron had been given the green light, the corporal had been found dead by the landlady of the flat he'd been sharing with an American postgraduate at Berlin University. Thereafter, it had become a matter for the Special Investigation Branch.

The SIB report ran to a hundred pages and had some pretty scathing things to say about the operation; it was also highly critical of the way it had been controlled by 261 Intelligence and Security Company. The coffee arrived when Radford was on page ten; it was stone cold by the time he finished reading it.

Iremonger caught his eye and smiled. "When it comes to a fuck-up, Heron takes a lot of beating, doesn't it?"

Radford nodded. "I think my partner should know about this. You got a phone I can use?"

"Be my guest."

"Thanks." Radford moved the phone nearer and lifted the receiver, then looked at Iremonger. "I'm sorry about this . . ." he said slowly.

"But you'd like a little privacy." Iremonger stood up and put on his beret, adjusting it so that the cap badge was an inch above the left eyebrow. "Don't give it another thought; it's about time I took a stroll round the block to see what's going on."

Radford waited until the warrant officer had left before he rang Headquarters Berlin and got through to the office they'd been allocated. When Drew answered, he gave him a résumé of Operation Heron.

"The whole thing was a disaster," Radford said, winding up. "Apart from the unit being undermanned and overstretched, there was a lot of turbulence among the senior NCOs, some of whom were being short toured. That corporal had no less than four case officers, finishing up with Harry Paine."

"Interesting." Drew's voice grated down the line. "What else have you got?"

"The American postgraduate vanished sometime before the corporal's body was found by the landlady. Efforts to trace him through Berlin University failed because none of the faculty had ever heard of him. However, he did leave some of his personal effects behind in the flat including a number of items which suggested he could be an American serviceman."

"And surprise, surprise, the US Provost Marshal assigned Sergeant Stefan Bartowski to the case."

"You want to make another guess?" Radford asked.

"No, I've had my flash of inspiration for the day. Let's hear the rest from you."

"When the MPs were finally given permission to search the flat, they found twelve ounces of pure, uncut heroin. The street value was estimated to be in the region of eight hundred thousand pounds."

"Some people would kill a man for a fraction of that."

"Forget it," Radford said tersely, "the corporal died from natural causes. A blood clot precipitated a massive coronary. I know he was only twenty but sometimes these things happen."

"So what are you suggesting?"

"I think there was more than twelve ounces of heroin in the flat. I think Paine got there first and stumbled upon another cache which he later split down the middle with Bartowski."

"And then he banked the proceeds in Zürich."

"I believe friend Stefan did the same." Radford paused, then said, "That's why I'd like to take another crack at Krystyna Bartowski."

"The hell you will. We've got a small army of Krauts watching that girl and you and I are going to play the waiting game."

Radford figured they had already shown their hand and had nothing to lose but Drew hung up on him before he could make the point. When he called back, the operator told him the extension he wanted was engaged. It was still engaged an hour later when he finally gave up and drove back to the Olympic Stadium.

Patience, an eye for detail, and the ability to spot anything that seemed at odds with the general pattern were qualities the armed forces expected from their photo interpreters. Sergeant George Elder possessed all three, though patience had never really been his strong suit and it had become even thinner since he'd been obliged to cover for Harry Paine. He also had to admit that for most of yesterday the other two qualities had temporarily deserted him. They had only begun to return after C.J. had made it very clear that he was required to go on looking at the mosaic of the Kirova Depression until he found a logical explanation for the bush fire Paine had originally noticed.

Had anyone asked him to estimate how long the job would take, Elder would have told them that some poor slob would still be grinding away at the task long after he'd left the RAF and was drawing his service pension. Then, suddenly, late yesterday afternoon, he'd spotted a tiny fire-blackened object on the periphery of the blaze. By six o'clock the printing section had grudgingly produced a twenty-fold enlargement of the exposure; by seven pm, having told his wife he would be late for dinner, Elder had identified the object in question.

This morning he'd deliberately come in early to study the enlargement again in the cold light of day. Two hours later, satisfied he hadn't been mistaken, Elder was ready to confront C.J.; armed with the photographic evidence, he tapped on the door and walked into his office.

"I've cracked it, C.J.," Elder announced boldly.

"You reckon?"

"I know it. Cast your eyes over this." Elder placed the enlargement in front of the chief analyst, then walked round the desk and leaned over his shoulder. "You see this collection of junk?" he said, pointing to a lot of wreckage scattered over a wide area. "That's what's left of a HARE-Mi-1 reconnaissance helicopter. It can carry up to four passengers over a radius of one hundred and fifteen nautical miles."

"Oh yes?" C.J. glanced up at him. "Are you saying the helicopter crashed and set fire to the grassland?"

"Well, the so-called grassland is mainly scrub and it would have been tinder dry last October when this picture was taken. If there had been a good stiff breeze, the Soviets would have had a major conflagration on their hands."

"Quite. Tell me something, George – have you compared this enlargement with the photographs taken of the same area when the fire was still smouldering?"

"Yes." Elder guessed what was passing through his mind and tried to head him off. "I know what you're thinking, C.J.," he said quickly. "The previous batch were taken five days earlier and the Russians could have planted the wreckage in between time."

"But?"

"But nothing. For all I know you could be right. The definition is poor on the first set of photographs; practically every exposure is obscured by drifting clouds of smoke and I can't be sure what I'm looking at even when the frame is enlarged."

There was a long, ominous silence. Knowing the chief analyst, Elder was expecting to be told to go back to first principles and start again, that the brush fire had been a smoke screen designed to capture their attention while something happened elsewhere and that he should plot the heart of the fire and then work outwards, studying the areas to the north, south, east and west at fifty kilometre intervals.

"Finito," C.J. said abruptly. "Show me your draft before it goes to the typing pool."

"Come again?" Elder said incredulously.

"I want this whole thing wrapped up as soon as possible. We can't afford to waste any more time looking for something that doesn't exist."

Dollmann's office was also on the second floor of the State Security building on Normannenstrasse, but Leber rarely visited it. Whenever he did, Dollman knew a particularly dirty job was coming his way. This morning was no exception and the older man's obvious reluctance to get to the point was an indication of just how messy it was going to be. Over the years, Dollmann had developed his own equivalent of the Beaufort and Richter scales for measuring the potential disturbance and in this instance, ten minutes of inconsequential chatter about the security arrangements for the forthcoming May Day parade equated to a hurricane force gale or a major tremor.

"We've just heard from Moscow, Erich," Leber said, finally broaching the subject.

"Oh, yes. What did they have to say?"

"Not a lot, but all of it was bad." Leber turned away from the window where he had been gazing aimlessly at a rain-washed pale blue sky. "They want us to eliminate Fräulein Bartowski. I tried to convince them it wasn't necessary but they wouldn't listen."

Dollmann was sure Leber was lying. Recalling how yesterday he'd been ordered to prepare a contingency plan for just such an eventuality, there were very strong grounds for believing the decision to neutralise the American girl had been taken before he'd returned to Berlin. There was, however, no point in making an issue of it; an order was an order, especially when it came from Moscow.

"How long have we got?" Dollmann asked matter of factly.

"Centre would like the job done as soon as possible, Erich, but they haven't set a deadline."

"It's just as well they haven't; we need a day or two to get things properly organised. To move against her with maximum hostility while she's still in Berlin would be a mistake and tantamount to fouling our own doorstep." The operation was fast becoming a small war but so far neither the Americans nor the British were aware of the blood bath, and Dollmann wanted to keep it that way. "I think we should point her in another direction."

"I agree with you," Leber said. "But how are we going to persuade her to move on?"

"I thought we might use 'The Actor' to deliver a personal message from her brother. Naturally, we'll use two Guardians to cover his back."

'The Actor' was a twenty-four-year-old bank clerk who lived in the Siemensstadt District of West Berlin and was a keen member of the local amateur dramatic society. Fluent in English, he had a mid Atlantic accent and could pass himself off as an American. There was one other plus factor; his record was so clean he hadn't even collected a parking ticket.

"He's a good choice," Leber said thoughtfully, "but it's conceivable the British are keeping Fräulein Bartowski under surveillance."

"So what if he does come to their notice? It won't be the end of the world; as a last resort, we can always put him out to grass until they lose interest. The same applies to his Guardians."

"All right, Erich. When do you think he'll be ready?"

"I put him on standby yesterday evening, and he knows he'll be playing the part of an American serviceman.

There's no reason why he shouldn't meet Fräulein Bartowski tonight, provided we can get the stage props to him in time."

"You're not going to put 'The Actor' in uniform, are you?"

Dollmann shook his head. "It won't be necessary; he'll be off duty and wearing civilian clothes. On the other hand, it's vital we give him some personal items belonging to her brother which she'll recognise – say a wristwatch, a key ring or a fountain pen."

"I'm sure we can find an appropriate keepsake," Leber said.

"Good. Of course, he'll have to explain where, when and how he met her brother."

"Naturally."

Dollmann waited expectantly. The operation had been broken down into a number of autonomous component parts. Until yesterday, he'd never heard of Monika Starnberg and apart from gathering that she had been the American's girlfriend, he still didn't know precisely where she fitted into the overall picture. Similarly, the team that had been assigned to deal with Monika Starnberg had probably never heard of the Paines either. Leber knew this and no one was better placed to appreciate the extent to which he was being hamstrung by a lack of information. The continuing silence seemed to suggest that the ex-Gestapo officer was not willing to enlighten him.

"Look," Dollmann said patiently, "if 'The Actor' is to be properly briefed, I need to know a great deal more about Bartowski's army career than I do at present."

"Bartowski is only part of the story, Erich, and I think the time has come for you to know as much as I do about this operation."

"May I ask why?"

Leber stared at him, the hint of a contemptuous smile on his lips. "Now you're being coy."

"I wasn't aware of it, Herr Direktor," Dollmann said, stung by the implied criticism.

"You mean you haven't been keeping an ear to the ground?" Leber shrugged. "I should have thought the news would have been all over the building long ago."

"Well, it hasn't reached me, whatever it is."

"Then let me enlighten you, Erich. The Minister of the Interior has decided that you will take over from me when I leave."

"I didn't even know you were thinking of retiring."

"I'm not." Leber grimaced and tapped his chest. "But I may not have much choice."

Manfred was retiring on health grounds; he had a heart condition and his doctor had advised him to call it a day. He clearly didn't like the idea and was living in hopes that he could carry on. Dollmann could think of no other interpretation for his gesture.

"Better lock your security cabinet and come along to my office, Erich. You've got a lot to learn, especially about Major General Vasili Petrovich Yagoda."

"Who's he?"

"Our link with Moscow Centre," Leber told him. "The man who's breathing down our necks."

In the event of war, Baku Military District became the 83rd Army and part of the Trans Caucasian Front which embraced the whole of the Soviet Socialist Republic of Azerbaijan. In peace time, the Headquarters was responsible for the standard of training and operational readiness of the 42nd Mountain, 93rd and 107th Mechanised Divisions and the 201st (Guards) Tank Division. Located within the district boundaries but not under command were the 8th Airborne Division belonging to the strategic reserve and the 11th Security Brigade. Of these two formations, it was the 11th Security Brigade who had almost given Major General Nikolai Andreyev an ulcer. They were a KGB outfit charged with guarding the frontier with Iran and answerable only to their own Chief Directorate in Moscow. Andreyev didn't like being excluded from the chain of command and in the past it had angered him every time he'd thought about it. But today, he could view the situation with some equanimity because at twelve noon he would cease to be the Commanding General of Baku Military District.

Promotion had come late and unexpectedly to Nikolai Andreyev. At the age of sixty-three, he was the oldest serving Major General in the Red Army and until the February '85 list had appeared, he'd given up all hope of further advancement. As the commander of Baku District, he should have been given the rank of Lieutenant General when he was originally appointed to the post in April '82, but despite a brilliant war record which had included service with the partisans operating behind the German lines, his annual fitness assessments had evidently not impressed the Soviet High Command. His sudden elevation owed more to the fact that he had known when to turn a blind eye and keep his mouth shut than any startling improvement in the performance of his military duties.

His successor was a Major General S. A. Ustenko, a Ukrainian from Kiev, who was some twelve years younger than himself. Widely regarded as a high-flier, Ustenko was bitterly disappointed that his name had not appeared in the February List. Although Andreyev had pointed out that it was not at all unusual for a District Commander and his subordinate Divisional Commanders to be of equal rank, Ustenko had still been irked by what he considered to be a grave injustice. Indeed, it had played on his mind to such an extent that he'd frequently paid very little attention to what those who were briefing him had to say during the two days the High Command had allowed for their handover. Now, half an hour before Andreyev was due to have a farewell glass of wine with the Headquarter's staff, Ustenko had cornered him in his office with a host of last minute questions covering every subject under the sun from the VD rate to the role of the fast patrol boats of the Caspian Sea flotilla in peace time.

"What about the frontier troops?" Ustenko asked,

taking one last glance at his field service notebook before he put it away. "Do we have much to do with them?"

"Not a lot. They take part in STORM CLOUD every year."

"That's the annual transition to war exercise?"

"It is." Even though the younger man had been preoccupied with the imagined setback to his career, Andreyev didn't see how Ustenko could have failed to hoist that one in. "11 Security Brigade send their post exercise report direct to Moscow but I saw every draft and my suggestions were invariably included in the final version. Of course, that was an entirely unofficial arrangement between me and the previous Brigade Commander, V. P. Yagoda."

"Ah yes, he left the District on promotion a few months ago." Ustenko nodded judiciously as though the posting met with his approval, then expressed his thoughts aloud in case Andreyev had misunderstood him. "One might say it was a just reward for the way he dealt with those reactionary Kurds in the Kirova Depression last October."

"They were Azerbaijanis, Shiite Moslems who considered themselves disciples of that lunatic Ayatollah Khomeini."

"My mistake," Ustenko said contritely.

Andreyev raised a hand and made a vague gesture which could be taken to mean almost anything. Ustenko's error was understandable; neither the incident nor the subsequent trial of the ringleaders had received much coverage in 'Pravda'.

"I seem to recall that the army suffered a number of fatal casualties." The younger man paused, then said, "Two staff officers from this Headquarters and a helicopter pilot from the aviation battalion?"

"That's right." Andreyev wondered how his successor had come by the information and just where their conversation was leading. "The helicopter was hit by a burst of machine-gun fire and the pilot had to make a deadstick landing in the immediate area when the engine seized up. They were trying to make their way out of the Kirova

83

Depression on foot when Azerbaijanis caught up with them."

The facts were broadly correct, but it had been the KGB frontier guards who'd murdered them, not the Shiite Moslems. The staff officers had been on a reconnaissance in connection with a series of tactical exercises planned for the Spring of '85. Although they had been warned not to enter the airspace of the 11th Security Brigade, they had spotted a fairly large fire in the south-east corner of the Kirova Depression and the pilot had announced that they were going in close to take a good look at it. Thereafter, no further message had been received from the helicopter. Subsequently, the Board of Inquiry had attributed the black-out to local atmospheric conditions even though the static recorded by air traffic control had sounded as though the frequency was being jammed.

"A heinous crime," Ustenko said pompously, "but at least the swine didn't get away with it. Seven of the terrorists were tried and convicted on the evidence of your Chief of Staff."

Andreyev nodded. "He identified certain personal items belonging to the staff officers which the KGB had found on the terrorists they'd captured."

Yagoda had come to him virtually demanding an independent witness whose neutral testimony would give added weight to the case the KGB were preparing against the Shiite Moslems. Yagoda had also made the point that it would be better received in Moscow if he could show that the Red Army had been actively involved. It had not been necessary for him to add that Andreyev would do himself no harm if he co-operated with the KGB. The Chief of Staff had been excluded from the conspiracy and the evidence he'd given in court had sounded all the more convincing for it. One month after the Shiites had been tried, convicted and executed, Andreyev's name had appeared in the annual promotion list.

"A most interesting case."

"Yes, indeed." Andreyev glanced pointedly at his wristwatch. Time was running on, the Headquarter's staff were waiting for him downstairs and he had a plane to catch. "Are there any other matters you'd like me to clarify before I go?" he asked, just in case Ustenko was too thick-skinned to take the hint.

"No, I don't think so." A smile made the briefest of appearances on his heavy features. "I hope you find life agreeable in Far East Command."

Andreyev didn't like Baku, this dreary city on the Apsheron peninsula which jutted out into the Caspian Sea like a thumb into the rectum of the Trans Caucasus. He didn't like the hot summers and the bitter winters, he didn't like the oil fields, he didn't like the environs of Chernyi Gorod and Belii Gorod, but most of all he hated the Kirova Depression.

"Vladivostok will suit me fine," he growled and moved towards the door.

"Oh, by the way, Comrade General," Ustenko said chattily, "did you ever discover what those terrorists had set alight in the Depression?"

Suddenly the whole purpose behind the questions became clear. Moscow still wasn't sure of him and Ustenko had been primed to ascertain if he could be trusted to keep his mouth shut.

"Scrub," Andreyev said, repeating the explanation he'd learned by heart. "The terrorists set fire to the scrub hoping the smoke would be seen and that the nearest border patrol would be ordered to investigate and report back. Having waited two whole days and nights for someone to walk into their carefully laid ambush, they were getting a little desperate."

7

Harper turned right outside the Athenaeum in Waterloo Place, crossed Carlton House Terrace and went down the steps by the Duke of York's monument in The Mall, then wheeled left towards Admiralty Arch. To lunch with an old friend was always a pleasure; it was even more so when the old friend was able to throw a beam of light into a dark corner.

He had met Louis Norman in January 1944 when the latter had rejoined the battalion after a long spell in hospital. A twenty-four-year-old captain, Norman had been one of the very few survivors from the old battalion who'd landed with General Anderson's 1st Army in Algeria and had been up at the sharp end throughout the Tunisian campaign. He had taken over command of Harper's company a month before they had been made up to strength and thrown into the slaughter house of Monte Cassino where, in a little over forty-eight hours, they had been cut to pieces again.

A friendship forged in war had survived forty years of peace largely because Harper had made sure they kept in touch. In the immediate post war years, they had seen rather more of each other than they did nowadays but their friendship had not yet reached the low point where they merely exchanged Christmas cards. Genuine feelings of friendship apart, there was no telling when the expertise of a merchant banker might come in handy and in the past Louis Norman had often given him sound financial advice whenever he'd had a small amount of capital to invest.

Today, his old friend had performed a different but equally rewarding favour by identifying the numbers Radford had found in Paine's notebook. The Neu Standard Gesellschaft of Zürich, the fastest growing secondary bank in Switzerland thanks to its finance director, Wolfgang Thierack. Harper experienced a warm glow of pleasure; Louis might be in semi retirement but he still had an ear to the ground. His euphoria lasted as far as Carfax House, then evaporated when he found Detective Chief Superintendent Marsh and Adrian Carpenter waiting for him.

Carpenter was one of the coming men in the Security Service popularly known as MI5, discreetly referred to as Box by those on the periphery of the trade who wished to impress the less well informed. Variously described as polished, smooth, articulate and clever, he had been a member of the Footlights Review when up at Cambridge and at one time had seriously entertained the idea of joining the acting profession. There were some people in Whitehall who maintained Carpenter had done just that even though he'd never held an Equity card. From 1976 to 1979, he had been seconded to the Foreign and Commonwealth Office as a security adviser and had fitted in so well that he'd frequently been mistaken for a career diplomat. Currently, he was the Assistant Director of Q1, the newly redesignated branch which was reponsible for counter espionage. As such, he'd given evidence before the Security Commission on a number of occasions and had now acquired a judicious manner. He'd also developed the habit of coming straight to the point, something he had rarely been able to do while he was with the Foreign Office.

"I understand you have a proprietary interest in a Staff Sergeant Paine?" he said, even as Harper waved him to a chair.

The way Marsh avoided his gaze and concentrated on the pigeons roosting on the ledge outside the porthole window told Harper that he had been talking out of turn. Knowing the Detective Chief Superintendent, it was unlikely he'd done so from choice.

"I wouldn't put it quite like that," Harper said casually. "In common with certain other branches of the Ministry of Defence, we were informed he was an absentee. Michael Radford, who runs the army desk for me, discovered that Paine was a photo interpreter with the highly sensitive Air Reconnaissance Interpretation Centre at RAF Church Fenton, and I decided we should make it our business to know a little more about him."

"And immediately involved Special Branch?"

"Paine was missing and his wife had been found dead. I merely contacted Detective Chief Superintendent Marsh to see if the army had asked Special Branch for their assistance and he told me they had." Harper raised his voice slightly and said, "Isn't that right, Bill?"

Losing interest in the pigeons outside the porthole window, Marsh turned to face Carpenter. "Absolutely," he said. "Mr Harper then asked me to keep him informed."

"And it didn't occur to either of you that we also should have been kept in the picture?" Carpenter looked from one man to the other, his face in harmony with the incredulous tone of voice.

"We didn't think it necessary," Harper told him cheerfully. "The RAF were satisfied there hadn't been a breach of security and once it had been established that Paine had gone to Switzerland, he was no longer within your jurisdiction."

"He's beyond everyone's jurisdiction now, Cedric."

"Are you trying to tell me something?"

"Paine is dead. His body was discovered yesterday in Arosa buried beneath the floor of a garage belonging to one of several chalets under construction. Someone had put four bullets into his head. Fortunately, a very bright pathologist in Chur realised he was a British soldier and persuaded the police to contact our military attaché in Berne."

The rest was self-evident to Harper. The MA had signalled the Attaché Liaison Staff at the Ministry of Defence and they in turn had contacted the army's Directorate of

Security. The latter had undoubtedly alerted Box who'd advised that news of the latest development in the Paine case should be restricted to those with a need to know. Clearly, Adrian Carpenter had not included the Department of Subversive Warfare in this category.

"Thank you for telling me, Adrian," he said blandly.

"You are, of course, already aware of Paine's friendship with a Master Sergeant Bartowski who is wanted for desertion."

Harper nodded. It was a statement of fact and he would gain nothing by being evasive. The Security Service would have received a full update from the army and they would know that Krystyna Bartowski had asked the Intelligence and Security Company in Berlin if they could put her in touch with Paine.

"You've probably heard of Monika Starnberg too?"

"I have."

"She also has been murdered. Her partially-clad body was found in an Audi saloon which had been left on a local training area near Münster. She had been strangled with a pure silk scarf and the pathologist who carried out the autopsy formed the opinion that death had occurred some forty-eight hours before her body was discovered in the evening of the thirteenth òf March. Furthermore, he was able to say with absolute certainty that the killer had tortured her with a pair of electrodes." Carpenter grimaced to show his profound distaste, then said, "There were extensive burns inside the vagina and rectum."

Killers, Harper thought, plural not singular. The man who'd dumped the Audi on the training area had evidently made a clean getaway and that meant someone had followed him out there in a second vehicle. According to Drew, Monika Starnberg had disappeared from her flat in Frankfurt on the twenty-fourth of February; seventeen days later, her body had been found on the outskirts of Münster, some one hundred and fifty miles to the north. He wondered where she had been held in the interim and what it was the killers wanted from her.

"What are your people doing in Berlin, Cedric?"

It seemed to Harper that Warrant Officer Iremonger had taken it upon himself to keep the world and his wife informed. He'd obviously sent another of his damned signals to the Intelligence Corps depot and they'd passed it on to half of Whitehall.

"Since Paine wrote Bartowski a letter and sent it care of his sister I thought we should find out what he'd said to him."

"And did you?"

Harper shook his head. "The letter was about as informative as a laundry list. It was written on plain notepaper and Paine had deliberately omitted his address. However, he did put his phone number on the back of the envelope, concealed within his service details and the post code of the Manning and Record Office at Exeter. Krystyna Bartowski claims she didn't spot it but she knew the name and was sufficiently worried about her brother to hop a plane to Berlin where she'd met the Paines in 1981."

"Am I to understand that your people have already questioned her?"

It wasn't so much the substance of the question that irritated Harper as the manner in which it was asked. Maybe he was getting touchy in his old age but Carpenter seemed to be inferring that he'd been incredibly stupid.

"How else would we have discovered that Monika Starnberg had been a courier?" he said coldly.

"Delivering what?"

"Money. We know she met Krystyna Bartowski in New York one weekend in the October of '83 and we've reason to believe a wad of dollar bills changed hands."

"Can you prove it?"

"Radford thinks we can."

Radford hadn't said anything of the kind but that didn't deter Harper. Faced with a take-over bid, he was prepared to stretch the truth like a piece of elastic in order to stay in the game.

"Are you sure he isn't still labouring under the illusion that he's a Detective Sergeant in Special Branch, Cedric?"

Carpenter was really enjoying himself; it showed in the arrogant smirk on his face and the barely suppressed crow in his voice. One of his minions had obviously been on to the Regional Crime Squad in Leeds shortly after they'd learned that Paine had been murdered. The County Police Force had then referred him in double quick time to Special Branch and Marsh had been forced to let the cat out of the bag. Carpenter had dragged the Detective Chief Superintendent along, partly because he enjoyed watching his discomfiture and partly because he wanted Harper to realise this was one time he couldn't bluff his way out of an awkward situation.

"I'm not going to apologise," Harper said tersely. "Paine was missing and his wife had apparently met with a fatal accident. We needed to get the feel of things, and I've yet to meet the police officer who'll take an outsider into his confidence. You of all people should know that."

A sharp intake of breath was all that betrayed Carpenter's anger and when he spoke his voice was cool. "Who's running the surveillance operation in Berlin?" he asked. "Drew or Radford?"

Somewhere, someone must have slipped up. As far as Harper could see, it was about the only thing they'd omitted to tell Carpenter. "Drew," he said.

"Then perhaps you would be good enough to let him know that we're taking over."

"You're going to do what?"

Carpenter sighed. "I know you have a reputation for being unorthodox," he said, "but this is ridiculous. You've asked a foreign power to spy on an American citizen. How you managed to persuade Abteilung I to do it beats me, but if word gets out, there'll be one hell of a row."

"Whereas you can guarantee to keep the whole thing under wraps?"

"No, of course I can't, Cedric, but if the Government is going to carry the can when things go wrong, they've every right to insist the operation should be controlled by someone like our Director General who's far more senior than you." Carpenter raised a hand to silence Harper before he had a chance to object, then said, "It's no use venting your spleen on me, I'm only the messenger boy. If you want to contest the decision, you'd better take it up with the Cabinet Office."

"When do you intend to assume control?"

"The British Security Service Organisation in Berlin will take over at 1800 hours local time tonight."

"Then there's not much point in my approaching the Cabinet Office, is there?" said Harper.

"Not a lot. But we'd like either Drew or Radford to stay on for a day or so to liaise with Abteilung I."

Harper wasn't sure what lay behind the request but he could recognise a golden opportunity when there was one in the offing. "I'll leave Radford behind," he said quickly, "he could use the experience."

"You know best, Cedric."

"I assume you'll be covering the Air Reconnaissance Interpretation Centre at Church Fenton?"

"We shall be giving it the full treatment," Carpenter told him. "Subject interviews plus a complete check of all classified documents."

"It would be interesting to know what task Paine was working on before he disappeared." Harper put on a wistful expression. "I'd also like to hear what his colleagues thought of him, but I suppose that's out of the question?"

"You know the form, Cedric."

He certainly did. Once the Security Service moved in, no other agency was allowed to question anyone belonging to the unit or establishment under investigation. Nor were outsiders allowed to sit in on an interrogation.

"Well, there's no harm in asking," he said.

"Quite so." Carpenter pursed his lips. "Of course, there are exceptions to every rule," he said presently, "and in this particular instance, I'm sure we can reach a compromise. If it's any help, we'll let you know who actually worked alongside Paine and you can have a word with them after they've been interviewed by us."

"That sounds very fair, Adrian."

Harper managed to hide a triumphant smile. Whatever Carpenter might like to think, he'd gained more than he'd given away. So what if the Security Service were going to run things in Berlin? Radford would keep him posted and if things went sour, the Department of Subversive Warfare would come out of it smelling like a rose. Furthermore, Carpenter had agreed he could interview the people he wanted to at RAF Church Fenton and he'd obtained that concession without ever mentioning a word about Wolfgang Thierack and the Neu Standard Gesellschaft.

The midfield player gathered the ball, looked up, saw that the right back had moved into an overlapping position and split the defence with a long through ball he could run on to. With no one marking him, the right back took the ball up to the by-line, then crossed it low into the penalty area. Timing his run to perfection, the tall red-haired striker beat the off-side trap and came in like a thunderbolt to meet the cross. All he had to do was make contact with the ball but he wanted to blast it and the goalkeeper into the back of the net. Instead of trapping the ball, he let fly in mid stride and from ten yards out, ballooned it high over the goal posts. His team mates and the dozen or so spectators watching the inter company match on one of the pitches outside the Olympic Stadium chorused their disbelief in no uncertain terms.

Beyond the sports fields a broad avenue linked the Olympic Stadium with Heer Strasse. From their office Radford could see the Coubertin Plaza where Hitler had alighted from his Mercedes limousine before strutting through the triumphant archway into the Roman amphitheatre, there to be captured for posterity by Leni Riefenstahl and her cameramen. Now, almost fifty years on, the home of the Xth Olympiad was just a backdrop for two teams of off-duty soldiers whose fathers in all probability hadn't even been born when Jesse Owens was winning his four gold medals. Radford was still trying to fathom the significance of this piece of homespun philosophy when he heard Drew replace the phone.

"You sounded very circumspect," he said, turning away from the window.

"You don't interrupt Harper when he's in full spate."

"Have we been given our marching orders?" It seemed at least a possibility judging by the odd question Radford had overheard.

"You could say that." Drew picked up his lighter and the packet of cigarettes he'd left on the desk and stuffed them into the pockets of his jacket. "The surveillance op is now under new management; we've been given the elbow and the BSSO is about to climb into the driver's seat."

"Who?"

"The British Security Service Organisation, MI5's away team. Harper wants you to stay on in Berlin as the link man."

"Where are you going then?"

"Zürich, to see a man called Thierack. Seems you were right about Paine; he did have a numbered account, only he's no longer around to enjoy it."

The rest came at breakneck speed. His body had been found in Arosa with four bullet wounds in the head and Bartowski's girlfriend, Monika Starnberg, had also been murdered after being brutally tortured.

"The away team takes over at 1800 hours," Drew continued. "Their controller will call you on this number shortly after six and the two of you can then arrange how to keep in touch."

"Does he have a name?"

" 'Electra'."

"Christ," said Radford. "Someone should tell him that World War Two ended forty years ago."

"Plenty of people already have, but he's not convinced." Drew reached into his trouser pocket, took out a bunch of car keys and played one-handed catch with them while he tried to make up his mind just what he was going to do with the Volkswagen they'd hired from Avis. "If I get a move on, I can catch the Pan Am evening flight to Frankfurt and the connection to Zürich," he said, thinking aloud.

"So why don't I drive you to the airport?" Radford suggested. "We can always leave a message for 'Electra' to let him know where he can reach me."

" 'Electra' is pretty elusive; he could be in any one of half a dozen places. Besides, they won't acknowledge our existence if you don't do things their way." The keys went back into his pocket. "You'd better stay on until you hear from 'Electra'. I'll check the Volkswagen in with the Avis desk at Berlin-Tegel; you can always hire another car if you need one."

"Right."

"And stay away from Krystyna Bartowski; we don't want you spooking her."

"You've already make that very clear," Radford told him, "several times over."

"Good. Then I guess that about covers everything." Drew moved towards the door, then stopped, his exit temporarily arrested by a last-minute thought. "One final thing," he said slowly, "there's no love lost between our department, the Secret Intelligence Service and MI5. For all I know, 'Electra' may be as nice as pie to you but that doesn't mean you have to take everything he tells you on trust."

"You're going to miss your plane if you're not careful," Radford warned.

"Don't you believe it," Drew said, and closed the door behind him.

The football match continued on the pitch below the office, the standard of play becoming more and more scrappy as the light faded in the gathering dusk. When the final whistle blew a few minutes before six, there were no spectators left and even one of the linesmen had pushed off.

'Electra' made contact at exactly 1800 hours, exchanged a few pleasantries with Radford and said he would keep him informed of any developments. He did not think it necessary to give him a contact number and was mildly amused when Radford insisted he should at least take down the name and address of his hotel.

"We're hardly faced with an international crisis," he said laughingly before hanging up on him.

But there was a crisis of sorts. Jiggling the contact breakers until he got a dialling tone, Radford phoned the liaison officer at Abteilung I and learned that the surveillance operation had been terminated at 1730 hours at the request of MI5.

8

Iremonger spotted a vacant space on the opposite side of the road beyond the Berlin Ambassador, figured there was just about enough room for his Opel Manta and cutting across the oncoming traffic, managed to squeeze past a large grey Mercedes and tuck himself in facing a BMW. With a distinctly audible sigh of relief, he then switched off the engine, withdrew the key from the ignition and leaned back in his seat.

"I'm afraid this is the best I can do," he said with all the enthusiasm of a man who had been looking forward to a quiet evening at home before Radford had phoned the office. "We aren't exactly spoiled for choice."

"This is okay," Radford told him. "We passed a place called Café Huber a few yards back down the road. We can watch the hotel from there."

"For how long, sir?"

"Until I've sorted things out."

Radford wished he could be more specific but he didn't know how long it would take him to contact Harper and whether or not he was going to be given credit for acting on his own initiative.

"What do you want the lad to do?"

The lad was a nineteen-year-old lance corporal named Garrold who'd happened to be in the wrong place at the wrong time when Iremonger had been trying to put a surveillance team together.

"He'd better come with us," Radford said. "He'll be too conspicuous sitting out here in the car." The trouble with Garrold was that he looked unmistakably English; he had the kind of features foreigners instinctively associated with the Anglo-Saxon.

The Café Huber was a coffee shop, a wine bar and a restaurant all rolled into one. The décor and atmosphere were intended to reflect the nineteen twenties, an illusion that was sustained by a Dixieland jazz band. In late spring, high summer and early autumn, there were tables and chairs on the sidewalk under an awning; at this time of the year, the only way of keeping the street under observation was from one of the booths in the window. Radford chose one just inside the entrance which gave them a peep view of the Berlin Ambassador diagonally across the street. Leaving Iremonger to order three beers from one of the look-alike blonde waitresses, he made straight for the pay phone outside the men's room.

Radford ducked under the plastic bubble dome, placed all the loose change he had on the shelf above the telephone directories and carefully followed the step by step instructions for making a direct dial international call. When the duty officer at Carfax House answered, he gave his name, read out the number of the pay phone and asked him to make certain Harper contacted him as soon as possible. Two minutes later and twelve Marks fifty pfennigs the poorer, he hung up and waited for the Director to call him back.

The Dixieland jazz band made their first appearance of the evening and ran through a couple of lively numbers. Their intro was greeted by a ripple of applause, then a girl with a sultry voice sang a slow blues number accompanied by a pianist and a double bass. She was just starting her carefully rehearsed encore when Radford had a spot of aggro with a middle-aged German businessman who wanted to phone for a taxi. Fortunately, Harper rang back from his house in West Byfleet before they actually came to blows.

Radford said, "This merger isn't going as well as we'd hoped. As a matter of fact, it looks as though the whole deal has fallen through."

"Are we being squeezed out?" Harper asked.

"It's worse than you think. Our former partners have told the Germans that we're no longer interested and the bottom's dropped right out of the market."

"When did this happen?"

"This evening around five thirty, but I didn't hear about it until after six." The full jazz band started up again and Radford had to raise his voice to make himself heard above the racket. "We're back in with a chance," he continued. "I've managed to recruit a couple of friendly surveyors but only on a very temporary basis."

Using veiled speech was all very well but more often than not it led to confusion and he wondered if the right message was getting through; then Harper said he would have a word with the German consortium in a bid to re-awaken their interest. They were still discussing how Harper would let him know what had transpired when the German businessman reappeared and started tapping on the plastic bubble like a demented woodpecker. In the end, Radford said he would call back whenever an opportunity arose and surrendered the phone.

The girl with the sultry voice was on the stage again when he returned to their booth. A petite brunette with a shapely figure, she was wearing a dark blue dress which clung to her like a second skin. Garrold, who was seated on the inside next to Iremonger, was trying to keep both eyes on the street but it was obviously a bit of an uphill struggle. The Warrant Officer wasn't interested in ogling the unobtainable and preferred the beer.

"Drink up," he told Radford, "I've ordered another round."

"How much do I owe you for the first one?"

"You don't," Iremonger said and aimed a finger.

The chit was peeping coyly out from under a dish of salted peanuts.

"Fifty-six Marks seventy-five for three beers?" Radford whistled. "What do they think they're doing? Giving us a mortgage on the place?"

"The first round always includes a cover charge for the band." Iremonger finished his beer, moved the empty glass aside and helped himself to a handful of nuts. "On top of that, you've got your sales tax plus fifteen per cent service charge."

"I should go easy on the peanuts if I were you," said Radford. "You may have to make the next beer last all night."

"Unless Krystyna puts in an appearance."

If she did, tailing her would pose a few problems for Iremonger and himself. Krystyna Bartowski had met them both face to face and was probably sharp enough to pick them out in a crowd. An awful lot was going to depend on Garrold and he was going to need all the help they could give him.

"We'll use a variation of the old three card trick," he said, sharing his thoughts with Iremonger. "If Miss Bartowski spots anyone, it had better be you or me. Our job is to screen Corporal Garrold. She doesn't know his face so he's the only one who has a chance of staying close to her. Agreed?"

Iremonger nodded. "He's a natural for the job."

"Two final points," Radford continued. "Firstly, if she does go walkabout tonight, I want to know who she meets and where, and secondly, if we have to split up for any reason, we rendezvous back here. Got it?"

Garrold said, "Excuse me, sir, but I think the lady's just surfaced."

Radford glanced over his left shoulder in time to catch a glimpse of Krystyna Bartowski before the hotel doorman moved in front of her to flag down a Mercedes taxicab. Telling the other two to follow her in the Opel Manta, he dug out his wallet and left three twenties under the ashtray to cover their drinks bill. By the time he reached the street, Iremonger had already pulled out from the kerb and was waiting for a break in the oncoming traffic before moving over to the correct side of the road. The black Mercedes taxicab already had a thirty yard lead on him and was disappearing towards Nollendorf Plaza.

Radford looked up and down the road, spotted another cab across the street which was heading in the right direction, and let go with a shrill ear-splitting whistle, then raised one arm aloft for good measure. The cab driver hit the brakes a split second after he'd gone past him, moved out to occupy the centre of the road and tripped the offside indicator to show that he was going to make a U-turn. Radford scurried after him making frantic tick-tack signs to indicate he didn't want the driver to change direction. The U-turn became a side slip that provoked a cacophony of discordant horns from the traffic heading the other way which was forced to move out and around the cab. As he drew abreast, Radford saw that Iremonger was going on round the Nollendorf Plaza and surmised the Mercedes was taking Krystyna Bartowski to the US airbase at Tempelhof.

The middle-aged German businessman appeared from nowhere and tried to shoulder Radford out of the way. He had an attractive Vietnamese girl in tow whom he'd picked up in Huber's and was now clearly intent on getting to know her more intimately in some back street hotel where the desk clerk was used to renting rooms by the hour. There was absolutely no doubt in Radford's mind that his need was the greater and the issue of just who had a prior claim on the taxi simply wasn't negotiable. Smiling apologetically at the Vietnamese girl over the German's shoulder, Radford hit him very hard in the belly, then catching his adversary under the arms, he gently sat him down on the pavement and calmly got into the cab.

Iremonger turned into Bülow Strasse, put his foot down on the accelerator and began to overtake everything in front of him. There was a black Mercedes cab up ahead but it wasn't the same one he'd been following from the Berlin Ambassador. Two converging lines of traffic had merged into one at Nellendorf Plaza and he had a lot of ground to make up. Or had Krystyna Bartowski told her cab driver to swing off into a side street shortly after they'd filtered into

Bülow Strasse? The possibility worried him; the fact that all black Mercedes looked alike and he couldn't recall the licence number made him doubly anxious.

Glancing speculatively at Garrold who was sitting beside him, he said, "I hope you know the licence number of the vehicle we're chasing."

"Not exactly, sir."

"What does that mean in plain English?"

"I remember there were a couple of nines and a three."

"Two nines and a three." Iremonger clucked his tongue. "I suppose that's better than nothing."

The road curved to the right, passed under the railway bridges of the Düppel and Wünsdorf 'S' Bahn lines and merged with Yorck Strasse. Two figure nines and a three; as they approached the intersection with Mehring Damm, Iremonger spotted the Mercedes and knew the driver was going to turn right before he signalled his intention of doing so.

"She's making for Tempelhof base," he told Garrold.

But he was only partially right. A hundred yards from the slip road leading to the original terminal buildings, the cab driver pulled into the kerbside and dropped her off at the U Bahn station. Iremonger drove on past the Mercedes for another twenty yards or so and then stopped. Glancing into the rear view mirror he watched Krystyna Bartowski pay off the cab and walk towards the underground station.

"You'll find a Minnox camera in the glove compartment, Corporal," he said. "Take it with you and get some pix."

"Yes, sir."

"Better get a move on then, lad."

The Mercedes pulled away from the kerb and continued on down Tempelhofer. Alighting from the car, Iremonger positioned himself behind the Opel Manta where he was silhouetted by the headlights of the overtaking traffic.

Radford spotted the familiar figure standing in the road and as the cab swerved round Iremonger, he told his driver to pull up. No one had to draw him a picture; thrusting a ten Mark note at the driver, he bailed out of the cab and started running towards the U Bahn station, Iremonger hard on his heels. Krystyna Bartowski had a head start of at least two minutes on him and although the trains weren't as frequent as they were in the rush hour, every second was vital. He pushed a handful of loose change at the clerk behind the window, told him he wanted two to the end of the line and passed one ticket over to Iremonger as they ran down to the platforms.

An up-train to Tegel was alongside and whoever checked out the down line was going to miss it. Dodging the passengers who were making for the exit, Radford boarded the last coach and stood there between the doors to prevent them closing. As a delaying tactic, it had its limitations but he was able to hold up the train long enough for Iremonger to double back from the other platform and signal a pair of zeros. No sign of the girl, no sign of Garrold, therefore they had to be somewhere on this train. Retreating from the doors, he moved to the other end of the coach far away from the irate guard and sat down.

The route map was displayed in a roof panel directly opposite him across the centre aisle. He noted there were three stops before the inter-zonal boundary with East Berlin, two of which, Mehring Damm and Hallesches Tor, were interchange stations for U Bahn lines 7 and 1 respectively. Radford glanced to his right and quickly sized up the dozen or so passengers in the coach: a typical cross-section of any city anywhere in the world. Preoccupied with their own affairs, not one of them paid the slightest attention to him.

At Mehring Damm, he checked to make sure they hadn't stopped opposite an exit, then got up and moved to the door. Only a few people got off the train and Krystyna Bartowski wasn't among them; leaving it to the last minute, he moved up to the next coach. Although there was still no sign of her in the adjoining car, he could see Garrold through the window in the communicating door and knew he could afford to relax a little.

Hallesches Tor came and went without incident. At

Kochstrasse the usual special announcement was broadcast over the public address system ordering all Allied military personnel to leave the train before it entered East Berlin. The announcement was repeated in French and German, then four minutes later, the doors closed and the train pulled out of the station. Wheels screeching in a nerve-grinding crescendo, it thundered into the tunnel as though the motorman was anxious to complete the short transit journey through the eastern sector in the shortest possible time.

Stadtmitte, Franzosisch Strasse, Bahnhof Friedrichstrasse, Oranienburger Tor, Stettiner Bahnhof and Schwartzkopffstrasse; Radford measured their progress on the route map as they swept through the defunct stations and breathed a little easier when they entered the western sector at Reinickendorfer Strasse. Just as he had anticipated, Garrold left the train at Leopoldplatz two stops further on. It was the last interchange on the line and he assumed Krystyna Bartowski would double back to the Zoo-garten near her original starting point. In doing so, she would be merely following the kind of routine security procedures which were observed by every agent before proceeding to the final rendezvous. A supposition became an established fact when he saw Garrold enter the subway leading to the Spichernstrasse line.

The man who came up behind Radford was wearing rubber-soled shoes and the noise of the departing train was simply an added bonus. He heard nothing, not even a faint swish from the black-jack before the rubber hose filled with lead shot smashed into his skull above the right ear and felled him like a tree.

Wolfgang Thierack left his Volvo in the car park at the Jardin Anglais in Geneva, then walked back over the Pont du Mont-Blanc and turned right. It had taken him just under two and a half hours to reach Geneva by way of Berne and Lausanne but although the motorway had made driving easy, he wished Kalin had chosen a more convenient rendezvous.

A chill breeze swept across the lake and he huddled inside his topcoat, drawing in on himself to seek further protection against the cold. In a few weeks' time, the city would be full of tourists but tonight the quayside was deserted and there was no sign of life aboard the pleasure craft moored alongside the floating pontoons. Across the lake off the jetty Eaux-Vives, the illuminated fountain sent a jet of water soaring thirty feet into the air. Thierack walked on, crossed over on to the opposite side of the road and made his way to the Au Fin Bec in the Rue de Berne.

Kalin was waiting for him at a table for two near the kitchen. As Thierack entered the restaurant, he smiled warmly and raising his right hand, snapped his fingers to catch the head waiter's eye. In the process, he effectively silenced the low background murmur of conversation and made Thierack a temporary focal point of interest for the other diners. Conscious that everyone was watching him, Thierack surrendered his topcoat to the hat-check girl and followed the attentive head waiter to the corner table.

"You found this place without difficulty then," Kalin observed in a loud voice.

Thierack sat down and tried to hide behind the menu. "I could hardly go wrong; you gave me very precise directions," he said quietly.

"Good." Kalin pointed to the bottle in the ice bucket and indicated he wanted the head waiter to fill their glasses. "I thought we'd have an apéritif first and order later."

"Sounds a good idea."

"Champagne, Wolfgang – nothing but the best for the finance director of the Neu Standard Gesellschaft."

Thierack shuddered. Short of actually naming him, Kalin couldn't have made it more obvious who he was. Considering the confidential nature of their business, Bartowski's legal representative was behaving in an irrational and potentially dangerous manner. Had he been drunk, the lawyer could hardly have been more indiscreet, but Kalin was stone-cold sober and knew exactly what he was doing.

"My client is very pleased with the way you've handled his affairs, Wolfgang. He was under the impression that it would take you at least a week to transfer his account to the Volksbank in Dresden. Now here we are two days later and everything's been signed, sealed and delivered."

Thierack glanced round the room. The head waiter had moved away from their table and he was relieved to see that the other diners had lost interest in them. "I was only doing my job," he murmured.

"I told him you'd say that." Kalin reached inside his jacket, took out an envelope and placed it in front of the banker. "Nevertheless, Herr Bartowski feels you should receive some small recompense for services rendered."

"What's in the envelope?" Thierack enquired cautiously.

"Why don't you open it and see for yourself?"

Thierack did so and found the envelope contained a bank slip which showed that an account had been opened in his name with Crédit Suisse in Geneva. The amount on deposit totalled thirty thousand francs and represented exactly half the sum drawn in cash by Kalin two days ago.

"There's more where that came from, Wolfgang. Of course, I know you were hoping I'd give it to you in a brown paper bag, but you're a banker and one must observe certain standards."

"I can't accept this."

"You already have. All you have to do now is transfer Herr Paine's account and the rest is yours."

"No." Thierack made a chopping motion to emphasise the point and knocked over his glass, spilling the champagne on to the tablecloth. The low buzz of conversation died a second time and his embarrassment was further compounded by the head waiter who insisted on replacing his glass along with everything else.

Then Kalin decided to make things even worse. "We were discussing a business proposition," he explained gravely, "and I'm afraid my friend got carried away by his excitement."

The head waiter nodded and smiled understandingly, but Kalin wouldn't let the matter rest. He prattled on, determined that everyone within earshot should know just what was at stake.

"I won't do it," Thierack whispered fiercely when they were alone once more.

"Staff Sergeant Paine is believed to have 378,500 Swiss Francs in his numbered account. This sum, less than the usual commission, is to be transferred forthwith to the Deutsche Volksbank in Dresden and credited to Herr Erich Dollmann."

"Save your breath. I've already told you I won't do it."

"You don't have any choice," Kalin told him calmly. "The deposit you made with Crédit Suisse is only part of the incriminating evidence we have on you. Theft, fraud, embezzlement; I wouldn't be surprised if the police charged you with all three offences."

"You're bluffing; accuse me and you accuse yourself."

"How wrong you are." Kalin smiled, then masked his face behind the palm of his left hand as though he found it almost impossible to restrain his laughter. Both shoulders quivered and when finally he did look up, there were tears in his eyes. "Forgive me," he spluttered, "but it's a long time since I've met anyone who's afforded me so much amusement."

"I doubt you'll be laughing after I've said my piece."

"I'll have left Switzerland long before then, Wolfgang. The police will be acting on information from an anonymous source; by the time they've completed their investigation, they will have all the documentary evidence they need to file charges. Whether their case will be strong enough to obtain a conviction is perhaps debatable but whatever the verdict, you'll never work in a bank again."

Thierack frowned; he still thought Kalin was bluffing, but he couldn't afford to take that chance. Once the police moved in, other banking irregularities would come to light and there was a very real possibility that he would end up in prison. There was however one obvious difficulty the lawyer had apparently overlooked which would allow him to wriggle out from under.

"Aren't you forgetting Herr Paine?" he asked.

"The Englishman will never know." Kalin went through his wallet and took out a small press cutting from the *Zürcher AZ*. "If you didn't confine your reading to the financial pages, you'd know he was dead."

"What?"

"Stefan Bartowski shot him. If you're not careful, the police might charge you with being an accessory." Kalin leaned forward, his manner suddenly very confidential. "After all, it was you who transferred his money to Dresden."

There was a lump the size of a pigeon's egg behind his right ear and the top of his skull felt as if it was about to lift off. In the circumstances, a crowded smoke-filled restaurant coupled with a bunch of jazz musicians doing their best to raise the roof were hardly calculated to relieve a blinding headache. Had Iremonger's Opel Manta not been parked in the vicinity Radford would have given Huber's a wide berth. Had the management refused to admit him, he wouldn't have been too upset about it, but it seemed the minor fracas with the middle-aged German had either gone unnoticed or had long since been forgotten for one of the blonde waitresses greeted him like a long-lost friend.

Iremonger was occupying a corner booth at the back of the restaurant near the swing doors leading to the kitchen. He was nursing a litre-size beer mug and his gloomy expression suggested the evening had not been a riotous success as far as he was concerned. When Radford joined him, he looked up slowly, his eyes eventually registering a double-take as they focused on the band-aid covering the swelling.

"What happened to you?" he breathed.

"The police say I was mugged."

"And were you?"

Radford shrugged. "They could be right. Whoever gave me this lump on the head also stole my wallet."

"When did this happen?"

"Around eight o'clock."

Radford had then spent the next three hours arguing with the doctor in charge of the casualty department at the Rudolf Virchow Hospital who'd wanted to detain him overnight. The X-rays had looked okay and Radford didn't appear to be suffering from concussion but the intern had wanted to play it safe and keep him under observation. Signing a certificate which absolved the hospital of all responsibility was the only way he'd been able to discharge himself.

"Miss Bartowski returned at nine twenty. I was sitting in my car watching the hotel when she arrived."

"She could have left again soon afterwards."

Iremonger shook his head. "I doubt it, I hung around until after eleven."

"What about Garrold?"

"I've not seen him. He hasn't checked in with the guard-room at Dempsey Barracks either."

There was always the possibility that he was still shadowing the contact Krystyna Bartowski had met but Radford was inclined to doubt it. One could hope for the best but it was more realistic to assume that he was at least three hours adrift and take it from there.

"This Lance Corporal Garrold of yours," he said thoughtfully, "how reliable is he?"

"Never known him not to be."

"Then I think you'd better alert the Military Police."

"Maybe we should give him another hour or so?" Iremonger suggested tentatively. "I mean, we'd look pretty silly if we hit the panic button and Garrold walked in here large as life a few minutes later."

Harper could certainly use the extra time to square things with Abteilung I. When Radford had phoned him from the hospital, he hadn't been having much luck with his German friends and until their stop-gap operation was officially authorised, they were all skating on very thin ice. But at the end of the day, this was only a minor consideration.

"We can't afford to sit on this." Radford jerked a thumb towards the street. "We've got a soldier out there who could be in serious trouble and we need all the help we can get."

9

A discordant jangle set his head throbbing again and woke him from a restless sleep. For a moment or two, Radford wasn't entirely sure where he was, then in the chink of grey light between the partially-drawn curtains, he recognised the solid-looking wardrobe that was so typical of the hotel furniture. Rolling over on to his left side, he reached out for the telephone and lifted the receiver.

Iremonger said, "They've found Garrold," then cleared his throat and fell silent as though he'd suddenly lost the thread of what he'd intended to say next.

"Is he all right?" Radford asked with a sense of foreboding.

"Garrold was still alive when they put him in the ambulance; he died before they could get him on the operating table."

While drawing the curtains in her bedroom, a housewife in the Siemensstadt District had seen the nineteen-year-old Lance Corporal run into a dimly-lit alleyway off the Altweg pursued by two men. A few minutes later, the same two men had reappeared and strolled off towards the 'S' Bahn station at Wernerwerk. At first, the housewife had allowed her husband to persuade her that the younger man had obviously outrun the other two and got clean away but the more she'd thought about the incident, the more uneasy she had become. Unable to get to sleep, she'd slipped out of bed and without waking her husband, had tiptoed into the hallway and phoned the police. A prowl car had arrived

111

on the scene at one thirty-five am, some three and a quarter hours after she had first seen Garrold.

"The police found him near one of the warehouses fronting the River Spree," Iremonger continued. "He'd been stabbed in the chest and stomach and dumped in a rubbish skip. The bastards who did it took everything he had – wristwatch, ID card, camera, wallet; even the loose change in his pockets."

"What's that about a camera?" Radford asked sharply.

"I gave him a Minox infra-red so that he could photograph the contact who met Krystyna Bartowski."

"Who else knows about it?"

"Jesus Christ," Iremonger said angrily, "one of my junior NCOs ends up on a cold slab in a mortuary and all you can think about is the fucking Minox – sir."

The 'sir' was an explosive punctuation mark and far more effective than any of the expletives.

"I asked you a question," Radford said icily, "and I'm still waiting for an answer. Get a hold of yourself and for God's sake act like a soldier. Tell me who else knows about the camera."

Iremonger took a deep breath. "No one," he said. "I'm sure of that. I was the one who had to identify the body. The Germans had tagged him as a John Doe until our MPs filed a missing person's report with the Polizei. It was me who told them that Garrold's wristwatch, ID card and wallet were missing."

"Who's handling the investigation? The Kriminal-polizei?"

"Yes, sir, but our Special Investigation Branch also wants a statement from you. You're supposed to report to the Provost Marshal's office at Headquarters Berlin at 08.00 hours."

Radford peered at his wristwatch, saw that it was ten minutes to six and reckoned he would be pushed to fit in a round trip to Siemensstadt in the time. "Are you going to pick me up from the hotel, Mr Iremonger?"

"I can do, sir." There was an infinite amount of weariness in his voice as though life in general and one officer in particular had become an intolerable burden.

"Good," said Radford. "I'll expect you at six fifteen. And bring an interpreter with you; my German isn't up to much."

"Something tells me we're going the long way round."

"Just a slight detour."

"The Provost Marshal won't like it if you're late, sir."

"He can always complain to London and see where that gets him," Radford said and hung up.

They were an hour ahead of England and he had a mental picture of Harper sound asleep in bed blissfully unaware that he would shortly receive yet another bombshell. Radford had disturbed him twice during the night; the first time towards midnight when he'd phoned him from the hospital and then again shortly after Iremonger had informed the military police that Garrold was missing. Now he was about to rouse Harper for the third and decidedly unlucky time. He dialled the international and area codes followed by the subscriber's number and then sat there on the edge of the bed listening to it ringing out. Some two minutes later a surprisingly alert Harper answered the phone.

Ever since the crisis had started yesterday evening, they had been forced to communicate in veiled speech and as a result had developed a fine understanding of one another's euphemisms. Still acting out the scenario that they were both executives of some international business corporation, he was able to inform Harper that the junior member of the negotiating team had been rendered non effective, which he hoped was a subtle way of telling him that Garrold had been murdered. In return, Harper gave Radford to understand that he would keep the army and the BSSO off his back and ensure the Kriminalpolizei co-operated with him.

Radford thanked him and put the phone down. Stripping off, he went into the bathroom and stood under a lukewarm shower before shaving with an open cut-throat. Returning

113

to the bedroom he took out a clean shirt from the chest of drawers and put on his second suit which, unlike the other, didn't look as though he'd slept in it. He unlocked his briefcase, took out the spare traveller's cheques he'd put aside for emergencies and making a mental note that he'd better report the numbers of the stolen ones to American Express as soon as they opened, went downstairs to the lobby. Iremonger arrived promptly at six fifteen and alone.

"I'm a Class 1 interpreter," Iremonger said, pre-empting any possible misunderstanding.

"Obviously a man of many talents."

Iremonger smiled grimly. "Just enough to get by, sir."

It had rained during the early hours of Saturday morning and the air smelt fresh and clean. Turning right on Spandauer Damm, they drove towards the city centre, then headed north on Fürstenbrunner Weg to run parallel with the inner ring motorway. Two miles farther on, the roads diverged and swinging north-west they passed over the 'S' Bahn and crossed the River Spree by the Rohrdamm bridge.

Alteweg lay on the fringe of the residential area directly behind the wharfs and to the right of the bridge. The alleyway where Garrold had been stabbed to death was closed to traffic and a uniformed police officer was on duty at the junction just in case anyone felt inclined to ignore the diversion signs. Leaving Iremonger to lock the car after parking it farther up the road, Radford walked back to the alleyway and stood there looking at the warehouses on either side. He tried to put himself in Garrold's shoes but couldn't fathom what had prompted the young lance corporal to duck into a blind alley where the only source of light came from a solitary lamp above one of the loading bays. However, it had been a dark night and perhaps he hadn't realised he'd turned into a cul-de-sac until it was too late.

"Beats me why he came this way at all," Radford said when Iremonger joined him. "He couldn't have been thinking straight otherwise he would have stuck to the residential area."

"Garrold was a first class athlete; he must have thought he could outrun them."

Krystyna Bartowski had returned to the Berlin Ambassador at twenty minutes past nine which meant she must have rendezvoused with her contact shortly after leaving the U-Bahn at Leopoldplatz. After they had parted company, Garrold had then followed the contact to Siemensstadt. Although there were a number of imponderables, it was the only explanation Radford could think of that fitted the known timetable of events.

"Did you happen to notice if Garrold's hands were bruised or swollen?"

"I didn't think to look," Iremonger admitted candidly. "I could ask the SIB when we get back if you like?"

"It's not that important; I was just curious to know if he'd tried to defend himself."

The rubbish skip where Garrold's body had been found had been taped off and a police photographer was busy shooting it from all angles. Directing his efforts was a muscular dark-haired man in a thigh-length black leather jacket who looked as though he might be a useful light heavyweight.

"I think we'll have a word with that man over there," said Radford.

"I doubt he'll welcome us with open arms."

"Tell him I'm a British Intelligence Officer and let's see where that gets us."

Iremonger nodded, took a deep breath and then in a loud voice that carried all of twenty-five yards, he introduced Radford in fluent German and asked if they could come forward to view the scene of the crime. The detective sergeant answered him in almost perfect English and said he had no objections provided they didn't get in his way.

"Bang goes your hope of a quiet tête-à-tête," Iremonger muttered as they moved forward.

"You want to bet?"

Radford walked on past the skip to the far end of the blind alley and turned about. There were no gutters but the pronounced camber of the cobbled roadway was a natural watershed and there were a couple of drains, one left and forward of the skip, the other right and to the rear. Crouching over the nearest drain, Radford slipped both hands through the grating, took a firm grip on the metal bars and lifted it clear. The early morning rain had washed everything away except for a soggy wrapper from a packet of cigarettes.

"What are you doing, Captain?"

Radford looked up and smiled at the detective sergeant. "Lance Corporal Garrold was on duty. He had a Minox infra-red camera and we believe he may have photographed one of the men who subsequently murdered him."

"The camera is missing?"

"It wasn't found among his personal effects."

"Then obviously they stole it."

"Not necessarily, Herr Wachtmeister." Radford replaced the grating and straightened up. "Mr Iremonger here tells me he was a very good NCO, the kind of young man who was unlikely to lose his head in an emergency. The way I see it, Garrold would have hidden the camera as soon as he realised he was trapped in a blind alley."

"And the drain would have made a good hiding place – yes?"

"No. The men who chased him into the alley were hard on his heels and they would have pounced on him as he tried to lift the grating."

Radford circled the skip. The steel container was chest high and measured some twelve feet by eight. It was full almost to the brim with bits of cardboard, packing crates that had been reduced to matchwood, strands of baling wire and umpteen plastic bags crammed with wood shavings. Garrold had been lying face down on top of a heap of plastic bags, his life blood staining the shavings a russet brown.

116

"That's the first place they would have looked," the German told him.

"And maybe they found the camera if it was lying on top of the rubbish," said Radford. "But if it had been buried underneath, they weren't here long enough to conduct a proper search. From what I hear, the Hausfrau who phoned the local police station said they were only in the alley a couple of minutes."

"You're a very persistent man, Captain."

"You reckon?" Radford climbed into the skip and began passing out the plastic bags.

"Searching this little lot could take us all day," Iremonger complained wearily.

But he was wrong there. Less than an hour later and long before they'd checked a third of the bags, Radford found the Minox. It had fallen almost to the bottom of the skip and was wedged into a corner where it was partially concealed by a cardboard box. There was a slight difference of opinion as to who should retain the camera. In the end, Radford persuaded the police sergeant that for technical reasons, the film should be developed by 261 Intelligence and Security Company on the understanding that a complete set of prints would be produced for the Kriminalpolizei.

Harper stirred the mug of instant coffee with a paperknife, creating a minor whirlpool that sucked in the last globule of powdered milk which until then had been floating on the surface. Normally he would have turned up his nose at such a pale imitation of the real thing, but he had come up to town on the first train from West Byfleet and had had to give breakfast a miss. Worse still, his PA had gone away for the weekend taking with her the only key to the cabinet where the electric percolator and the ground coffee were kept. The instant variety he owed to the Duty Officer and he was pleasantly surprised to find the coffee tasted better than it looked.

His first act on reaching the office shortly after seven

fifteen had been to phone the Police President of West Berlin. They had met at an international symposium on counter terrorism in May 1979 which had been sponsored by Interpol Headquarters at St Cloud and had kept in touch ever since, exchanging Christmas and birthday cards. On a more practical level, the Police President was aware that he owed the Department of Subversive Warfare a favour. In July 1981 he had circulated a description of Gudrun Ehrhardt-Bach, a prominent member of the Baader-Meinhof group, who had disappeared from West Berlin after participating in the murder of two American servicemen, and it had been Drew who had eventually tracked her down to a College of Further Education where she had been teaching German.

Berlin was one hour ahead of London and the Police President was invariably at his desk by seven forty-five, Saturdays included; when Harper phoned, it transpired that he'd arrived even earlier than usual. The fact that the Police President had already been briefed about the Garrold case by his own people had made it that much easier for Harper to obtain the kind of tie-up with the Kriminalpolizei that Radford had hinted at.

Taking the appropriate steps to ensure the army kept off Radford's back was, however, a much more complex business. From the outset, Harper had known that a direct approach to the proper staff branch at the Ministry of Defence would get him nowhere. The Provost Marshal's Department would refer any such request to the Adjutant General and he in turn would take it up with the Permanent Under Secretary. Apart from the fact that Harper had precious little influence at that rarefied level, the PUS was not one of his more ardent fans, something he had made abundantly clear on several previous occasions. He had therefore chosen the indirect approach and had briefed his friendly acquaintance in the Cabinet Office in sufficient detail to ensure the weekend started badly for the Director General of MI5. And in this instance, if the weekend started badly for the head of the Security Service, it

118

wouldn't be long before Adrian Carpenter, the assistant director of Q1 heard about it.

Had he been a gambler, Harper would have wagered that Carpenter would be knocking at his door between ten minutes to and ten minutes after nine o'clock. Had Harper found any takers, he would have lost his bet. One minute before eight thirty, a puzzled Duty Officer came through on the office intercom to announce that Mr Adrian Carpenter had just entered Carfax House and was on his way up to the sixth floor.

Yesterday, Carpenter had rubbed his nose in the mire, this morning he was about to eat humble pie. A lesser man would have savoured the moment but Harper hastily swallowed the rest of the coffee, left the mug in his PA's office and walked down the corridor to meet Carpenter as he stepped out of the lift.

He looked decidedly out of sorts and acted like it. "I've just had my head bitten off, thanks to you, Cedric," he said testily. "I'm not denying that our BSSO people in Berlin made a monumental cock-up but as a matter of common courtesy I think you might have had the decency to have it out with me face to face instead of going behind my back."

"I'm not in the habit of going behind anyone's back," Harper told him without batting an eyelid. "The situation was taken out of my hands once the army learned that one of their soldiers had been murdered. How do you suppose the MOD feels about me? Before the day's much older, I'll have the PUS breathing down my neck." He walked Carpenter into his office, steered him to a chair and closed the door. "I'm sorry to hear your Director's been gunning for you," he continued, "but I see no point in wasting time on mutual recrimination. We either stand together or we go under, it's as simple as that."

"What do you suggest we do?"

"Well, we certainly don't want the military police and the SIB putting their big feet into it, do we?" Harper smiled fleetingly, then went on as though they were of a like mind. "So I recommend you instruct the head of BSSO to have a quiet word with the General Officer Commanding British Troops Berlin to impress upon him that Her Majesty's Government will regard it as a very serious breach of security if any of his minions question Radford too closely about the surveillance operation. As far as the army is concerned, Lance Corporal Garrold was robbed and murdered while off duty. Furthermore, they're not to take any disciplinary action against Warrant Officer Iremonger."

"What about the civilian police?"

"I've already taken care of them."

"They're not likely to make any waves then?" Carpenter wanted to be assured that every 'i' had been dotted and every 't' crossed before he committed himself.

"Not after their President has made his views known."

"One could hardly ask for more."

"I can," said Harper. "For a start, I want a much tighter rein kept on Krystyna Bartowski."

"No. No, that's out of the question."

"You're not going to give me that old Foreign Office routine again, are you, Adrian? In view of what's happened in the last twelve hours, they've got nothing to fear from the US State Department. We've every reason to put Krystyna Bartowski under surveillance."

"I thought we'd agreed to allow the Kriminalpolizei to handle this case? If they catch us following the American girl, it will cease to be a straightforward murder investigation."

Carpenter was fighting a rearguard action. His superiors wanted the girl left alone until they'd had time to check her out with the US Intelligence agencies and he'd been detailed to warn everyone off. Even if he was privy to all the facts, Harper doubted if he would be able to extract the truth from him. The way Carpenter had used the police investigation as an argument for doing nothing was an example of his outstanding ability to think on his feet and extemporise. Besides, Radford would now have a pretty free hand in Berlin and there were other concessions to be had for the taking.

"You have a point," Harper said agreeably. "After all, we don't want a repeat of yesterday's fiasco when the left hand didn't know what the right was doing. That's why it's essential we define our respective areas of operational responsibility. Logically, my Department should have a free hand in Europe while you concentrate on the UK. Agreed?"

"It seems a tidy arrangement," Carpenter said cautiously.

"Of course, you and I will have to ensure there is a constant two way flow of information, otherwise the whole set-up will come unstuck."

"Quite."

"And, in this connection," Harper continued remorselessly, "I shall want a cassette of every interview your investigators have with Paine's former colleagues at the Air Reconnaissance Interpretation Centre."

"Surely a résumé of each one would be sufficient?"

"I don't think so, Adrian. My people may uncover certain facts that need to be verified and it would be a ridiculous waste of time if we went over the same ground again." There was a second's pause, then Harper delivered the final knife thrust. "I know I have the backing of the Cabinet Office on this," he said quietly.

"Then there's nothing more to be said, is there?"

"Only that you might like to use my secure telephone to call Berlin. The sooner your man out there has a word with the GOC, the happier we'll all be."

"Right."

"And while you're doing that," said Harper, "I'll have my Duty Officer type out a brief memorandum to the Cabinet Office outlining the division of operational responsibilities we've agreed to."

The images began to appear. A sphere gradually became a round, moon-like face; a shadowy figure, a man in a light topcoat; rimless glasses, short dark hair that was barely visible beneath a snappy fedora. Definitely a Yank, the corporal decided. And the blonde with him was a bit of all right if her shapely legs were anything to go by. Hard to tell where Garrold had taken the shot, but there were others, though the girl wasn't in any of them. A small apartment house on a street corner that could be anywhere in Berlin, the man in the fedora about to use his pass key to enter the building.

The corporal peered a little closer, noticed the oblong plate on the wall above the second floor windows to the left of the entrance and smiled to himself, knowing that if he blew that section up, the street would no longer remain anonymous.

10

The dentists were departing when Radford arrived at the Hotel Berlin Ambassador. Some of them were still ebullient but most of those who were sitting in the lobby surrounded by their luggage looked subdued and somewhat hungover as though they'd had one too many drinks the night before and were now thoroughly regretting it. The small scrum which had formed around the reception desk were just plain impatient and aggressive with it. Every man seemed to think he had only to ask for his bill in a loud voice and wave a credit card at the two harassed girls behind the counter to get immediate attention. Avoiding the crush, Radford positioned himself on the fringe, directly opposite the filing cabinet containing the individual accounts, waited until one of the girls opened the top 'A' to 'F' drawer and then pounced.

"My name's Rushmore." He leaned across the counter, placed a hand on her right elbow to detain her and smiled apologetically. "Henry H. Rushmore, US Consular Office, West Berlin. You have a Fräulein Krystyna Bartowski staying here – room 518 or some such number?"

The ruse worked just the way he'd hoped it would. The girl was rushed off her feet and didn't know if she was coming or going. In the circumstances, it was hardly surprising that hotel security went by the board; the right drawer was open in the filing cabinet and it was all too easy to flip through the individual accounts filed under the initial letter 'B'.

"Room 429," the girl said, correcting him.

Radford thanked her and moved away towards the lifts before she thought to ask him what he wanted. Alighting at the fourth floor, he followed the directional signs to the left and tapped on the door of 429. In fluent German, Krystyna Bartowski told him it wasn't locked and to come on in.

Her bags were stacked in the narrow entrance awaiting collection and it was evident she'd assumed he was one of the hotel porters. Closing the door behind him, Radford pushed the button in the handle to lock it, then moved into the room.

Krystyna Bartowski was seated at the dressing table packing her make-up into a vanity case. Her eyes widened and did a double-take when she caught sight of him in the mirror.

"What are you doing here?" she asked him calmly.

"You invited me in."

"That was a mistake. I thought you were the porter to collect my bags."

"Seems I arrived only just in time then."

If the Special Investigation Branch had had their way, he would still be at Headquarters Berlin fielding their questions as best he could. The officer in charge of the detachment had become increasingly annoyed with his constant references to the Official Secrets Acts and had finally threatened to charge him under Section 69 of the Army Act with 'Conduct Prejudicial to the Maintenance of Good Order and Military Discipline' unless he adopted a more co-operative attitude. Then the General Officer Commanding British Troops Berlin had intervened through the person of the Deputy Assistant Provost Marshal and the SIB officer had been obliged to let him go, much to Iremonger's relief.

"You want to tell me about this man?" Radford showed her one of the photographs Lance Corporal Garrold had taken.

"You've been following me." Krystyna Bartowski managed to sound both indignant and amazed.

124

"How did you guess?"

"I don't think I like your attitude, Captain Radford."

"You're the second person this morning to tell me that," he said. "But I'm not asking for a testimonial, I just want you to tell me what you know about this man."

"Give me one good reason why I should?"

"Because the NCO who took this photograph was subsequently stabbed to death in an alley off the Alteweg in the Siemensstadt District."

"And you think there's a connection?"

Her cool, almost insolent detachment angered him. A nineteen-year-old soldier had snuffed it before the ambulance men could get him to a hospital and she had taken the news as calmly as if she'd been listening to a weather forecast.

"You bet I do," he snapped.

"Yes, well, I guess I'd feel the same in your shoes." Krystyna avoided his gaze and looked down at the contents of her vanity case as if to satisfy herself she hadn't forgotten anything. "I'm sorry one of your noncoms has been murdered," she said quietly, "but I don't see how I can help you. The man in the photograph is a complete stranger, he just stopped me to ask the way to Finkle's."

"Don't give me that crap; it was a pre-arranged meeting. You took a cab out to Tempelhof, then rode the U Bahn, switching from one line to another to see if anyone was following you."

"There's a much simpler explanation, Captain Radford, but I haven't the time to waste telling you."

"How would you like it if I called the police?"

"You'd be doing me a favour." Krystyna closed the lid of her vanity case and pushed the catch home, using more force than was strictly necessary. "I'm tired of being harassed by you and I'm going to put a stop to it right now."

"You're going to swear out a complaint?"

"That's the general idea."

"You don't mind missing your plane?" Radford said artfully.

A tiny frown and a surreptitious glance at her wristwatch gave him the clue to what Krystyna Bartowski was thinking. Any moment now, one of the hotel porters would arrive to collect her baggage and with a plane to catch, she didn't want any unnecessary complications.

"I don't know what I'm getting so uptight about," she said eventually. "Sure, I asked the doorman to get me a cab but I didn't tell the driver to take me to Tempelhof. I wanted to go to the Tiergarten and when I realised we were heading in the wrong direction, I made him stop the car and I got out. We just happened to be near the U Bahn and it seemed a good idea to use it."

"To get to the Tiergarten?"

"Yes."

"Via Leopoldplatz?"

"So I went the long way round. So what? I got on the wrong train at first and had to switch."

"Why were you going to the Tiergarten at that time of night?"

"Jesus, you don't give up, do you?" Krystyna went over to the wardrobe and began checking the drawers. It allowed her to turn her back on him so that he couldn't see her expression. "If you must know, it was my last night in Berlin and I was tired of eating in the hotel. One of the desk clerks suggested I try the Café Wisemann in the Bellevue Allee and I thought I'd see what the place had to offer."

"You were back here by nine-twenty."

"I didn't have much to celebrate."

"You've heard the news about Monika Starnberg then," Radford said.

"What are you talking about?"

"She's dead, so is Harry Paine – someone put four bullets into his head. Your brother's girlfriend had been strangled with her own scarf."

"When did this happen?" This time her voice sounded

126

as though she was making a determined effort to stay cool and collected.

"We're still waiting for the post mortems," Radford told her. "However, it appears Monika Starnberg was found in her car which had been left on the local military training area outside Münster. Paine, on the other hand, had been lured to a partially-built house in the Swiss ski resort of Arosa."

"And you think Stefan is responsible?"

"He's the most likely candidate."

"You're crazy."

Krystyna closed the wardrobe and walked into the bathroom, ostensibly still checking that she'd packed everything while continuing to tell him exactly why Stefan was innocent and why the Berlin trip had been such a fiasco. She was still going strong about the latter when the porter arrived to collect her bags and found he couldn't get into the room.

"I locked the door," Radford informed her.

"Then you'd better unlock it pretty damn quick."

Radford went out into the hall, let the porter in and stood there while he collected her bags. There was no way he could detain Krystyna Bartowski against her will. He might think her story was pure fabrication but proving it was a different matter and the Kriminalpolizei weren't going to arrest an American citizen unless they had something they could pin on her. They had made that very clear when he and Iremonger had delivered the prints. Besides which, they were far more concerned to trace the man whom Garrold had photographed with her and again when he was about to enter an apartment house on Wernerwerk. The order in which the photographs had been taken made him a prime suspect and provided enough circumstantial evidence for them to bring him in for questioning.

"Now are you satisfied?"

The question intruded upon his thoughts and brought him back to reality. "No, I'm not," he said.

"I guess there's no pleasing some people."

127

Krystyna put on a thigh-length reefer jacket, then tucked the vanity case into a holdall and zipped it up. Watching her, Radford found himself wishing that she was just an attractive schoolteacher from Chicago, Illinois.

"I'm about to check out." She straightened up and looked him in the eye. "I don't think you can stop me, much as you'd like to."

"There'll be another time."

"Don't hold your breath, Captain."

Radford followed her along the corridor, rode down to the lobby in the same lift and parted company without saying another word. Leaving the hotel, he turned right and walked down the street towards Nollendorf Plaza where Iremonger had parked his car and got in beside him.

"How did you get on?" Iremonger asked.

"Not too well. As a matter of fact, the lady was very unco-operative."

"So what do we do now?"

"Miss Bartowski will be leaving the hotel any moment now," Radford told him. "I'd like to follow her out to the airport to see where she's going."

Radford was not the only one to see Krystyna Bartowski off at the airport. An elderly man loitering near the TWA check-in desk watched her enter the departure lounge, waited until her flight was airborne, then strolled over to the bank of pay phones in the main concourse and made a call to a woman living in the Wilmersdorf District of West Berlin, ostensibly to let her know that her niece had just left for Frankfurt. A few minutes later, the woman spoke to a second cut-out in Neukölln and from there the message eventually reached Dollmann via a third intermediary in the Pankow District who in turn walked it along the corridor to Leber's office on the second floor of the State Security Building.

"Our pigeon has just taken off," he announced baldly.

"'The Actor' must have given an award-winning performance," Leber observed with considerable satisfaction.

"It would seem so, but we'll know that for sure if she goes on to Paris."

"Has he told you how it went?" Leber asked.

"No, he was told that we would get in touch with him in due course. On the other hand, we've received a report from one of the guardians to the effect that everything went off without a hitch."

"So what are you worried about, Erich?"

It was impossible to hide anything from Leber. Even if you were outwardly calm, he had an uncanny instinct for sensing the tension and anxiety lurking beneath the surface more accurately than any polygraph test ever could. It was this faculty more than anything else which had made his reputation in the Gestapo during World War Two.

"It's probably nothing," Dollmann said reluctantly, "but the operator who was monitoring the West Berlin Police waveband last night picked up a flash report from a prowl car in the Siemensstadt District. The officers concerned were responding to an emergency call from a housewife living in a block of flats on the Alteweg. Shortly after arriving in the neighbourhood, they found a young male Caucasian with serious stab wounds lying in a rubbish skip. The victim, who had apparently been robbed, died on the way to hospital."

"And this should concern us?"

" 'The Actor' lives nearby and I wondered if there might be a connection."

"Not two minutes ago, you said that according to one of the guardians everything had passed off without a hitch."

"He could have been lying," Dollmann said quietly.

Leber picked up a pencil and keeping the point uppermost, tapped it against his desk making a sound like a metronome on a slow beat. If the guardian had lied, then something must have gone terribly wrong and that opened up a whole range of new possibilities, none of which appealed to him. The KGB in the person of Major General Vasili Petrovich Yagoda had embroiled his department in a small clandestine war which was rapidly expanding and had to be contained before it got completely out of hand.

"Put 'The Actor' in quarantine, Erich," he said, finally reaching a decision. "I don't want any of our people to approach him unless they have my express permission to do so."

"I'll pass the word on to his guardians."

"Of course, I'm only thinking aloud," Leber ruminated, "but suppose we didn't warn them off and they were picked up by the opposition? How much damage would we suffer if they talked?"

"We'd lose a cut-out and she in turn could give Abteilung I the names of one or two other small fry." Dollmann frowned; those were the irrefutable facts but there were others which were harder to evaluate. "You can bet the opposition will make the most of it," he said thoughtfully. "They will build up a minor setback for us into a major victory for them. There's no telling how that will affect the morale of our people on the other side of the wall."

"Do you know what angers me most about this operation?" Leber stopped using the pencil as a drumstick and tried flexing it like a ruler instead. "The fact that it's being executed for the benefit of a few greedy men in the Kremlin who've been lining their own pockets and now have the effrontery to expect us to save their skins. The operation is entirely unofficial; it has been badly planned and mounted in a hurry by Yagoda who's probably just as big a crook as his masters are. Furthermore, it started to go badly wrong from the moment it was launched." Leber looked up and met Dollmann's gaze unflinchingly. "The English have a saying, Erich – don't throw good money after bad."

"We're going to abandon our people," Dollmann said and was mildly surprised to discover he didn't care.

"It would be more accurate to say that we're going to allow matters to take their natural course. If Bartowski's sister takes the bait we've laid, we'll deal with her but if she doesn't like the smell and walks away from it, we won't go after her."

"Dare we back off?" Dollmann asked, smiling. "I mean, from what you've told me, this Yagoda is a real poisonous shit and I certainly wouldn't like to be in your shoes if he got the impression we'd sold him short."

The pencil Leber was flexing suddenly snapped in two making a noise like a small pistol shot. "Nor I in yours, Erich," he said in a harsh croak.

The lakeside villa was eight miles south of Zürich on the road to Kusnach. The neighbouring properties on either side were a good fifty yards away and were hidden from view by tall conifers. Moored alongside the private landing-stage was a cabin cruiser which Drew estimated was worth at least sixty thousand pounds. Like the Porsche sports car parked next to the Volvo in the double garage, the boat was one of the expensive toys Wolfgang Thierack had acquired in the six years he had been the finance director of the Neu Standard Gesellschaft.

Drew had made his acquaintance earlier that morning. He had simply walked into the bank, told one of the cashiers behind the counter that he represented Rand and Goodbody, diamond merchants of Hatton Garden, and that he wished to see Herr Thierack about opening an investment account. Rand and Goodbody had acted on behalf of the Department of Subversive Warfare on a number of occasions in the past and although this informal association had been terminated by mutual agreement a long time ago, Drew had retained one of their business cards with his name printed on it. Still in mint condition, it had helped to get him into Thierack's office; his second-hand knowledge of the diamond market had done the rest and he had been able to discuss a business proposition without arousing the banker's suspicion. The subterfuge had enabled Drew to put a face to the name Harper had given him; he had then kept the bank under observation and had tailed Thierack back to his lakeside villa in an anonymous Renault which he'd rented from the Hertz agency on arrival at Zürich airport.

Leaving the car where he'd parked it on the grass verge beyond the entrance, Drew walked back to the villa and rang the bell inside the front porch. Moments later, the door was opened by a slim, greying man neatly attired in a pair of very dark navy slacks and matching waistcoat over a white shirt and black tie.

"Herr Thierack is expecting me," Drew said in bastardised German and stepped past him.

There were four doors off the square-shaped hall, two facing one another left and right of the entrance and two more beyond the centrally positioned open staircase. The rooms at the front of the house didn't have much of a view but those at the back obviously looked out on to the lake. Mentally flipping a coin, Drew tried the one facing him on the right and walked into the dining room, the elderly manservant still plucking at the sleeve of his jacket while nervously asking him who he was and what he wanted.

Wolfgang Thierack was seated at a refectory table, his back to the serving hatch from the kitchen, the french windows to the patio and landing-stage to his right. He was about to have lunch and had changed out of the conservative business suit he'd worn to the office into a pair of checked pants and a sports jacket. More than a little surprised to find he had company, he sat there gaping at Drew, temporarily lost for words. So too was the plumpish woman who was standing by the sideboard with a ladle in one hand and the lid of the soup tureen in the other. Then suddenly everyone started talking at once, the servants in German wanting to know if they should send for the police, Thierack in stilted English demanding to know what gave him the right to invade the privacy of his home.

"I'm here on behalf of Staff Sergeant Harry Paine," Drew told him above the noise.

He didn't have to say anything else. After a momentary hesitation Thierack nodded his head as if the brief explanation had made perfect sense to him; then turning to his housekeeper, he told her to lay an extra place at the table.

"We're having clear soup followed by charcoal grilled

steak and a green salad," Thierack informed him. Although his voice sounded calm enough, there was a nervous facial tick directly below his right eye.

"Sounds fine to me," Drew said.

"So how do you like your steak done?"

"Black on the outside, blood-red on the inside."

Thierack repeated the order to his housekeeper in German, waited until both servants had left the dining room, then said, "Who sent you? Was it Kalin?"

The name meant nothing to Drew. "Kalin or Stefan Bartowski," he said casually, "does it matter who I take my orders from? Right now, all that should concern us is Paine's numbered bank account."

"It's no use trying to pressurise me. Kalin must know that the instructions he gave me can't be effected overnight."

"You're not going to give me that old banking procedures routine, are you?"

He'd already learned a lot by pretending to know more than he did but Drew knew by the way Thierack narrowed his eyes that he'd overplayed his hand.

"I think you are a confidence trickster, Mr Drew."

The choice of words was a trifle quaint but there was nothing cute about his demeanour. His attitude had hardened and Drew realised he would have to put the fear of God into him if he was to loosen his tongue again.

"You're really something, Herr Thierack. I mean, you sit there looking down your nose at me as though I'm a bad smell and all the while you've got blood on your hands."

"Don't be ridiculous . . ."

"Harry Paine was a client of yours; the day before yesterday some builders in Arosa happened to come across his grave. Someone had put four bullets into his head at close range and then buried him under the floor of a garage."

"I read about it in the newspapers; there was a small paragraph on page two of *Zürcher AZ*." Thierack shrugged. "Naturally I was sorry to learn that Mr Paine had been murdered but I can't be held responsible for his untimely death."

"Apart from the fact that it's illegal, Staff Sergeants in our army aren't paid enough to have a numbered account with a Swiss bank. The cash he deposited with the Neu Standard was funny money and something pretty nasty usually happens to people who deal in that."

"I've no idea how much the British pay their soldiers, Mr Drew, nor do I care. I didn't know Mr Paine was in your army; he approached me with references from two of our most highly reputable customers and I had no reason to doubt his integrity."

"Who were these highly reputable customers?" Drew enquired scornfully.

"I'm not prepared to disclose their names; to do so would be a breach of confidentiality."

Drew cast his mind back and came to the conclusion that he'd rarely met anyone who was quite such a smug, hypocritical son of a bitch. Dipping his soup spoon into the consommé, he filled it to the rim then flicked the contents into Thierack's face.

"Now you listen to me, asshole," he said in a low menacing voice. "Maybe we can't prove that you were an accessory to murder before or after the fact, but we sure as hell can show you've been wheeling and dealing in hot money. Perhaps your government would have turned a blind eye to this a few years back; after all, it was the unique customer services provided by Swiss banks that gave the country such a sound economy. But times change and the good burghers are becoming a mite sensitive about their country being labelled the tax evader's paradise. So the word's gone out; improve your image and be a little more discriminating about the kind of people you choose to do business with." Drew paused to lend emphasis to what he was about to say. "I don't say you'll end up in prison but believe me, your co-directors will dump you overboard before you can blink. Then you can kiss this

134

place goodbye along with the cabin cruiser and the nifty little Porsche you have as a second car."

Thierack placed the napkin he'd been using to clean up his face on the table. "What is it you want from me?" he asked.

"Everything you know about Paine, Bartowski and Kalin." Drew took out a handkerchief, moistened a corner with his tongue, then leaned across the table to sponge off the soup stain Thierack had overlooked on his cream-coloured shirt. "When they first came to you, what you did for them and so on. You get the picture?"

"Yes."

"Good." Drew gave him a friendly pat on the cheek. "You know something," he said, "I have a feeling we're going to get along like a house on fire from now on."

11

His name was Horst Winkler. He was twenty-four years old, single, weighed approximately one hundred and twenty-eight pounds, stood five foot seven and had dark hair which was trimmed short back and sides in a style akin to an old-fashioned crew cut. He was bilingual, English being his second language which he spoke with a noticeable American accent. Saturday had not been his lucky day. He had gone to the local supermarket in the morning to buy his usual week's supply of groceries and had returned home just before noon to find two officers from the Kriminalpolizei waiting for him in the entrance hall of the apartment block on Reisstrasse where he lived. They had informed him they had reason to believe he could assist them with their enquiries and had invited him to accompany them to police headquarters, a request they'd indicated he was in no position to refuse.

The Kripos had taken Winkler down to the Kluckstrasse precinct which was close enough to the former Gestapo headquarters on Prinz Albrecht Strasse in the eastern sector to arouse a certain amount of trepidation in those who knew their history. Although no one had laid a finger on Winkler, the manner in which the Kripos had informed him of his rights had suggested they would put his balls in a vice and close the jaws if he gave them any trouble. While, so far, he had denied all knowledge of the British soldier who had been stabbed to death in an alleyway after following him to his apartment house, Winkler was perspiring freely and looking very sorry for himself when Radford was finally allowed to see him some twenty-six hours after he'd been arrested.

"You're in big trouble, Horst." Radford smiled at him across the table in the interview room. "If the police don't get you, we will. One of our side got himself killed because of you and we don't like that."

"I want to see a lawyer," Winkler muttered sulkily.

"You may well need one if I don't get some answers." Radford took out a photograph and slapped it down in front of the German. "Krystyna Bartowski," he said, "also known as Krystyna Kukiel, a Polish American girl about your age, claims to be a schoolteacher from Chicago, Illinois, but is really a KGB operative in the First Chief Directorate and holds the shadow rank of Major. You're her link man in Berlin."

The identity and legend Radford had woven about Krystyna Bartowski was a product of his imagination but it sounded authentic and Winkler seemed ready to believe it.

"Yesterday evening you rang the Berlin Ambassador," Radford continued, "and shortly after, Krystyna Bartowski left the hotel to rendezvous with you. You then gave her a message; I want to know what it was, word for word."

"There was no message. The lady merely stopped me to ask the way to . . ."

"I'll tell you something," Radford said, interrupting him, "you're lucky to be alive. Everyone else I know who's been involved with Krystyna Bartowski has been terminated – Staff Sergeant Paine, his wife Jackie, brother Stefan's former girlfriend, Monika Starnberg, and Lance Corporal Garrold who took that photograph. Frankly, I don't give much for your chances if the police allow you to walk out of here. Either Abteilung I will ensure you spend the next twenty years behind bars for espionage, or your own side will dispose of you because your services are no longer required."

"But you can get me a better deal?" Winkler said, not without a trace of irony.

"I can offer certain fringe benefits – immunity from prosecution, a small pension for services rendered and basic physical protection until you're out of danger."

Although he hadn't discussed it with him, Radford thought Harper would go along with the offer, at least as far as the cash side of the deal was concerned. Just who was going to obtain the necessary immunity and provide Winkler with a bodyguard was another matter. If he could show there was a KGB or East German connection, the British Security Service Organisation in Berlin might well take Winkler under their wing and run him as a double agent.

"Have you got a cigarette?" Winkler asked. "The Kripos took mine when they made me empty my pockets."

"And now you're dying for a smoke." Radford took out a packet of Benson and Hedges, removed the cellophane wrapper and offered one to the German.

"You ever been to Paris, Captain?"

"A couple of times."

"Everyone should see Paris in the Spring."

"Is that where Krystyna Bartowski has gone?"

"She may have mentioned it in passing." Winkler smiled apologetically. "Trouble is, my memory isn't what it was."

"How much will it take to jog it?"

"I don't know, but I'm open to suggestions."

Radford pocketed the cigarettes and stood up. "Stop wasting my time," he said. "You won't get a better deal than the one I've offered."

"How do I know it's not all talk?" Winkler contemplated the glowing ember of his cigarette, then drew on it and slowly exhaled. "What's to stop you walking out on me after I've told you what I know?"

"You give me something to prove your good intentions and we'll leave this place together."

Radford knew the Kriminalpolizei wouldn't object; they had already told him they had nothing on Winkler and were about to turn him loose. They would mark Winkler's card and keep an eye on him for a time but if he kept his head and went about his business, they would eventually lose interest. Like any other force policing a city with a high crime rate, there was a limit to the amount of time they could devote to a particular case.

"You want something on account?" Winkler said.

"That's the general idea," Radford told him.

"I showed Miss Bartowski an engraved lighter belonging to her brother so that she would know the message was genuine."

"What message?"

"The one that sent her to Paris." Winkler gave him a sly smile. "You'll have to raise the ante if you want to hear the rest, Captain."

"All right, let's go."

"Just like that?"

"Why not?"

Radford tapped on the door to gain attention, told the duty policeman that he had previously seen the Kommissar and now wanted the suspect released in his custody as had been tentatively agreed. The tentative agreement had to be verified of course, but in the end Winkler collected his personal valuables from the desk sergeant and they walked out of the precinct building into the late afternoon sunlight.

If the German was impressed his face didn't show it and he kept his thoughts to himself during the short time it took Radford to drive out to Headquarters Berlin. No match was in progress on the pitch below the office he and Drew had been using but half a dozen soldiers were having a kickabout at the far end. Parking the rented Volkswagen in one of the many vacant slots, Radford switched off the engine and turned to face Winkler.

"All right," he said, "let's hear it."

"Hear what?"

"The message you gave Krystyna Bartowski."

Winkler rubbed the index finger of his right hand against the thumb. "Where are the greenbacks then?" he asked, trotting out an expression he'd obviously acquired from watching old Hollywood movies on late night TV.

"You don't get cash in advance for an itty bitty message."

"I think I'm losing my voice, Captain. I get these attacks of laryngitis now and again."

Radford sighed. "How would it be if I dropped you off at Dempsey Barracks on your way home? Lots of guys there who knew Garrold would be only too happy to help you find it again."

"You wouldn't do that."

"Try me."

Winkler searched his face. "Yes, I rather think you might." He shook his head as though lamenting the demise of the British officer and gentleman, then said, "Stefan Bartowski doesn't want his sister looking for him; he's got enough problems without her adding to them and he would be a whole lot happier if she just got the hell out of it and went back to Chicago. But he knows Krystyna won't do that unless she hears it from him – at least, that's the story I was given. Anyway, he's holed up somewhere in Paris and there are certain rules Krystyna has to follow if she's to see him. So starting today, she has to spend every afternoon between three and four at the Georges Pompidou Centre. If the weather's fine, she's to sit on one of the bench seats in the plaza facing the main entrance; if it's raining, she is to wait in the rooftop cafeteria."

It looked as though Bartowski intended to check his sister out to see if she was being followed before he approached her. When satisfied that she was in the clear, he would either use an intermediary to get a message to her or have her tailed back to her hotel.

"Did she take everything you told her on trust?" Radford asked.

"Yeah." Winkler grinned. "I introduced myself as Sergeant Frank Minotti of Company G, 66 Military Intelligence Battalion and she believed me."

"Why?"

"Because she knows Frank Minotti and her brother were business partners. Minotti was Bartowski's representative here in Berlin; he had a finger in every racket going – soft and hard drugs, prostitution, porno movies and extortion. He used the information passing across his desk to lean on people."

"So where's Minotti now?"

"The other side of the wall," Winkler said laconically. "Things got too hot for him when the Provost Marshal's department began to crack down on the drug pushers. Bartowski would probably have gone with him only he was on the staff of battalion headquarters and Württemberg is a long way from the East German border."

The story had some semblance of truth about it and if nothing else, confirmed a suspicion that Bartowski was involved with a hostile Intelligence service. So was Winkler, which made him a valuable acquisition.

"You wait here in the car," Radford said. "I shan't be long."

There wasn't a secure telephone in the office Headquarters Berlin had allocated them and the information he wanted to pass to Harper couldn't be said over an unguarded link which was habitually monitored by the Russians. Obtaining the key to his office from the duty clerk, he found a message pad in the bottom drawer of the desk and drafted a signal to the Department of Subversive Warfare paraphrasing everything he'd learned from Winkler. He also tactfully suggested that 'Electra', the BSSO Chief in Berlin, might be interested in running him as a double agent. Classifying the message Secret, he gave it an Emergency precedence, then signed and dated it before walking the flimsy to the communication centre at the other end of the corridor.

The only NCO on duty in the comcen was a WRAC corporal. Encoding the message was not a problem; what shook her was the precedence. Over sixty per cent of the signals she handled were Routine and the rest were usually Priority. She could recall a few that had been Op Immediate but an

Emergency precedence was only one step below Flash which in itself practically amounted to a declaration of war. Unwilling to accept the message as it stood, she telephoned the duty staff officer who happened to be the Deputy Assistant Provost Marshal. Mindful of the flak they'd caught from London the last time they had tried to assert their authority over Radford, he told her to stop belly-aching and get on with it.

The Georges Pompidou Centre resembled a chemical plant set down in the heart of Paris on a ten acre site in the Third Arrondissement. Everything that would have been on the inside of a conventional building was on the outside so that the exterior was a lattice-work of steel beams, air ducts and convector pipes, some functional, others merely decorative and painted either white or sky blue. Also on the outside fronting the southern aspect were the up-and-down escalators which were enclosed within a translucent plastic skin and looked like a pair of giant caterpillars. Part of life's rich tapestry in the plaza below included a sword swallower, an escapologist, a party of Zen Buddhists in saffron robes and a young woman in jeans playing a lute to the accompaniment of a full blown orchestra on her portable Hi Fi.

The girl whom Radford knew as Krystyna Bartowski was sitting on one of the bench seats near the steps leading down to the plaza, almost but not quite opposite the main entrance to the arts centre. It was a warm Sunday afternoon and the dark sunglasses she was wearing did not seem wholly inappropriate. They obscured her features just enough to get by at a distance, which was about the most she could reasonably hope for. Although they were not look-alikes, there was a superficial resemblance; she was roughly the same shape and size, had the same ash blonde hair and even shared the same Christian name, but close up, no one who knew the real Krystyna Bartowski would be fooled for a moment, even though she had been equipped with an identical wardrobe.

The dice, however, were not entirely loaded against her. Bartowski had already used one emissary to contact her and given his cautious nature, he was likely to do so again. And since she had succeeded in fooling Sergeant Frank Minotti, there was no reason why she shouldn't get away with it a second time. Alternatively, if Bartowski came in person, he would expect to find his sister on the next bench but one to her left and the fact that she had apparently failed to obey his instructions to the letter might well be enough to throw him. Chances were he would want to make sure his eyes hadn't deceived him and that would be his big mistake because, long before he realised she was an impostor, she would recognise him from his mugshot. The rest would then be up to the Office Central pour la Répression du Banditisme, the serious crimes task force whose headquarters was located on Rue du Faubourg St Honoré.

Krystyna resisted the temptation to look for them amongst the crowds milling about in the plaza. The Chicago office hadn't let her down yet and the 'flicks' would be there somewhere in the background. As a theorem it was long on hope, short on facts and she couldn't help wishing they had confirmed that everything was okay or had got back to her with a contact number. Trouble was, everything had happened too fast. The forty-two hours Chicago had had to make all the necessary arrangements from the time she had received the message from Bartowski's courier in Berlin to the moment when she was supposed to rendezvous with him here in the Third Arrondissement looked pretty thin once you took the weekend and the differing time zones into account.

Just thinking about the implications made her feel isolated and exposed. Instinctively, Krystyna glanced at her wristwatch, saw that it was a couple of minutes after four, and got to her feet. Bartowski was certainly playing it cool; she had followed his instructions virtually to the letter and waited an hour at the rendezvous, but no one had come near her. She wasn't exactly disappointed; the dress rehearsal had indicated a need for a short-range voice net and the extra twenty-four hours would give the Bureau and their French counterparts sufficient time to iron out all the wrinkles.

Krystyna left the plaza, cut through the pedestrian precinct to the Boulevard de Sébastopol and turning right, walked towards the Métro station at Strasbourg St Denis. At that hour on a Sunday afternoon, there wasn't a taxi in sight. The service on the Métro was spasmodic and it took her almost three quarters of an hour to reach the Hotel Caravelle near the Crimée station.

The Hotel Caravelle was at the bottom end of the market and was described in the Michelin Guide as quite comfortable. A completely anonymous building in the Rue de Joinville, it was off the beaten track and lacked many of the amenities tourists the world over had come to expect. Well over half the rooms did not have a private bath and the only TV set was in the minute bar across the lobby from the almost equally small restaurant. Krystyna had chosen this modest hotel hoping to avoid the kind of attention she had received at the popular Berlin Ambassador. Collecting her key from Reception, she took the lift up to her room on the second floor.

The telephone was another facility that left something to be desired. To obtain a number other than the restaurant, room service or reception, it was necessary to go through the hotel switchboard. Lifting the receiver, Krystyna waited for the operator to answer, then told the girl she wanted a person to person call to Chicago, Illinois and gave her the name and private number of the local Bureau chief. A feeling that she might well have to wait for ever was confounded when the operator called her back a couple of minutes later.

"Hi, Nick," she said brightly. "Guess who?"

"Krysia?"

"Right. I arrived in Paris yesterday afternoon and checked into the Hotel Caravelle."

"Paris, huh? You're certainly getting around Europe. Question is, are you having a swell time?"

Krystyna smiled. Nick was no slouch; aware that she hadn't dialled straight through, he'd automatically assumed the hotel switchboard operator was listening to their conversation and had slipped into the rôle of old friend and confidant.

"You bet." Krystyna paused for effect, then said, "I had some time to kill this afternoon, so I decided to look up your friends, the ones who are supposed to be expecting me."

"What about them?"

"They didn't seem to know who I was. Do you think they got your letter?"

"Your guess is as good as mine, Krysia. The mail's subject to all kinds of delays these days, especially when it's routed through Washington."

She had called Nick between flights at Frankfurt to let him know that Bartowski had contacted her to set up a meeting in Paris and would the Bureau therefore kindly liaise with the French. Specifically, she'd wanted their serious crimes squad to watch her back; now Nick was telling her that the people on Pennsylvania Avenue were dragging their feet.

"I guess you won't have received the letter we wrote you either," Nick continued. "I don't know how this will affect your plans but your old classmate, Monika Starnberg, has been killed in a traffic accident."

Krystyna sat on the edge of her bed and stared at the flower-pattern wallpaper around the window. "When did this happen?" she asked.

"Last Wednesday. We did our best to let you know as soon as we heard the news."

They undoubtedly had, but it worried her that British Intelligence in the person of Radford clearly knew a great deal more about Bartowski than the FBI did.

"Yeah, well, like you said, the mail just isn't getting through all that fast these days."

"So what are you going to do, Krysia?"

Nick hadn't known that Monika Starnberg was dead

when he'd given her the green light to rendezvous with Bartowski, nor had he foreseen that the people in Washington would approach the French for help with the speed of a snail. Now he was having second thoughts about it but had made it clear that the ball was strictly in her court.

"I don't see any reason to change my plans," Krystyna said, and began to regret her decision the moment the words were out of her mouth.

The message was unambiguous and relatively brief. Classified secret, addressed to Headquarters Berlin and carrying an Op Immediate precedence, it read:

PERSONAL FOR RADFORD FROM HARPER(.) YOUR OPS 1 DATE TIME GROUP 171605Z MARCH 85 REFERS(.) FIRST(.) AGREE WINKLER MAY BE SUITABLE FOR EMPLOYMENT ON LINES YOU SUGGEST(.) CONTACT ELECTRA ON 918370604 SOONEST AND ARRANGE HANDOVER OF MERCHANDISE(.) ELECTRA HAS BEEN WARNED BY BOX LONDON TO EXPECT CALL FROM YOU(.) SECOND(.) APPRECIATE INFORMATION FROM SOURCE IS OUT OF DATE COMMA BUT YOU SHOULD MOVE TO PARIS BY FASTEST MEANS AFTER COMPLETING REQUIREMENT DETAILED IN PARA 1 ABOVE(.) DREW WILL JOIN YOU IN NEW LOCATION TO ASSIST WITH SURVEILLANCE(.) ACTION ALREADY IN HAND TO RELIEVE HIM IN ZÜRICH AND HIS ETA PARIS IS 1400 HOURS LOCAL TIME(.) YOU SHOULD CONTACT HIM THROUGH HEAD OF CHANCERY BRITISH EMBASSY ON RUE DU FAUBOURG ST HONORÉ(.) THIRD(.) ACKNOWLEDGE(.)

In Harper's opinion, any crypto trained date telegraphist who was halfway efficient should have decoded the message in next to no time but here he was, still waiting for an acknowledgment nearly three quarters of an hour after it had been transmitted.

There were, Harper thought, better ways of spending a Sunday evening than being cooped up in his office unable to pass the time profitably. Without in any way being over-confident, he was sure that everything that needed to be done had been done. Adrian Carpenter had reluctantly driven into town from Richmond after he had phoned him at home and had then subsequently departed for his office in Curzon Street happy as Larry, having acquired a double agent without lifting a finger. Dennis Whattmore, a former security officer with the Foreign and Commonwealth Office, had been detailed to relieve Drew in Zürich, and the Head of Chancery in Paris, another of Harper's small army of acquaintances, had agreed to act as a go-between. Briefing Drew had not been without its difficulties but the duty officer had finally managed to catch him at the contact number he'd given soon after arriving in Zürich on Saturday morning.

Harper glanced at his wristwatch for the umpteenth time that evening and wondered what the delay was. As if in answer to his unspoken question, the duty officer tapped on the door, entered his office and placed a teleprint copy in front of him.

"From Berlin," the duty officer said unnecessarily.

"So I see." Harper could also see that it was the acknowledgment he'd been waiting for, but it was the precedence which took his breath away. "Deferred," he said incredulously, "they sent it deferred."

"That's standard procedure with a routine acknowledgment," the duty officer told him, then noticed the expression on Harper's face and wished he'd kept his mouth shut.

12

Dennis Whattmore passed rapidly through Customs and Immigration, then followed the signs pointing the way to the escalators and the Bahnhof. Offhand, he couldn't remember visiting Zürich before but he supposed he must have done so at some time or other during his varied career. Whattmore had started off in the Metropolitan police force which he'd joined as a cadet at the age of seventeen. In the space of ten years, he'd risen to the rank of Inspector and had come to the notice of the Foreign and Commonwealth Office shortly after being assigned to the Diplomatic Protection Group. A tentative suggestion that he might like to consider joining them had been made at a time when his marriage had been faltering and when the promotion board had recently decided he needed to broaden his experience before they could see their way to advancing him to Chief Inspector.

The invitation from the Foreign and Commonwealth had seemed the answer to all his problems. The new job rated a much improved salary, appeared to be confined to regular office hours except when he was required to carry out on-site inspections, and was a salve to his injured pride. In the event, the change of employment had led him to spending two weeks out of every four abroad and while the job had certainly restored his self-esteem, it had failed to save his marriage.

Harper, in turn, had poached him from the Foreign and Commonwealth Office in November '82, a few days after his fortieth birthday, by which time it had become abun-

148

dantly clear that he was destined to spend the rest of his working life dealing with the physical protection of individual embassies. Apart from the improved conditions of service, the new appointment was much more satisfying; instead of defending a building, he now spent the great part of each working day studying ways and means of attacking one. Until Harper had alerted him to relieve Drew, he had been studying photographs of the East German Legation in Beirut with a view to effecting a break in.

Drew was waiting by the bookstall a few yards from the escalators. According to the briefing he'd had from Harper, they were supposed to meet up at the Hotel Weinberg in town, but the senior desk officer had always been a law unto himself. As he veered towards him, Drew signalled he should follow on, then made his way to the cafeteria beyond the duty free shop.

"Why the change in plan?" Whattmore asked when he caught up with him.

"I'm working to a tight schedule," Drew said. "This way, I can catch an earlier flight and be in Paris on time."

"So who's keeping an eye on Thierack?"

"No one, he's doing the job for us. Wolfgang arrived at the bank at seven forty-five, like he always does every morning, and he won't leave his office without our permission." Drew pressed a thumb against the flat surface of the table as though squashing an insect. "It's like this, Dennis, he knows I've got him where I want him."

"You hope."

"I know so." Drew walked over to the service counter and returned a few moments later with two cups of coffee. "What have you been told about Thierack?" he asked, resuming their conversation.

"Not a lot, only that he was in the process of transferring Paine's account to the Volksbank in Dresden where it's to be credited to a Herr Erich Dollmann, and that he claims to be taking his instructions from someone called Kalin who's alleged to be Bartowski's tax lawyer. I gather we're talking about a small fortune?"

Drew nodded. "Paine was good for roughly one hundred and twenty-six thousand pounds and Bartowski had well over half a million in his account before he had it transferred to the same bank in Dresden, less the sixty thousand Swiss Francs Kalin drew in cash."

"For himself?"

"So Thierack would have us believe. Personally, I think the money ended up sticking to his fingers."

Whattmore opened the small plastic thimble of UHT milk and poured it into his coffee. "What do you reckon Kalin got out of the deal?" he asked.

"One hundred and twenty-six thousand if he and Dollmann are the same man."

"Harper's running both names with Century House and Box."

"Is he?" Drew looked sceptical. "I doubt if the Secret Intelligence Service or MI5 will come up with anything. There's no one by the name of Kalin practising as a tax lawyer in Switzerland."

In his new-found desire to stay within the law, Thierack had checked the listings of every Canton and had drawn a blank. He'd also told Drew that he'd never once seen Bartowski and Kalin together. He had talked with the lawyer on the phone and Kalin had called in at the bank a couple of times but after a fleeting visit to Zürich towards the end of October '84, he had never again met the Polish American.

"I'll tell you something else, Dennis – the first time Kalin put in an appearance was four days after Bartowski had gone AWOL. Before that, he'd never had a lawyer; then suddenly he needs one to help him convert good Swiss Francs into rubbishy East German Marks so that he can enjoy a decent standard of living in Poland. Anyone who can smooth the way for a transaction involving a lot of technical difficulties has got to have connections with a hostile Intelligence service. Chances are we'll discover that Kalin works out of Normannenstrasse."

"That's a bit far-fetched, isn't it?" Whattmore observed hesitantly.

"It's one of the reasons you're here." Drew produced a snapshot from his wallet and gave it to Whattmore. Printed on the back was a physical description which did not relate to the man in the photograph. "The would-be sailor on the private landing stage is Wolfgang Thierack; the physical characteristics on the back is how he described Kalin. He's going to phone you as soon as the lawyer gets in touch with him again to check that the Paine account has been transferred to Dresden."

"How will Thierack know where to reach me?" Whattmore asked, then silently cursed himself for being so stupid because Drew had obviously booked him in at the rendezvous. "The Hotel Weinberg," he said, lamely answering his own question.

"Right. What we want from you is a photograph of Kalin if it's at all possible." Drew downed the rest of his coffee and pushed the cup aside. "One other thing," he said. "You're invited to dinner at Thierack's place tonight at seven thirty sharp – the Villa Seefahrer, eight miles south of Zürich on the road to Kusnach. He'll be giving you two print-outs showing every transaction that has passed through the accounts belonging to Paine and Bartowski since they were opened."

"That should make interesting reading."

"You got any questions, Dennis?"

"I don't think so."

"Good. That's us finished then," Drew said, and walked away.

Whattmore stood there gazing after the blond man until he'd disappeared into the departure lounge, then turning away, he retraced his steps to the bookstall and went down the escalator to catch a train into town.

The Box and Century House checks failed to produce a trace on either Erich Dollmann or the man simply known as Kalin. Both MI5 and the Secret Intelligence Service were, however, anxious to know why Harper was interested in the two men and what, if anything, he had on them. Although for once Harper could truthfully say he had precious little, neither agency had been inclined to believe him. His insistence that Kalin and Dollmann were just a couple of names which had cropped up during enquiries into the business activities of the late Staff Sergeant Paine had been received with a stony incredulity that boded ill for the future.

Harper had enjoyed better luck with Sergeant Frank Minotti. Through the Military Attaché at the US Embassy in Grosvenor Square, he'd learned that the details Radford had included in his signal were broadly correct. Minotti was a sergeant in Military Intelligence and had been stationed in Berlin with Company 'G' of the 66th Battalion before he'd deserted on the eleventh of December 1984. The Military Attaché had also informed him that up till the beginning of April '84, Minotti had been the senior clerk in charge of the card index system at Battalion Headquarters in Württemberg and it was there that he'd obviously met and got to know Stefan Bartowski.

Unfortunately, the rest of Radford's information had proved incorrect; far from being into drugs, prostitution, porn and extortion, Minotti was merely a womaniser. Nemesis had finally caught up with him when a young French woman from Strasbourg had walked into 7th Army Headquarters seeking news of her husband whom she hadn't seen or heard from in eight months. Like a great many other bigamists, Minotti had married her under an assumed name and it had taken the Military Police several days to identify him from the sketchy service details and physical description she had been able to furnish. Had she known Minotti's correct serial number, they could have tracked him down on their computer in a matter of seconds; instead, the MPs had been obliged to circulate a 'wanted' bulletin to every unit in the theatre.

Although they couldn't prove it, the Provost Marshal's department believed that when the bulletin had reached the 66th Military Intelligence Battalion, some wellwisher there had tipped Minotti off. Harper was in no doubt that the wellwisher had been Master Sergeant Stefan Bartowski.

The airport bus left the Boulevard Périphérique just beyond the Cité Universitaire and headed into town on the Avenue de la Porte d'Orléans. Half a mile farther on, it ran straight into the kind of snarl-up Paris was famous for. If proof were needed to support Radford's theory that when things started to go wrong, they usually progressed from bad to worse, the traffic jam provided it. As far as he was concerned, the day had got off to a bad start in Berlin when a ground mist had delayed the departure of his flight by some three hours and the 'embuggerance' factors had simply multiplied from there on. A strike of baggage handlers at Charles de Gaulle had led to his flight being diverted to Orly along with just about every other plane in the sky. They had then spent almost an hour orbiting the airport waiting their turn to land and when finally their plane had touched down, they'd disembarked to find that the strike had spread to the porters at Orly. By the time Radford had collected his baggage and passed through customs, every taxicab in the rank had been commandeered and he'd been forced to use the airport bus.

Two forty-three. Although Radford had vowed to refrain from constantly looking at his wristwatch, the temptation to do so proved irresistible. In another seventeen minutes, Krystyna Bartowski would arrive at the rendezvous, provided her brother hadn't already contacted her yesterday afternoon. That had always been on the cards and Harper had known it when he'd decided to pull Drew out of Zürich. He wondered if Drew had been dogged by a similar run of bad luck and immediately came to the conclusion that that line of thinking would get him nowhere.

Suddenly and for no apparent reason, the traffic started moving again. Turning into the Avenue du Maine, the bus driver put his foot down and did his level best to overtake every other vehicle on the road. A little over ten minutes later, he pulled into the underground terminal on the Esplanade des Invalides.

One of the first to alight from the coach, Radford checked his bag into a twenty-four hour lock-up and in contrast with his earlier frustrations, was lucky enough to flag down a passing cab as soon as he reached street level. By two fifty-nine, he was heading across the river towards the Place de la Concorde, but there was no way he was going to reach the Georges Pompidou Centre ahead of Krystyna Bartowski.

Drew strolled through the rooftop cafeteria and went out on to the terrace. Even though Easter was still almost three weeks away, it seemed the tourist season had started early and the Georges Pompidou Centre was more crowded than he'd expected to find it.

Jinking past the crowded tables, Drew moved up to the balustrade and looked down into the square. The scene below was like a three-ring circus with jugglers, contortionists and a sword swallower competing for the largest audience with a troupe of Israeli folk dancers. There was, however, no sign of Krystyna Bartowski as yet; even though Drew had never met the American girl, he'd seen her at a distance in Berlin and Harper had told him exactly where to look for her in the square. There was no sign of Radford either but Drew knew he was held up somewhere along the way. When he'd phoned the embassy just before leaving his hotel for the Georges Pompidou Centre, the head of Chancery had told him that ground mist in Berlin and the strike at Orly had fouled up Radford's flight.

Two fifty-nine; his eyes zeroed in on the bench seat directly opposite the main entrance. Three o'clock: a tall girl with ash blonde hair, wearing jeans and a denim jacket over a floppy sweater entered the periphery of Drew's vision and sauntered towards an ice cream van where she tagged on to the end of a short queue. He watched her buy an ice lolly, then move to the appropriate bench and take the space a young mother wheeling a pushchair had just vacated. Her features were not easily discernible from where he was standing and were further obscured by a pair of dark sunglasses but even so, he knew beyond a shadow of doubt that it was Krystyna Bartowski.

So far so good, he thought, but there was still no sign of Radford and without him he was in a bind. If they went their separate ways after the meet, he could either follow Krystyna Bartowski or the courier who'd contacted her. No matter who he plumped for, it no longer made sense to keep the square under observation from the rooftop cafeteria. Retracing his steps, Drew rode the escalator down to ground level while contriving to keep the American girl in sight at the same time. His vision was constantly interrupted by the constant stream of visitors passing him on the up escalator so that it was something of a relief to find she hadn't moved from the bench seat when he reached the entrance hall.

Drew moved towards the rear of the hall and positioned himself where he had a clear view of the girl. Even though she was gazing directly at the entrance, he knew she couldn't see him. It was the old principle of sunlight and shade; Krystyna Bartowski was out in the open silhouetted by the sun directly behind her back while he was standing in the shadowy interior of a building merging into the background.

He watched the people around her; the children and adults at the ice cream van to her right and rear, the Israeli folk dancers in the square left and forward of where she was sitting. Students, pickpockets, tourists, vagrants, young mothers with their children and the aged passed each other on the steps leading from the esplanade to the square below. Black, white, brown and yellow; occidentals, blackamoors and orientals; Drew stood there watching the world go by.

Then, out of the corner of his eye, he spotted Radford. The younger man was ten minutes late and seemingly in a hurry to make up for lost time. He appeared from the right and was moving diagonally across the square towards the steps while waving his arms above his head as if deliberately trying to catch Krystyna Bartowski's attention. Drew saw him put a finger to his lips and heard a shrill whistle above the chanting of the Israeli folk dancers.

Krystyna Bartowski heard it too, saw Radford advancing purposefully in her direction and immediately left the bench seat. Her pace was deceptive; without breaking into a run, she covered a lot of ground in a few strides and rapidly disappeared from sight behind the ice cream van.

"You stupid fucker." Drew mouthed the words silently at Radford and moved towards the entrance. As he left the building, he noticed a thin plume of black smoke rising from one of the concrete litter bins on the esplanade near the steps. A split second later, he rocked back on his heels as though someone had caught him with a sucker punch under the heart. Then he heard the dull crump of an explosion.

Although Radford was closer to the bomb, he had thrown himself flat a millisecond before it detonated so that the blast wave passed harmlessly above him. The rushing noise died away and was followed by a momentary silence, then there was a high-pitched scream and the crowd in the immediate vicinity scattered in all directions.

It was always difficult to gauge the size of an explosive device merely by the noise level but in this instance, Radford had seen the man who'd planted it and knew from its shape and size that it had been made up with no more than two or three pounds of plastic. The charge had been concealed in a disposable carrier bag from a supermarket and the concrete litter bin had briefly contained the kinetic energy like a bomb casing. When finally the bin had fragmented, the ice cream van and the queue of people waiting to be served had stopped most of the debris.

There were four dead, including a schoolgirl whose features were now indeterminate. A woman lay halfway down the flight of steps, one arm reduced to a bloody stump, her left foot all but severed except for a single tendon. She was already in deep shock, her face so pinched and grey that Radford could tell at a glance that she was past saving. In a situation where every second counted, his training had taught him not to waste valuable time on the dying; he moved on to help a teenage youngster who was sitting on the top step contemplating his mangled right hand as though trying to figure out why some of the fingers were missing. As Radford removed the belt around his slacks and used it as a tourniquet, the answer came to the lad and he passed out.

A familiar figure raced past Radford heading towards the pedestrian precinct which linked the square with the Boulevard de Sébastopol. Looking up, he recognised Drew and called to him to lend a hand with the injured, but the blond man ignored him and ran on. Away in the distance, he could just hear the discordant warble of a police car as it sped towards the scene of the incident. Closer at hand, a number of people were running about in a blind panic calling for a nurse or a doctor to attend to their wounds. A man in his mid thirties, his left trouser leg at half mast, tried to drag him away from the youngster, insisting that he do something about the gash on his kneecap. Reaching out with his free hand, Radford grabbed the man by his shirtfront, pulled him down on to his knees, then struck him hard across the face.

A woman joined Radford at the boy's side, inspected the tourniquet with what seemed a professional eye and using sign language, indicated that she would take over. Directly to his rear, a man with a harsh voice gabbled at him in French, then jabbed something hard into his back. Glancing over his shoulder, he saw that his assailant was an angry-looking gendarme armed with a MAT 49 sub-machine gun.

It didn't take a Mensa intellect to realise the Frenchman had seen him waving to Krystyna Bartowski seconds before the device had exploded and had drawn the wrong conclusion. However, he did need an interpreter to get that message across to the gendarme, especially as by now a second officer had arrived on the scene and neither was inclined to heed his protests. Between them they managed to cuff his wrists behind his back; then a police van appeared on the promenade and they bundled him into the back and locked the door. Drew, of course, was nowhere to be seen. Neither was Krystyna Bartowski.

13

Krystyna went into the adjoining bathroom, found a spare glass on the shelf above the washbasin and filled it from the cold water tap. She had spent a good three quarters of an hour criss-crossing Paris on the Métro to cover her tracks, but even now her limbs were still shaky and she knew, without looking at her reflection in the mirror and from what the receptionist who'd given her the key to her room had said, that her face was the colour of paste.

She drank from the glass and rinsed out her mouth but it didn't make any difference; the sour taste clung to her palate and wouldn't go away. She hadn't been caught up in a terrorist outrage; Bartowski had simply tried to kill her. That was the plain, unvarnished truth, even if it did look as though the Israeli folk dancers had been the target. And she wouldn't be here now if it hadn't been for Radford, though she hadn't seen it that way at the time. As a matter of fact, her one thought when she'd spotted him advancing towards her had been to make a dignified exit before he ruined everything. The penny should have dropped after the blast wave had knocked her flat, but her brain had been less than ice cool and had been affected by a kind of paralysis.

The blond man had spooked her. Moments after the explosion, Krystyna had found herself in the pedestrian precinct without any clear recollection of how she came to be there. She had immediately turned about to see what she could do for the injured and while still a good thirty yards from the square, had spotted him on the steps. He had seen her at roughly the same time and she had known instinctively that he was coming after her. The one thought that had been uppermost in her mind had been the conviction that he meant to succeed where the bomb had failed. It was this premonition that had prompted her to run back into the precinct where in a matter of a few seconds she had been swallowed up by a crowd of people surging towards the square.

Krystyna returned to the bedroom, found a pack of cigarettes in her shoulder bag and lit one, then flopped into an easy chair and hooked one leg over the arm. There was a hole in the right leg of her jeans that hadn't been there before and she had skinned her kneecap. On closer inspection, Krystyna discovered that she had also grazed both palms, but that was the least of her worries. In a long list of foul-ups, the Bureau's failure to get the backing she'd asked for was top of the list. Had the French been covering the square, they might have grabbed the bastard who'd planted the bomb; they might even have prevented the outrage altogether.

The indiscriminate way Bartowski had chosen to eliminate her didn't make sense either. It lacked the clinical efficiency she had come to associate with a professional hit ordered by the Mafia. If they were going to blow the target up, they usually wired the bomb to the ignition of the victim's car. They just didn't plant the charge in a place where there was a good chance it would take out a lot of innocent people. Not that morality had anything to do with it; their over-riding consideration was to ensure they blew away the right target.

Another thing Krystyna couldn't understand was how Radford had managed to track her down. Although grateful that he had, it didn't stop her questioning why he'd happened to be in the right place at the right time. Radford could have gotten the information from Frank Minotti, though why the sergeant should have been so obliging was hard to figure. One thing however was crystal clear; the coat trailing operation to lure Bartowski out into the open was now a dead duck. She hadn't fooled anyone, his friends had made that very evident this afternoon at the Georges Pompidou Centre.

Bad news invariably travelled fast and the Bureau chiefs in Washington would keep their heads well down once they learned what had happened. Their first priority would be to contact the agent they had reputedly sent over to liaise with the French. Unless it was already too late, Krystyna thought it likely that he would be instructed to back off.

They would expect her to do the same, quietly and discreetly. The last thing they wanted was one of their agents at the centre of a diplomatic row. Exactly when she could leave Paris depended on how much coverage the incident was given by the media and whether anyone had given a description of her to the police. Any precipitate move on her part might well result in all kinds of complications. Staying put for the next day or so was about the best thing she could do in the circumstances.

Radford got to his feet and began to pace up and down the six-by-six detention room. Neither the Inspector who'd questioned him at the Préfecture de Police following his arrest, nor the detectives of the Serious Crimes Squad who'd subsequently moved him from the Ile de la Cité to their headquarters on Rue du Faubourg Saint Honoré had believed his voluntary statement. He didn't altogether blame them. None of the other witnesses the detectives had talked to recalled the man he'd seen walking away from the litter bin and they wouldn't accept that Radford had simply acted on a hunch when he'd shouted a warning.

But he had. The youngish man who'd dumped a plastic bag in the litter bin had been listening to a pocket-size Hi Fi and ordinarily Radford wouldn't have paid much attention to him. It was Krystyna Bartowski's presence that had made the difference and had led him to put two and two together; the police might have understood that had he been able to give them all the facts. But he and

161

Drew were running an illegal surveillance operation on French soil and to have named Krystyna Bartowski would have brought it all out into the open.

Radford had no idea what the French intended to do with him. They had taken his passport and the officer in charge of the interrogation had nodded sagely when one of his detectives had pointed out that on page two the Englishman was described as a government official. It was the all-embracing description for anyone who was a servant of the Crown, but the Serious Crimes Squad wouldn't have it. They were convinced that 'government official' was merely a coy way of saying he was an Intelligence agent. The loose key they'd found in his jacket pocket had also excited them. They knew it belonged to a left luggage container at the air terminal and had promptly sent one of their clerks over to the Place des Invalides to collect his bag. Right now, they were probably sorting through his dirty laundry.

A key turned in the lock and the door opened. Deliverance had arrived in the form of a very smug-looking Drew.

"About time," Radford said. "What kept you?"

"You're not the most popular visitor in town," Drew told him. "It took a lot of wheeling and dealing to secure your release."

Whatever bargain had been struck, it was apparent that the Serious Crimes Squad hadn't come out ahead. His clothes had been stuffed back into the case any old how and the officer who'd led the interrogation warned Radford that he didn't want to see his face in Paris again for a very long time.

"Nice of them to let you know the score," Drew said acidly when they were safely outside on the pavement.

A Peugeot saloon with CD plates was parked at the kerbside. Unlocking the trunk, Drew told him to dump the case inside, then got in behind the wheel, started the engine and switched on the quartz headlights.

"This jalopy belongs to one of the Second Secretaries in the British Embassy," he said, anticipating the question.

"Decent of him to lend it," said Radford.

"For one reason or another, there are any number of people willing to do Harper a favour."

"Including someone in the Police Nationale who has plenty of clout?"

"Wrong department," Drew said laconically. "The man you have to thank is with the Service de Documentation Extérieure et de Contre-Espionage, popularly known as the SDECE."

"The French Secret Intelligence Service," Radford said in a flat voice.

"So they tell me." Drew pulled out from the kerb and drove past the Elysée, heading towards Rue Royal. "You got anything against them?"

"I'm not sure I entirely approve of some of their methods."

Since their inception in the early sixties, the SDECE had been accused of every crime in the book – narcotics, blackmail, extortion, dealing in counterfeit currency, kidnapping and murder. They had acquired a reputation for being totally ruthless in Algeria, first against the FLN, then the OAS. Their hard-nose image hadn't mellowed with the passage of time.

"Krystyna Bartowski is staying at the Hotel Caravelle. We wouldn't have found that out if it hadn't been for the SDECE."

"They did us a favour?"

"You could say that. Every tourist who stays in Paris fills out a hotel registration card, a copy of which goes to the Préfecture de Police. I gave them her name, they leaned on the police."

"What do they want from us in return?"

"First crack at the girl."

"You've got to be joking," said Radford. "They don't need our permission to question her. This is their territory, they can pick up Krystyna Bartowski any time they want."

"That's just what they're going to do now." Drew checked the rear view mirror, then made a left turn into

163

the Rue d'Anjou. "With a little help from us," he added.

"I smell something rotten."

"There are times when you have to take a few short cuts," Drew said angrily, "and this is one of them. Do things the nice, legal way and you end up with the US Ambassador demanding to know why the Police Judiciaire have arrested an American citizen. Next thing you know, we're in the middle of a tug of war and Krystyna Bartowski isn't saying anything because she knows the Frogs can't prove anything and the worst they can do is put her on a plane for New York. But if you're there to hold her hand, she won't give us any aggro."

Drew had taken leave of his senses; Radford could think of no other explanation for what he had in mind. No matter how he dressed it up, they were going to help the SDECE abduct her.

"Does Harper know what's going on?" Radford asked him.

"Are you trying to tell me how to do my job?"

Drew's defensive attitude said it all. He had got in touch with Harper as soon as he knew the police were holding Radford and the Director had subsequently contacted the SDECE but only to ask them if they would spring one of his officers as a personal favour. On his own initiative and almost certainly unbeknown to Harper, Drew had then taken things several stages farther.

"I wouldn't like to be in your shoes when he finds out," Radford said.

"In our game you often have to go out on a limb to get results." Drew pulled into the kerb and stopped a few yards beyond the Precinct House of the VIII Arrondissement. "This is where we collect our friend from the SDECE," he said.

In the stillness of the room, the sudden jangle from the telephone made Krystyna jump. Reaching out, she lifted the receiver in time to hear the switchboard operator say, "You're through, Monsieur."

Then a strange voice said, "Miss Bartowski?"

"Yes, who's calling?" she asked.

"My name's Oliver. I'm an old friend of Nick's. I believe he suggested you should look me up when you were in Paris?"

"Indeed he did." The go-between from Washington had finally arrived in town, a little late in the day perhaps but none the less welcome for all that. Though she tried to hide it, the sense of relief was present in her voice.

"Nick called me from Chicago to see if I'd got his letter and of course I hadn't, the mail being what it is these days. Anyway, he told me where you were staying and I decided to call you straight away."

In a roundabout fashion, Oliver was telling her that there had been some kind of foul-up in Washington that had delayed his departure. Someone in the Bureau had probably thought they should seek the advice of the State Department before they approached the French and there had been a lot of coming and going before State gave them the green light.

"Nick said that when he talked to you on Sunday, you were thinking of curtailing your vacation because of some family problem back home?"

"That's right." The message was loud and clear; Oliver was ordering her back to Chicago. The only thing left unsaid was how soon he wanted her to leave.

"So what are your plans, Krysia?"

"Well, I don't see how I can stay on over here, the way things are," she said.

"No, I guess not. My wife's going to be disappointed; she was looking forward to meeting you as much as I was."

"There'll be another time."

"Sure there will." There was a slight pause, then Oliver said, "Listen, if you have any trouble getting a flight tomorrow, give me a ring on Trinité 509888. My company does a lot of business with TWA and they owe me."

"Thanks."

"You're welcome."

Krystyna heard him put the phone down and slowly replaced the receiver.

Drew parked the car outside the Hotel Caravelle and switched off the headlights, then sat there gazing steadfastly to his front. Words, it seemed, were no longer necessary, something Radford thought was a blessing considering he hadn't stopped talking from the moment the gendarme had joined them. If they didn't know what to do now, they never would, and any last minute instructions would only serve to confuse them. Opening the door, Radford got out of the car, waited for the gendarme to join him on the sidewalk, then walked into the lobby.

The gendarme marched straight up to the desk, informed the receptionist that a Mademoiselle Krystyna Bartowski was staying in the hotel and demanded to know the number of her room. He was a tall man and the uniform added to his already commanding presence. Completely overawed, the receptionist checked the register and told him the American girl was in Room 208 on the second floor.

Krystyna Bartowski was more surprised than overawed when she opened the door to them. Her eyes flickered briefly, registering a double-take that Radford had seen once before, only this time it was followed by a slow smile.

"I don't know how you found me," she said warmly, "but I'm glad you did."

Radford doubted if she would be once she learned why they were there but the bogus gendarme was in no hurry to break the news. He just stood there openly admiring her, his eyes taking in the black calf-high boots and the stone coloured suede two-piece she was wearing.

"I wouldn't be here now if it wasn't for you, Captain. You saved my life."

Radford glared at the SDECE man, silently willing him to get on with it, but it seemed he'd temporarily lost the power of speech. "We're under arrest," he said, filling in for the Frenchman. "The authorities mean to deport us."

"What?"

Radford moved forward, forcing her to retreat farther into the room. "The Serious Crimes Squad wanted to charge us with murder but they realised they couldn't make it stick."

"This is ridiculous." Krystyna walked across the room to the telephone on the bedside table and lifted the receiver. Flashing the operator, she asked for Trinité 509888.

"Is Mademoiselle perhaps seeking the advice of an advocate?" The gendarme had finally come to life. His English, though reasonably fluent, was inclined to be stilted and occasionally included the odd word in French.

"I don't need to consult a lawyer," she said angrily. "I'm calling an official from Washington who can vouch for the fact that I'm an FBI agent."

Radford had never found the anxious sister role convincing. Initially, he'd thought Krystyna was probably as crooked as Bartowski but he'd begun to see her in a different light the day she'd left Berlin. He wouldn't have been surprised to learn that she was working for Army Intelligence; the fact that she was with the Federal Bureau of Investigation was something he was not expecting.

"I took a similar line," he said. "I told the Police Judiciaire I was a captain in the British Army but they didn't want to know."

"They'll find themselves in big trouble if they try anything with me . . ." Krystyna broke off, frowning. "Oliver?" One eyebrow rose in a quizzical arch. "It's me – Krysia. Listen, the French police are giving me some aggro and I'd like you to put the record straight. Tell them who I am and what I'd doing over here in Paris."

Suddenly her face turned to stone and it wasn't difficult to guess the kind of line Oliver was taking. As Radford prised the phone from her grasp, he heard him say, "I don't recognise your voice and I'm sure we've never met."

"I'm glad you're not on my side," Radford said in a cold voice. "I'd hate to have to depend on you in a tight corner." He put the phone down and smiled sympathetically at

Krystyna. "Seems like friend Oliver doesn't want to know you," he said.

"I'm with the Chicago office of the FBI," Krystyna said in a level voice.

"And you told Iremonger you were a schoolteacher."

"My name is Krystyna Zander. My great grandfather was born in Poland and came to America in 1881. He couldn't speak a word of English and the immigration authorities on Ellis Island couldn't spell Zandarowski so they Anglicised it."

"What name are you travelling under in your passport?"

"Bartowski."

"Then I guess you're stuck with it," said Radford.

"I'm supposed to be Bartowski's sister; the passport is part of the legend."

"Try convincing the police and see how far it gets you."

Short of nudging him in the ribs, Radford couldn't have given the Frenchman a broader hint that it was time he got the show on the road.

Slowly, as though they had all the time in the world, the 'gendarme' opened the wardrobe and leisurely examined the clothes hanging on the rail. "These can be collected later," he said pompously.

"Like hell," Krystyna said.

"We go now." The 'gendarme' snapped his fingers. "This minute, you understand?"

"I think he means it," Radford said and stepped aside so that Krystyna could go first, but she wasn't willing to leave just yet.

"This is crazy," she said. "Bartowski's friends set out to kill me, you try to clear the area in the immediate vicinity of the bomb, and we're the ones who end up getting arrested."

"There was a troupe of Israeli folk dancers performing in the square; the police think they were the target."

"Rubbish. The man I'm hunting is into heroin, not the Palestine Liberation Front, and he's running scared from the Mafia. They didn't mind him running a drugs operation in a small way so long as he confined his activities to the US Army in Europe, but they took grave exception when he tried to muscle in on the home market."

Although Krystyna was looking directly at him, Radford was pretty sure she was equally interested to see how the gendarme reacted to her story.

"Are you saying that Bartowski thought the Mafia were using you to draw him into the open?" he asked.

"You bet I am. The Israelis weren't in the square yesterday, but I was. Sunday was just a dry run to see if I had swallowed the bait and to check me out. Whoever planted that bomb knew exactly where I would be sitting."

"It's an interesting theory but there are a number of flaws."

Krystyna shrugged. "So okay, it may be a little rough in parts but I think it holds together. A sergeant called Frank Minotti got in touch with Bartowski and told him that some woman claiming to be his sister was running around Berlin asking after him. He was deeply suspicious so he ordered Minotti to get in touch with me and arrange a meeting."

"Did this Minotti know Krystyna Bartowski?" Radford asked.

"Of course he didn't. You don't think I would have gone into this thing unless I knew exactly who Krystyna had met when she visited Berlin in July '81, do you?"

"If Sunday was a dry run, Bartowski could have followed you back to the hotel. He could have taken you out any time he liked with a single pistol shot in the head, he didn't have to blow away a lot of innocent people."

"I told you it was a bit rough in parts."

It was all of that. The Frank Minotti whom Krystyna had met was Horst Winkler and he was an East German Intelligence agent pure and simple.

"Let's go," the 'gendarme' said, "we're wasting time."

Radford gritted his teeth, inwardly seething with anger. Instead of helping the SDECE abduct Krystyna, they should be sitting round a table exchanging information.

But this lunatic manoeuvre Drew had cooked up with the French Secret Service had developed a momentum of its own and was now unstoppable.

Radford followed her out of the room, the 'gendarme' closing the door behind them as they walked towards the lift at the other end of the corridor. They rode down to the ground floor in silence and went through an almost deserted lobby to the Peugeot waiting by the kerbside. Radford got in beside Drew; the 'gendarme' ushered Krystyna into the back, then joined her and pointedly locked both rear doors from the inside. Checking the rear view mirror to make sure the road behind was clear, Drew started up and pulled away from the kerb.

"Do you mind telling me where we're going?" Krystyna asked calmly.

"The detention centre at Ecouen on the outskirts of Paris," the 'gendarme' told her.

"Just so long as Oliver knows where to find me," she said.

There was a fat chance of that, Radford thought.

14

The mist came down suddenly and hung there like a wet, grey blanket so that his headlights were more of a hindrance than a help. Overshooting the Villa Seefahrer in the poor visibility, Whattmore had to drive on for almost half a mile before he could make a U-turn in safety. Approaching the house from the opposite direction, he signalled a left turn, swept into the driveway and halted in front of the double garage.

A light was on over the front porch but no one answered the door when he rang the bell. He rang it again, loud and long to no effect, then moved back several paces and looked up at the rooms above. Although most of the house was in darkness at the front, he could see a pale shaft of indirect light reflected in the window above the porch.

Thierack was definitely expecting him; he had phoned the Hotel Weinberg just before he left the bank to confirm their dinner date for seven thirty. Perplexed to know why he couldn't get an answer, Whattmore strolled round to the back. The private landing stage was invisible in the swirling mist but he could hear the water gently lapping against a boat and assumed it was the cabin cruiser in the snapshot Drew had given him. To his left and slightly forward of where he was standing, a chink of light showed through a narrow gap between the drawn curtains in one of the downstairs rooms. Trying the back door, he found it wasn't locked and walked into the kitchen.

A plump, middle-aged woman was lying on the floor in

one corner of the room, her legs outstretched and wide apart, her head propped against the refrigerator in a semi-raised position. Her attitude suggested she had fallen down in a drunken stupor, but she hadn't; whoever had put a bullet into her head above the right eye had held the pistol close enough to leave a powder burn around the lip of the entry hole. Her face was warm to the touch and a certain amount of blood was oozing from the exit wound behind the right ear. Death had certainly occurred in the last hour and the killer might still be lurking somewhere in the villa. The thought sent a shiver down Whattmore's spine.

He moved into the hall and quickly stepped to one side to avoid being silhouetted by the light from the kitchen. He listened attentively, straining his ears to catch the slightest sound but the only thing he seemed to hear was the thumping of his own heart. As his eyes adjusted to the gloom, Whattmore could see the outline of a man lying face down on the carpet halfway between the front door and the staircase. He was in his middle to late fifties, had thin grey hair and was over six foot. He was wearing a pair of striped pants, a black waistcoat and a white shirt. Turning him over, Whattmore found that the front of his waistcoat was soaked in blood from a bullet wound in the left side of his chest directly in line with the heart. The butler must have answered the door, taken one look at the pistol levelled at him and retreated into the hall. Before he had a chance to cry out, the gunman had moved in close and shot him at point blank range.

The intruder had moved swiftly, killing the manservant and housekeeper before either could raise the alarm; then he'd undoubtedly murdered Thierack. Was the body upstairs or downstairs? Whattmore craned his neck trying to peer round corners in order to see if the landing above was clear. Testing each wooden step in turn to satisfy himself it would bear his weight without creaking, he slowly climbed the staircase.

The light he'd seen earlier was coming from the master

bedroom overlooking the lake at the back of the villa. There was no sign of Thierack, but every drawer in the fitted wardrobe had been removed and up-ended on the king-size bed. The large, ornate trinket box on the dressing table hadn't been overlooked either; it had been forced with a carving steel and the contents scattered over the floor. Further investigation revealed that the other bedrooms had been ransacked in a similar fashion in what Whattmore had to admit was a pretty convincing attempt to make it appear the house had been burglarised.

He checked out the servants' quarters in the attic, then went downstairs, his nerves still tight as a drum. As he moved across the hall, the utter quiet was shattered by a clock which began to chime the hour in a deep bass tone that made his flesh crawl. Four, five, six, seven, eight; he counted off the individual chimes to himself, suddenly realised it was eight o'clock and wondered where the time had gone. He opened the door facing him, entered the room cautiously and feeling for the switch, put the light on. The table had been laid for two – silver cutlery from the hand-carved rosewood canteen near the serving hatch, crystal wine glasses. Error number one, he thought; a real burglar would have lifted the silver. Convinced he was right in thinking the burglary was a sham, Whattmore pushed the folding partition back and walked into the drawing room.

The landscape which normally hung below the picture light on the inner wall had been dumped in the nearest armchair and the safe it was intended to conceal had been opened and cleaned out. Just what had been taken was likely to remain a mystery because Thierack was in no position to tell him. He was lying on the floor curled up like a foetus on his left side. He had been changing for dinner when the killer had walked into his bedroom and was in his shirt tails, boxer shorts, dark grey nylon socks and black suspenders. How the killer had obtained the combination to the wall safe was not a mystery; one of

173

Thierack's eyes was closed to a narrow slit and both his cheeks were badly bruised from the pistol whipping he'd obviously been given.

Kalin. Suddenly the killer had a name even if Whattmore couldn't put a face to him. Kalin had beaten up Thierack and had then put a bullet into his head as he lay there cowering on the floor. There were other conclusions to be drawn. Thierack had completed the transfer of Paine's account to the Dresden branch of the Volksbank and had told Kalin this when the latter had contacted him. The finance director had sworn he would call him at the Hotel Weinberg the moment he heard from Kalin but in the event, he'd reneged on his word. Thierack had only received half the sixty thousand francs Kalin had drawn in cash and had wanted to lay his hands on the rest; offhand, Whattmore couldn't think of a better reason to explain why the dead man had decided to double-cross him. At the same time, it didn't necessarily follow that Thierack had played it straight down the line with Kalin.

There were two other rooms he hadn't checked – the study and the downstairs cloakroom. The study had also been turned over but in a very haphazard manner as though it had been the last thing Kalin had done before leaving the villa, and in his haste, he'd overlooked the one thing that really mattered – a thin document wallet containing the computerised records of two numbered accounts.

A faint spluttering noise greeted Whattmore when he returned to the kitchen and on investigation, he saw that one of the saucepans that had been left to simmer was gently boiling over. Pausing just long enough to switch the oven and the hob off at the mains, he then let himself out of the house and walked round to the front. The mist had all but lifted in the last forty minutes and the Renault he'd hired was clearly visible from the main road. When the bodies were eventually discovered, some passing motorist might well remember seeing a car parked in the driveway.

Someone who was exceptionally observant might even recall the make and colour but it was highly unlikely they would have made a note of the vehicle registration number. If his assumption was correct, Whattmore persuaded himself that the police wouldn't be able to trace him through the rental agency.

He heard a car in the distance, waited until it had gone past the house, then got into the Renault and made a three point turn in the drive. Turning left on the main road, Whattmore drove back to Zürich, parked the car in the hotel garage and went up to his room.

Nothing in life was ever simple and the computer print-outs were no exception; much to his annoyance, they did not produce the clear-cut picture he'd hoped they would. Paine had made two cash deposits, one on the twenty-fourth of June 1981 for the sterling equivalent of £41,750 and another for approximately £75,000 on the seventeenth of September '84. Except for five quite insignificant with-drawals, the capital had been left to accumulate a low rate of interest.

Bartowski had been much more active. Large sums of money had passed through his account at irregular intervals and in some instances the individual withdrawals amounted to the sterling equivalent of several hundred thousand. The transactions were recorded in a code which seemed to be peculiar to the Neu Standard Gesellschaft; cracking it proved to be beyond Whattmore's capabilities even though he worked on it through the night.

Radford heard the muffled sound of footsteps, then the door opened inwards and a voice he was getting to know quite well told him to look lively. Reluctantly, he opened his eyes and sat up rubbing the crick in his neck that was the result of cat-napping in an armchair.

"That's more like it."

Harper had not been in the best of tempers when he'd arrived in the safe house at Ecouen shortly after ten thirty; now, almost nine hours later in the first cold light of day,

175

his abrupt manner suggested he was still walking around like a bear with a sore head. The head of Subversive Warfare had seemed urbane enough on the surface last night, but his ice-cold anger had shown itself every time Drew opened his mouth. Thanks to Drew, his department had been involved in the bizarre abduction of an American citizen, as a result of which the French Secret Service had now got him over a barrel.

"What's happening?" Radford asked.

"Miss Bartowski hasn't budged from her original story and our friends have decided to call it a day."

"Her real name is Zander."

"So she would have us believe." Harper walked over to the window, drew back the curtains and stood there gazing at the faint streak of dawn on the horizon. "The trouble is she can't prove it and the French aren't inclined to take her word on trust. They still think she's working for the Palestine Liberation Organisation."

"And I suppose the bomb was intended to wipe out the Israeli folk dancers?"

"That's the way the SDECE sees it. Those Israeli students were scheduled to spend five days in Paris; Sunday they were at the Eiffel Tower, today they were going to the Louvre. It would not have been too difficult for the PLO to discover their itinerary."

It was a sight more difficult to read Harper's mind. The whole place was wired for sound and there were TV cameras everywhere, some obvious, others more expertly concealed. Knowing this, Harper had deliberately kept his voice neutral and his back towards the hidden eye.

"They may think she's involved," said Radford, "but what proof have they got?"

"None."

"So what are they planning to do with her?"

"The French Foreign Minister will inform the American Ambassador that she is no longer welcome here and they'll put her on the first available flight to New York this afternoon." Harper turned away from the window and looked up at the camera above Radford's head. "On the other hand, no one will raise any objection if she asks to go to London instead."

Too right they wouldn't. The SDECE were bluffing, they couldn't deport Krystyna Zander unless they were willing to risk the attendant publicity, and they wouldn't do that because the newspapers might find out that they'd virtually kidnapped her in the first place.

"It would be to her advantage," Harper said, underlining the point. "Apart from anything else, you can reach Berlin a lot quicker from Heathrow than you can from Kennedy Airport."

"She can't return to Berlin, her cover's blown."

"All right, make her see that it's not going to look good on her record if she's deported from France. It won't be her fault of course but her superiors will infer she failed to take proper evasive action."

"You never give up, do you?" said Radford.

"Build on that special relationship you've established, Michael. You saved her life; that's something she won't forget."

There were a number of other things Krystyna Zander might not forget. There was, for instance, the little matter of the Peugeot. If Krystyna had noticed the diplomatic plates, she would know the British and French Intelligence Services were acting in collusion. Then there was Drew; she must have wondered why he was in civilian clothes when his companion was in uniform. Although he hadn't opened his mouth throughout the entire journey, the fact remained that on one occasion, the 'gendarme' had been forced to use sign language in order to make him understand which road they should take. At best, Radford figured he would be dealing with a very suspicious lady.

"It's not going to be easy," Radford said, frowning. "If we want Krystyna Zander to accompany us to London, we've got to make it worth her while."

"You can tell her about the Neu Standard Bank in Zürich and what additional information we expect to get from Thierack shortly. Test her to see if she's heard of Kalin; if she has, try to give the impression we know more than we're letting on. Finally, you can also hint that she'll have a place at the table when we question the people who knew Paine at RAF Church Fenton. All right?"

"I'll give it a try on one condition."

Harper raised both eyebrows. "I wasn't aware that we were striking a bargain, Michael?"

"A request then. If we're going to pull the wool over her eyes, Krystyna has to believe we're the good guys and the French are the villains. I don't want there to be any confusion on that score. That means Drew has got to stay out of her sight until further notice."

"I guarantee he'll be invisible." Harper pointed a finger at the ceiling. "Now suppose you do your bit," he said.

The room the SDECE had been using was on the second floor to the left of the staircase. Except for the familiar figure of the 'gendarme' standing guard on the landing, there was no sign of the Intelligence officers who'd been grilling Krystyna Zander. The interview room was, however, pungent with the smell of their cigarettes and the metal ashtray on the table was brimming over with stubs. After a question and answer session lasting all of eight hours in a smoke-laden atmosphere, Krystyna looked all in, her eyes red-rimmed and sore.

"Hi," he said quietly. "How are you feeling?"

"Pretty bushed." Krystyna smiled. "But I'm glad to see you. Pull up a chair."

He thought she had a nice smile, the kind that wasn't merely confined to the mouth. Until yesterday evening, he'd only seen the artificially hard exterior and this new Krystyna was very disarming. He felt that if she put her mind to it, she could really bewitch a man.

"I only came to say goodbye before we go our separate ways," he heard himself say, then promptly sat down.

"Are you getting the old heave-ho too?" she asked.

"I am now. Until my boss intervened, the French were all in favour of locking me up and throwing away the key. The most I'll get now is a rap over the knuckles or maybe a letter from the Army Board expressing their displeasure."

"Will that be the kiss of death for you?"

"No. The Military Secretary will lodge a copy in my personal file but it'll be so much water under the bridge in a few years' time." Even though Radford appreciated it was necessary, lying to her left a nasty taste in his mouth. "How will this business affect you?" he asked. "Will you lose any Brownie points?"

"I'll survive."

"It's been suggested that we should get together and pool our information."

"You scratch my back and I'll scratch yours?" Krystyna smiled again but this time her eyes stayed cynical.

"That's the general idea," he said. "For instance, I can give you the name of the bank in Zürich where both Paine and Bartowski had numbered accounts."

"I think the Bureau would be interested to know that."

"There's more. Very shortly we'll have a print-out for both accounts which will show every transaction they've made. We're hoping some of these entries will lead us to various associates of Paine and Bartowski."

"And you'd pass on their names to the FBI?"

"Right."

"In exchange for what?"

"Everything you have on Bartowski and the late Monika Starnberg."

"Seems reasonable." There was a momentary pause and her furrowed brow suggested that some minor point had occurred to her which didn't add up. "One thing puzzles me," she said eventually. "Why isn't your boss talking to my boss? The kind of deal you're proposing is usually thrashed out between the Chiefs, not the Indians."

Krystyna was a very bright, very sharp lady. In no time at all, she had seen through the charade and was going to make the most of it unless he cut her down to size.

"My Director thinks we'll get more out of you than we will from your people in Washington," Radford said bluntly. "They won't part with any more information than they have to because that's the American way of doing business."

"And I'm different?"

"I think you're ambitious and want to do more than just survive. What happened yesterday afternoon can't have done your reputation a lot of good and I reckon you'd welcome an opportunity to restore it."

"I don't see how a couple of bank statements could put me in a good light."

"I never said they would. But it would be a hell of a feather in your cap if you discovered why Paine was so anxious for Bartowski to get in touch with him."

"You mind telling me how I'm going to do that?" she demanded.

"By questioning the people who worked alongside him at RAF Church Fenton. Paine was a photo interpreter, one of the best the Intelligence Corps had and I've always believed he stumbled upon something that put the fear of God into him."

"I'd have to come to England," she said thoughtfully.

"Right."

"Now there we have a problem seeing the French are determined to put me on a plane to New York."

"I think we can persuade them to change their minds."

Krystyna Zander avoided his gaze and looked down at the floor. Her shoulders didn't actually shake but a slight twitch at the corners of her mouth made it obvious she was finding it difficult to contain her laughter.

"I bet you can," she said at length.

"Do we have a deal?" Radford asked, holding back a grin with equal difficulty.

"So long as I'm allowed to call the Chicago office first."

"No one's going to stop you doing that."

"Good," said Krystyna. "I wouldn't like the folks back home to get the impression I am acting under duress."

15

Number 16 Tetbury Gardens belonged to the Department
of Subversive Warfare and was a gift from the Sultan of
Muscat and Oman in appreciation of services rendered.
The kind of elegant Islington town house featured in 'Ideal
Homes', it consisted of two self-contained flats situated
above and below the sitting room, study and two spare
bedrooms on the intermediate floor. Although nothing
like as sophisticated as the SDECE house at Ecouen, the
large sitting room was wired for sound and included a
number of well-concealed cameras. These enabled anyone
in the adjoining study to video tape as well as observe
whoever was being debriefed or interrogated. On the
advice of a consultant psychiatrist who believed it wasn't
necessary to furnish the place like a prison cell in order to
turn a man round and squeeze him dry, there were pictures
on the walls, a full-sized Axminster carpet on the floor and
comfortable chairs to sit in.

But not everything was sweetness and light. Of the
two bedrooms across the landing, one had been specially
adapted to cater for the more recalcitrant guests of the
department. Apart from being windowless and completely
soundproof, day could be turned into night at the touch
of a button so that an inmate could rapidly become dis-
orientated.

Harper's financial vote from the Treasury did not allow
him to employ a fulltime housekeeper. To overcome this
problem, the flat on the ground floor was always allocated
to the desk officer seconded from the Armed Services.

Invited guests were accommodated in the self-contained flat in the garret while those who would never have gone anywhere near 16 Tetbury Gardens had they been free agents were held in the small bedroom on the first floor which had all the comforts of a prison cell.

Krystyna Zander was an invited guest. From the safe house in Ecouen, the same bogus gendarme together with an equally bogus woman police officer, had driven her back to the Hotel Caravelle where she had packed and settled her bill before going to Charles de Gaulle airport in the unmarked SDECE car. In accordance with their pre-arranged plan, Drew and Harper had gone ahead to catch an earlier flight, leaving Radford to keep an eye on Krystyna. With the aid of the sensitive mike probe he'd first used in Berlin, he had monitored her conversation with someone called Nick when she had got through to Chicago from one of the pay phones in the departure lounge. After that, the rest of the journey had been uneventful.

Thanks to the arrangements Harper had made when he'd passed through Heathrow ahead of them, Radford had been able to whisk her through Customs and Immigration in double quick time. A little over an hour and a half later, she was having coffee with him in the sitting room of number 16 Tetbury Gardens, having moved into the top flat, unpacked her clothes and freshened up.

"So when do I get to meet this Cedric Harper you work for?" she asked, coming straight to the point.

"Just as soon as he can escape from the Joint Intelligence Committee," Radford told her. "They meet every Tuesday morning to compare notes."

In fact, Harper had gone straight round to MI5 at Leconfield House from the airport to warn Adrian Carpenter that unless he produced the NCO who'd shared an office with Paine at Church Fenton forthwith, the Cabinet Office would be breathing down his neck.

"What are we supposed to do in the meantime?" Krystyna asked.

"Harper thought we might get together and pool our information."

"That's not a bad idea, Mike. Why don't you lead off?"

The 'Mike' was a sign of the new relationship between them that had been forged on the flight from Paris. Occasionally she would also call him Radford as though it too was a first name.

"How about ladies first?"

"You're the host," Krystyna said calmly. "You invited me here."

Her father, she had proudly told him on the flight over, had been one of the toughest and most uncompromising cops to pound a beat on Chicago's North Side. Radford supposed it was only natural that his daughter would have a lot of the father in her.

"Have you ever heard of Operation Heron?" he asked.

"No."

"It was a low level, coat-trailing op dreamed up by an officer in 261 Intelligence and Security Company who should have known better. He took a twenty-year-old corporal who'd done a bit of undercover work in Northern Ireland and turned him loose on the streets of Berlin in the hope that he would flush out some IRA sympathisers amongst the foreign workers. The kid took up with an unknown American student who was said to be doing a postgraduate course at the University of Berlin, and Paine was his case officer, the last of a small army that had been assigned to Heron at one time or another. Anyway, the corporal has a heart attack and dies alone in the flat. It was Paine who found his body and naturally he was heavily involved in the subsequent investigation. The Provost Marshal's department of the US Army was called in because the American postgraduate, whom none of the Brits had ever met, had disappeared and the faculty at the University of Berlin had never heard of him. Guess who your compatriots assigned to the case?"

"Bartowski?"

184

Radford nodded. "Some weeks after the corporal's death, the military police found twelve ounces of pure uncut heroin concealed in the apartment he'd been sharing with this American postgraduate. That much is fact, the rest is largely conjecture, but I'm pretty sure Bartowski knew about the heroin and helped himself to most of the cache before the military police discovered it."

"You're right," Krystyna said. "Without any supporting evidence, it is pure conjecture."

"Except that personnel belonging to Military Intelligence do not come within the jurisdiction of the Provost Marshal's office other than for disciplinary reasons. That means they didn't have the power to assign Bartowski to the case. He must have convinced them that our graduate friend had come to the notice of Military Intelligence and they agreed he should be on the team."

"Yes, I think I'd buy that," Krystyna said.

"I also think he waited until he was sure of Paine before he went to the cache."

"Are you saying Bartowski split the heroin down the middle with him?"

"I don't see how else Paine could have put enough money together to open a Swiss bank account on what the army paid him."

"Well, you should know, Radford." Krystyna frowned. "When was this Operation Heron?" she asked.

"It started in September 1979 and folded some nine months later."

Radford could guess what she was thinking. If Bartowski had known where to find the cache, it followed that he and the postgraduate had been business partners. And when the latter had disappeared, he would have been forced to look for another supplier.

"Somehow I don't think Sergeant Frank Minotti was the man who stepped in to fill the breach," Krystyna said, as though she was also in tune with his thoughts.

"The man you met in Berlin was not Minotti."

"What?"

"His real name is Horst Winkler and he's an East German Intelligence agent."

"My God." She said it slowly, extending both words as the full import began to sink in. "What the hell is a spy doing mixed up with a drug pusher like Bartowski?"

"I wouldn't know. We got involved because a senior NCO with constant access to top secret material had apparently gone absent." Radford smiled. "What's your excuse?"

"Routine police work." Krystyna pursed her lips, then said, "Well, maybe not quite so routine. My father got to know Ms Bartowski when she was teaching my seven-year-old nephew. My sister and brother-in-law both work and he used to meet him from school. Anyway, one day last Fall, he decided to have a word with Ms Bartowski about the bullying going on in the schoolyard and how the younger kids were being terrorised."

Her father had found Ms Bartowski alone in the classroom and she'd made it patently obvious she wasn't pleased to see him. School had finished for the day, the kids had all gone home and she had every intention of following their example. It had been a bad day one way and another and to have to stand there listening to an old man sounding off about the complete absence of any kind of discipline in the school had been the final straw. Her offhand manner and apparent lack of interest had also been the final straw for ex-Sergeant Zander.

"Pops is apt to wave his arms around when he gets angry," Krystyna continued, "and he was good and mad that afternoon. He made a sweeping motion with his right arm to emphasise a point and accidentally swept her music case on to the floor. It was one of the old-fashioned kind made of leather and open at the top like a shopping bag. Among the contents which spilled out was an old one pound packet of self-raising flour that had split open at one end. Pops didn't have to taste it to know the powdery substance was heroin. By rights, he should have handed

Ms Bartowski over to the cops, but he wanted to give me a break."

Just how big a break ex-Sergeant Zander had given his daughter had only become apparent after Krystyna had had the contents of the packet analysed. Instead of the usual four per cent substance found on the streets, this particular packet of 'self-raising flour' had been a hundred per cent pure, unadulterated heroin. If purchased in Bangkok or Landi Kotal up on the north-west frontier of Pakistan, it would have cost the buyer $7375 or £4915 sterling at 1985 prices; by the time it had been cut with talcum powder, quinine, or lactose, its street value would have been increased a hundred and fifty fold to close on three quarters of a million pounds.

"Ms Bartowski had a boyfriend who was a chemist," Krystyna continued. "She was going to meet him after school that afternoon and hand over the packet on the understanding that he would receive forty per cent of the profits after the heroin had been cut."

"They must have made themselves a fortune," Radford said.

"Uh huh." Krystyna shook her head. "They were just getting started."

Although Monika Starnberg had delivered the heroin in June 1984, it had taken Ms Bartowski three months to find someone with the necessary skills who didn't have a police record. Indeed, the whole operation had been so inept that she hadn't even recruited a single pusher when Zander had grabbed her.

"There was enough evidence to send Krystyna Bartowski and her boyfriend up for a five to ten stretch and that's how it would probably have ended but for the lab report. The experts who'd analysed the sample were convinced the heroin hadn't originated from the so-called Golden Triangle between the Mae Sai and Mekong rivers on the borders of Laos, Thailand and Burma: apart from anything else, the colour wasn't right. Nor in their opinion, had it been produced from the opium poppies grown in the

187

Iranian and Afghanistan crescent. Colombia too was ruled out, and that meant there was a new and as yet unidentified source of supply."

The fact that Stefan Bartowski was in Military Intelligence hadn't greatly excited the FBI. If a master sergeant was pushing drugs they figured it was basically the army's problem, not theirs. What did concern the Bureau was the fact that a new face was trying to establish himself in the US market.

"Even so, I doubt Washington would have authorised an undercover operation if your Staff Sergeant Paine hadn't written to Bartowski care of his sister in Chicago. He added a whole new dimension. Until we intercepted his letter, the Bureau chiefs in Washington had assumed we were simply dealing with a trio of bungling amateurs, the Master Sergeant in Military Intelligence who'd somehow gotten hold of a limited quantity of pure heroin, his girlfriend the Lufthansa air hostess who'd smuggled it to the States, and the little sister who was expected to hawk the stuff around Chicago. Paine made it an international operation."

"Was he supposed to be running the UK market?" Radford asked.

"That's the way we saw it."

"And Monika Starnberg?"

"She was the link between Bartowski and the source. Until she switched to the New York run in June '83, Monika Starnberg was flying the Mid East route to Ankara, Beirut, Damascus and Tehran. We think her task was to recruit and train the couriers who smuggled the heroin into the Federal Republic of West Germany. Once the Mid East route was functioning efficiently, it was only natural that Bartowski should think of branching out into the States."

"He wasn't exactly quick off the mark," said Radford. "I mean, Monika Starnberg had been flying the New York route for a good twelve months before she made the first and only delivery."

"Stefan is a very cautious man," Krystyna said wryly. "Which is why he went AWOL when he heard the Mafia had put out a contract on him. They didn't like it when he tried to muscle in on their territory."

"Is that a fact?"

"No, but it seemed a convincing explanation at the time." Krystyna shrugged. "Anyway, I convinced Nick we should try to contact Bartowski and turn him round. Naturally, his friends were unlikely to point us in the right direction if they knew the FBI were looking for him, but they might just be inclined to do his sister a favour. I figured I could get away with impersonating Krystyna Bartowski provided I steered well clear of anyone who'd actually met her. Discovering where Paine was hiding himself was my number one priority, which is why I approached your Intelligence and Security Company in Berlin."

Undercover work demanded nerves of steel, a cool head and a special brand of courage. Radford thought Krystyna Zander possessed more than her fair share of all three.

"I never dreamt I would end up meeting an East German spy." She gazed at him speculatively. "Question is, Radford, where do we go from here?"

Answering the phone in the adjoining study was not what she had in mind but its insistent trill demanded attention. Although Harper hadn't said he would call him at the house in Tetbury Gardens, Radford didn't see how it could be anyone else. When he returned a few minutes later, it was evident the same thought had occurred to Krystyna.

"The Man?" she asked.

Radford nodded. "Which would you like to hear first, the good news or the bad?"

"The good."

"The good news is that we get to question Sergeant George Elder this afternoon. He's the RAF NCO who worked alongside Harry Paine. The bad news is that the Finance Director of the Neu Standard has been murdered,

189

we've lost the only lead we had on Bartowski's tax lawyer, and the desk officer Harper sent over to Zürich can't make head nor tail of the bank statements he's collected."

Kalin left the key to his room at the Hotel Duma with the desk clerk and walked out into the street. Turning right, he headed towards the Parliament buildings beyond the Roosevelt Gardens, then made his way down to the river and the bookshop opposite the Adam Clark suspension bridge. From Zürich, he had caught the Swissair flight departing at 08.50 hours for Vienna where he had arrived in time to connect with the Malev Airlines shuttle to Budapest and points east. It had been an uneventful journey and he anticipated that the debriefing session he was about to attend would prove equally mundane. Pushing the door open, he walked into the bookshop, told the middle-aged saleswoman that Mr Josef was expecting him and was immediately shown into the small back room.

Mr Josef was Major General Vasili Petrovich Yagoda, former commander of the 11th Security Brigade, Baku Military District. A squat, uncouth-looking man with bulbous eyes, he had been promoted over the heads of thirty-seven more senior colonels in recognition of the brilliant counter-insurgency operations he'd conducted against the dissident tribesmen in the Kirova Depression. Andrei Kalin too had not gone unrewarded; he had jumped from senior lieutenant to major after commanding the firing squad which had executed the seven Azerbaijani peasants convicted of terrorist crimes. Like the General, he'd known the prosecution's case had been a complete fabrication; like the General, the knowledge hadn't bothered him one bit. Moscow Centre had ordered them to wind up the experiment in such a way that no one would ever know it had taken place and being dedicated professionals, they had done just that. The subsequent executive action against external targets had been merely an extension of the original assignment. Kalin just wished a little more time and thought had been given to the problem. The use

190

of surrogate Intelligence agencies and the emphasis on speed smacked of panic in high places. The terse almost perfunctory way Yagoda greeted him suggested that some of the panic had rubbed off on to the General.

"Everything went off according to plan," Kalin told him, anticipating the obvious question. "The American, Stefan Bartowski, was particularly co-operative."

"He didn't give you any trouble then?"

"He came running as soon as he got my message, Comrade General. Of course, later on he offered a certain amount of resistance but we soon overcame that."

Contacting Bartowski hadn't been a problem; he had known the American's favourite off-duty haunts in Württemburg and a few well-chosen words in his ear had done the rest. The same tactics had been equally successful with Monika Starnberg especially when Bartowski himself had passed the message.

"You are satisfied he told you everything?"

It seemed Yagoda wanted a blow by blow account of what they had done to the girl when Bartowski had refused to disclose the location of his warehouse. Whether the General's curiosity was entirely normal or healthy was something Kalin did not care to think about too deeply.

"Fräulein Starnberg helped to concentrate her lover's mind wonderfully well," he said matter-of-factly. "She started screaming before we'd even inserted the electrodes, but I think it was the knowledge that we would do the same to him which eventually loosened his tongue. Bartowski had stored most of the heroin in a lock-up garage he'd rented near his girlfriend's apartment in Sophienstrasse. The rest he'd concealed around the engine compartment and chassis of his Mercedes."

The American had been like putty in their hands from then on. He must have suspected that they intended to kill him yet he'd made no attempt to escape and had willingly accompanied them to Switzerland. He had set things up with Thierack and had lured Paine to Arosa. Without anyone prompting him, Bartowski had even set Paine's mind at rest when the Englishman had referred to a letter which neither he nor Kalin had known anything about.

"And you had no problems with Wolfgang Thierack either?"

"None whatsoever."

Kalin had no reservations on that score. Bribery had secured Thierack's initial co-operation, simple blackmail had ensured he continued in the same vein and a bullet in the head had guaranteed he wouldn't talk out of turn. The bank account Kalin had opened for him with Credit Suisse of Geneva would provide the kind of mute testimony the KGB desired; its existence would help to persuade the Swiss police that the financial director of the Neu Standard had been doing business with the underworld.

"So I can assume that the sum of 378,500 Swiss Francs, less commission, has been transferred to the Deutsche Volksbank in Dresden where it has been credited to the account of Herr Erich Dollmann?"

"One does not have to assume anything, Comrade General." Kalin produced a slip of paper from the inside pocket of his jacket and gave it to Yagoda. "This is the telex he received from the Volksbank confirming the transaction."

"I wish certain other matters had been dealt with as efficiently."

Kalin wondered if the General was making a thinly veiled reference to Paine. It was scarcely his fault the body had been discovered so quickly; everything had had to be done in a hurry and the garage had been the only secure hiding place for the corpse. He had calculated quite correctly that the cement would have dried out by the time the workmen returned to the site on the Monday but luck, good or bad, was a random factor no one could take into account. The General, however, was not interested in excuses.

"I am sorry about the Englishman, Comrade General," he said hesitantly. "We should have found somewhere more remote to bury him."

192

Yagoda stared at him, his fish-like eyes cold and expressionless. "Will they find Bartowski?" he demanded.

"Absolutely not. There is nothing left to find; we cremated his body in a disused pottery outside Chur."

"Then there's nothing to worry about. All the evidence will lead the police to assume Paine was murdered by the missing American." Yagoda paused, his head inclined as if straining to hear the distant sound of a tram in the parallel street behind the bookshop. Then in a voice that sounded curiously remote, he said, "I was referring to the antics of our German colleagues in Berlin."

Until that moment, Kalin hadn't been aware that Krystyna Bartowski had been in Berlin looking for her brother. The more Yagoda told him, the more he was convinced that the 'apparatchiks' who ran Moscow Centre were reacting to the situation like a bunch of headless chickens.

"I want you to go to Berlin and be my eyes and ears," Yagoda told him. "I want to know what Bartowski's sister is doing in Paris and why Leber's men went after her with a bomb. So far as the girl is concerned, the job is to be finished and finished quickly. Do I make myself clear, Comrade Major Kalin?"

"Perfectly."

"Good. Once the girl has been dealt with, action should be put in hand to neutralise Erich Dollmann."

Although the name meant nothing to him, Kalin assumed he was the East German agent who'd eliminated Paine's wife. Then suddenly he found himself clutching the same slip of paper he'd given the General a few minutes earlier.

"When the time is ripe, you are to give that transfer slip to Leber. He will then do the rest."

"Yes, sir. When do I leave?"

"There's a GDR Luft Air flight departing at 18.35 hours tonight. Be on it."

"As the Comrade General wishes."

Kalin was conscious of sounding like a robot programmed to respond in an unemotional and strictly functional manner. Behind the impassive exterior, however, the adrenalin was pumping furiously with the realisation that what the KGB proposed to do to Dollmann, they could equally well do to him.

16

Sergeant George Elder arrived by taxi from King's Cross Station at three twenty-five; barely five minutes later he was holding forth in the sitting room of 16 Tetbury Gardens as though he had known Harper, Radford and Krystyna all his life. A bouncy, slightly overweight man in his late thirties, he was wearing a cheviot tweed suit which helped to foster the image of a cheerful bookmaker who'd had a good day at the races. He was one of those extroverts who got along with most people, the late Harry Paine being one of the few exceptions.

"I've got to be honest with you," Elder said. "I didn't like the guy. He wanted a commission so badly it hurt. And he was so two-faced about it; when he was having a beer with the likes of me, he was one of the boys and didn't have a good word to say for any of the officers. But it was a very different story when the Lieutenant Colonel commanding the army element at Church Fenton walked into our office. Then it was all yes sir, no sir, three bags full sir. I tell you, Harry really liked the taste of boot polish."

"And his wife – Jackie?" Harper asked quietly.

"She was very ambitious too but better at hiding it. Jackie enjoyed the good things in life."

"Like what?" Radford said.

"Dining out at least once a week, a fortnight's holiday in the sun. Last summer they went to Majorca."

"How about weekend breaks in Zürich?" Harper put in.

"If they went anywhere at weekends it was usually to stay with her mother in Blackpool. Harry only went to Zürich the once that I know of."

Elder was only confirming what Detective Chief Superintendent Marsh had already told him. At Harper's request, Special Branch had asked the airline desks to check their records to see how many times a Mr H. Paine had flown to Zürich in the previous twelve months. A similar approach had been made to all travel agents within a twenty mile radius of Riccall with equally negative results.

"Let's talk about his job," Harper said, abruptly changing the subject. "What was Paine working on before he disappeared?"

Elder glanced at Krystyna and shifted uncomfortably in his chair. "I'm not sure I'm allowed to," he said. "The stuff we get is highly classified."

"Everyone here has been positively vetted." Harper smiled. "We've also been cleared for Signal Intelligence and every other caveat under the sun."

The blanket clearance didn't apply to Krystyna but no one had told Elder that she was a law enforcement officer and he naturally assumed she was included.

"Well, okay," he said. "Just over a month ago, the Yanks sent us a batch of satellite photographs of the Baku Military District that had been taken on the fourteenth of October '84. They featured the Kirova Depression which is a triangular-shaped area abutting the Caspian Sea roughly sixty miles from the Soviet–Iranian border. The Yanks had already looked at the photographs and merely wanted a second opinion from us. It was the kind of boring task no one wanted to do, so we drew lots for it and Harry lost."

"Are you saying it was a waste of time?" Harper asked.

"Yes. The Americans had already told us there was nothing there and we saw no reason to disbelieve them. Harry never stopped bitching about it and did just enough to get by. It was a good job he was blessed with an inventive mind and a glib tongue to go with it because he certainly needed both when our head man paid us an unexpected visit."

"When was this?" Krystyna asked.

"I'm not exactly sure." Elder frowned. "Must have been about the sixteenth or seventeenth of February, roughly a week after the photos arrived. Anyway, Paine was sitting there in a dream when the Squadron Leader walked into the office and asked him what he was doing. That's why Harry made this big song and dance about an unnatural fogbank over the Kirova Depression."

"Was he nervous or excited?"

Elder gave the question some thought, then said, "A bit of both. I do know he had second thoughts later on about his discovery. Before he flew to Zürich, Harry made a point of telling me he wished he'd kept his mouth shut because there was nothing mysterious about the fogbank. It was just a scrub fire."

"How big a one?" Radford demanded.

"It covered all of eighteen square miles. 'Sandpiper' was on the twelfth alternate pass by the time the haze began to clear."

"I think you'd better explain what that means," Harper said. "Preferably in terms a layman can understand."

Elder did just that. 'Sandpiper' was the codename of a military satellite which normally observed the missile silos around Baku as well as certain other installations within its orbit. From time to time, however, 'Sandpiper' was instructed to look at other areas of possible interest of which the Kirova Depression was only one example. The satellite completed an orbit in seventy-eight minutes and had been programmed to photograph the Depression on alternate passes; the fire had therefore taken over thirty-one hours to burn itself out.

"It wasn't until the final batch of photographs arrived last Tuesday that the cause of the fire became apparent. They were from a second aerial reconnaissance carried out on the nineteenth of October and I noticed a few bits of

197

debris on the southern periphery of the fire. After the exposures had been enlarged, I was able to identify the remains of a Mi 1 recce helicopter. That was enough to satisfy the Chief Analyst of our section."

"You stopped looking?" Harper said.

Elder nodded. "There was nothing of military significance in the area."

"So no one would mind if you gave me a couple of prints?"

"Not if you signed for them."

"Good. I'll look forward to receiving them by courier post first thing tomorrow morning."

Elder had been given his marching orders and knew what was expected of him. If there was any lingering doubt in his mind on either score, it was rapidly dispelled when Harper thanked him for all his help and stated quite blandly that if necessary the prints were to be delivered by hand of special messenger. It was left to Radford to phone for a minicab and see him off the premises.

When he returned, Harper greeted him with a peremptory, "Well?"

"No one's ever going to know what really happened," said Radford, "but I reckon Paine must have had the shock of his life when he started to examine those photographs. He knew the Russians were supplying Bartowski with heroin and suddenly he's looking at the destruction of last year's opium crop. If I were a gambling man, I'd take bets that Paine stopped dealing in heroin when he left Berlin in '81 and had deliberately distanced himself from his former business partner. However, they had this private code for use in an emergency and he fired off a number of letters to various addresses with the aim of contacting Bartowski as quickly as possible. How he happened to know Ms Bartowski's new address in Chicago is more difficult to explain. My guess is she was the fall-back link and probably sent Paine a card last Christmas to let him know she was moving to a new apartment on the North Side."

Harper glanced inquisitively at Krystyna. "What do you think, Miss Zander?" he asked.

"I'd go along with everything Mike has said. What I don't understand is why the Soviets would bother to run such a small scale operation."

"Small scale?" Harper reiterated.

"We're talking about twelve thousand acres under cultivation," Krystyna told him. "I don't pretend to know the yield per acre, but taking other areas as a yardstick, I'd be surprised if the Kirova Depression was producing more than fifteen tons of raw opium per annum. Distilled in a laboratory with acetic anhydride, they'd end up with a ton and a half of heroin. The Golden Triangle in Siam produces well over seventy-five tons a year and that's nothing compared with what's coming out of the so-called Islamic Crescent."

"Look at it from a different angle," said Radford, "and it was a very ambitious operation. You find a crooked soldier like Bartowski and set him up in business by supplying him with uncut heroin at a knockdown price, then when he's raking in the shekels, you put the arm on him for classified information. Furthermore, you make Bartowski do the same to his middlemen. Perhaps the quality of information wasn't always top grade but Moscow could have had few complaints about the quantity."

"Then why dismantle the whole set-up?" Harper asked.

"Your guess is as good as mine. Maybe when Mikhail Gorbachev was Minister for Agriculture he heard a whisper that something pretty odd was going on down there in the Kirova Depression?"

"With heroin there's always corruption," Krystyna said. "While he was alive, J. Edgar Hoover kept the FBI out of the drug scene because he knew the enormous profits there were to be made in the trade and feared some of his agents would be tempted."

"So if certain people working in Dzerzhinsky Square became contaminated," Harper said, developing Krystyna's theme, "they would need their own Swiss numbered accounts to buy luxuries unobtainable in Russia." He smiled. "Perhaps they also bank with the Neu Standard?"

"I'll tell you this," Radford said, "it would be a hell of a joke if Bartowski and Monika Starnberg were purchasing the stuff at their behest. Bartowski would be off the hook and there wouldn't be a damn thing his case officer could do about it."

"Except kill him when they realised just how ill Chernenko was." Harper paused briefly, then said, "And for once the name of the heir presumptive wasn't in doubt which is probably why the KGB decided to destroy every trace of the operation."

The clean up should have begun and ended last October with the destruction of the opium poppies and the laboratory where the heroin was produced but Chernenko had gone into an irreversible decline at an inconvenient time when Gorbachev's star had still been in the ascendancy. Suddenly, fear had been the inspiration and driving force behind the second purge which had rapidly spiralled out of control. It also occurred to Radford that the men who'd launched the second purge were now incapable of stopping it and the killing would probably go on until no one was left who could remember how it had all started.

"It would be helpful to know the Soviet Order of Battle in the Transcaucasus at the beginning of October last year." Harper looked up at the ceiling as if seeking further inspiration. "I'd certainly be interested to know the names of the various formation commanders."

There was a distinct possibility that the Secret Intelligence Service or the Armed Forces Intelligence Directorate in the Ministry of Defence would have the relevant information, but Harper would already know that. There was however another source which Radford thought the Director might not be quite so familiar with.

"We used to monitor that part of the world when I was a Special Telegraphist in 9 Signal Regiment," he said, broaching the subject.

"And you think there's some particular area we should examine?"

"Yes, the air traffic control net of Baku Military District. Specifically we should ask the Government Communications Headquarters at Cheltenham for a transcript of every transmission we captured on the fourteenth of October. You never know, the pilot of that Mi 1 helicopter might have put out a mayday before he went into the deck."

It was one of those evenings in early March when it was hard to believe that Spring was on the way. A cold front moving in from the east had turned a light shower into sleet which a gusting wind then splattered against the window in Dollmann's office. Although not usually given to philosophical reflections, he thought the atrocious weather provided a fitting end to what had been a very bad day. Right from the moment late on Monday afternoon when the first reports of the explosion at the Georges Pompidou Centre in Paris had come through on the tickertape machine, Dollmann had had a premonition that the job had been bungled. Now, twenty-four hours later, his worst fears had been confirmed. He looked at the latest message he'd received from the clandestine relay station in West Berlin and reluctantly decided he'd have to brief Leber.

Everyone else who worked on the second floor of the State Security building had gone home except Leber. Although his filing trays were empty, the ex-Gestapo officer was still at his desk and did not seem the least bit surprised to see Dollmann.

"Come in, Erich," he said almost jovially and waved him to a chair. "I've been waiting to hear how much damage has been done."

Details of the incident had been coming through on the tickertape machine and Leber would know the Polish American girl was not mentioned in the list of dead and injured. Yet his manner suggested he was privy to very much more. Dollmann couldn't understand how this was possible when every message relayed through the clandestine station had come straight to him marked 'Exclusive For'.

"There's no way the incident can be attributed to us," Dollmann said tersely.

"I'm relieved to hear it, Erich."

"We used one of Gaddafi's assassins to plant the bomb and he believed the Israelis were the target."

"Excellent," Leber said, a shade too enthusiastically.

"Their presence was purely fortuitous."

"Luck is a very fickle lady, Erich. You should not complain when she looks upon you with favour."

"Our man waited until the Libyan was clear of the area," Dollmann said, ignoring the homily. "As he was about to radio activate the device, he caught sight of a tall, dark-haired man advancing towards Krystyna Bartowski. He says the stranger was definitely trying to warn her. Immediately after the explosion, he observed a second man running across the square in hot pursuit of the target."

"Is that an assumption or a plain statement of fact, Erich?"

"Fact. On Sunday afternoon he followed Krystyna Bartowski back to the Hotel Caravelle where she was staying in Paris. Last night, some five hours after the incident, a Peugeot saloon with diplomatic plates pulled up outside the hotel. Two men got out, a French gendarme and the tall, dark-haired man. Approximately fifteen minutes later they re-appeared with Krystyna Bartowski and drove off. The man who'd been seen running across the square was driving."

Leber opened the cigar box on his desk and helped himself to one of the Burma cheroots he favoured. Taking his time, he pierced the cigar with a matchstick, then lit it and leaned back in his chair.

"The Peugeot with diplomatic plates is a bit sinister," he said presently.

Dollmann licked his bottom lip. "There's been no press

release about the police arresting a suspect either. Those two facts taken in conjunction would seem to indicate that either Bartowski's sister has been turned round and is working for some government agency or else the woman we've been tracking is a plant."

"An impostor?"

"Why not?" said Dollmann. "Which of us has even seen a photograph of the sister? A young woman calls at Monika Starnberg's apartment in Frankfurt and the surveillance team who are watching the place assume she's Krystyna Bartowski. Too many people have made too many assumptions; that's why there have been so many foul-ups . . ."

"It doesn't matter who the woman is or what she is," Leber said interrupting him. "She has touched base and is now out of our reach."

"What happens if she re-surfaces?"

"Nothing, we're not going anywhere near her."

"Good. Let's hope Moscow Centre will go along with your decision." Dollmann stood up. "I might as well go on home," he said. "There's nothing more I can do tonight."

"Yes, you run along, Erich."

"You fancy a drink at the bar down the street?"

"I do but I can't." Leber smiled apologetically. "I'm expecting Major Andrei Kalin."

"Who's he?"

"Yagoda's right hand man. He's flying in from Budapest."

Dollmann lingered, hoping the older man would tell him more but Manfred was in one of his enigmatic moods and was about as communicative as a Trappist monk. Finally he said goodnight to Leber and left the building to drive a couple of blocks to the bar he sometimes frequented.

Ordering a beer and a Schnapps to chase it down, he parked himself in one of the booths and tried to figure out what had prompted Yagoda to send his trusted lieutenant to Berlin. The solution to the puzzle proved elusive and the alcohol failed to help him relax. A phone call to a lady friend living in the outer commuter belt took care of that particular problem, however, and in a slightly happier frame of mind he left the bar and continued on down the old east-west axis which led out of town.

The lady friend whose name was Ilse, was in charge of the typing pool on the second floor and had been security cleared by Dollmann himself some four years ago when she'd been in the process of joining the Department. A member of the Communist Party from the age of twenty-one, her references had been impeccable and there had been an imposing number of friends and acquaintances who'd willingly vouched for her loyalty and integrity. She'd also interviewed well but Dollmann had sensed that lurking beneath the demure exterior, there was a very earthy woman whose sexual tastes might incline to the kinky. Although fully aware that anyone who had such predilections was vulnerable to pressure, he had nevertheless cleared her for access to highly classified material.

Ilse was married to a news presenter on the overseas service of DDR Rundfunk whose foreign language broadcasts to Ethiopia were transmitted live between the hours of midnight and three a.m. four days a week. There were no children to complicate matters and their house was on the outskirts of Hoppegarten roughly ten minutes' walk from the 'S' Bahn station. Better still, it was the only one in a poorly lit, narrow lane which led to a market garden.

Dollmann swung into the drive and parked his car in front of the garage. Ilse had heard the tinny sound of the Wartburg's exhaust as soon as he'd turned into the lane and was waiting for him at the door when he got out. In the time it had taken him to motor out to Hoppegarten, she had changed into a severe-looking black suit and calf-length boots. The jacket was fastened by a single button at the waist to reveal a deep cleavage. From past experience, he knew she also had nothing on under the brief skirt, a thought which excited him and stirred a hitherto flaccid member into life.

"Hello, Ilse." His eyes fastened on the length of picture

cord she was holding in her right hand. "It's going to be like that, is it?" he said in a voice that sounded curiously submissive.

"But of course. We both know it's what you want."

Dollmann stepped into the hall and shucked off his raincoat, then following Ilse into the sitting room, obediently removed his jacket at her command. Again at her command, he faced the wall and crossed his hands behind him, passively allowing her to bind his wrists.

The games they played were always complicated and Ilse, who was eighteen months older than Dollmann, was invariably cast in the dominating role. However, a theme common to all their sessions was a bizarre interrogation concerning some quite facile but unspecified crime.

"I want your confession," she told him fiercely.

"What am I supposed to have done?" Dollmann asked in a meek voice.

"Now you're being insolent."

Ilse grabbed a fistful of hair and banged his head against the wall, then turning him round, she sank a clenched fist into his stomach. Working herself into a rage, she cuffed him about the head and slapped his face but not hard enough to leave the telltale impression of her fingers. Physical force was permissible so long as there was no visible evidence; that was one of their unwritten rules she punctiliously observed no matter how excited she became. But there were no restrictions where verbal abuse was concerned and Dollmann was often hard pressed to decide which he enjoyed the most.

The couch was to his right and he side-stepped towards it. In a matter of seconds now, she would mount him and they would simultaneously reach a shattering climax which neither of them ever experienced with their respective partners. He felt the couch behind him and fell back on to it; then just as they were about to couple, the telephone rang.

"Don't answer it," Dollmann said harshly. "Whoever's calling will soon get tired of waiting and will hang up."

But they didn't. The shrill summons continued, peal after peal, till in the end the intrusive noise ruined everything and Ilse went out into the hall to still it. A few moments later she returned, her forehead creased in a puzzled frown.

"It's your wife," Ilse informed him. "She wants to speak to you."

His stomach lurched as though he was in danger of falling from the roof of a high-rise building. "Tell her I'm not here."

"She knows you are."

Dollmann stared at Ilse. The curve of her mouth suggested that she found the situation amusing but he was damned if he could see the funny side of it. He twisted round on to his left hip, presenting his back to her.

"Untie me," he snapped.

Ilse had done a better job than either of them had anticipated and the knots were too tight for her to undo quickly. Knowing the longer his wife was kept waiting, the more suspicious she would become, he struggled to his feet, told Ilse to follow him and went out into the hall. The receiver was lying on the small table; picking it up, Ilse held the instrument for him while he spoke to his wife.

"Hello, Heidi," Dollmann said calmly.

"What are you doing in that woman's house?"

"I'm here on official business," he said.

"You lying little shit. Since when has fucking a whore been official business?"

It was her language more than her anger which rocked him back on his heels. In all the years they'd been married, he couldn't ever recall her using a swear word, never mind the gutter filth that had just fallen so easily from her lips.

"Now you listen to me," he said firmly. "It's my job to interview every employee of our section whenever their security clearance is due for renewal."

"Liar. I know what you've been doing. Every time you

supposedly went to Dresden to see your parents, you've been in Hoppegarten humping that bitch from the typing pool."

Dollmann tried to convince Heidi that she had got it all wrong, that if she telephoned his parents they would confirm his story, but his wife was in no mood to listen to him. Shouting at the top of her voice, she told Dollmann she never wanted to see him again and then hung up.

Ilse put the phone down. "You'd better go, Erich," she said nervously, then added, "Whoever told Heidi about us may also have told my husband."

"This isn't one of your little games, is it?" he asked.

"Are you mad? Of course it isn't."

"No, I didn't think it was." Dollmann followed her into the kitchen and waited patiently while she found a pair of scissors and cut the cord binding his wrists. "Would your husband have any reason to suspect anything?"

It was an idiotic question. Ilse had always been very discreet and they'd treated each other like polite strangers at the office.

But someone had arranged to have them watched. Who, why and when? The answer to the first part of the question came to Dollmann as he finished dressing. Leber had to be the one who'd put him under surveillance. He was the only man who had the necessary authority and could select the best operatives for the job. The agent must have shadowed him out to the house one night, then returned the next day to bug the place from top to bottom while Ilse and her husband were at work.

"It's going to be all right," Dollmann said and patted her on the cheek. "I know who put us under the microscope and I can deal with him."

"How can you be so sure?"

"Because I know where the skeletons are hidden," Dollmann told her.

Somewhere the spools were winding, recording every word, but he didn't give a damn. He wanted Leber, the ex-Gestapo officer, to know that if anything happened to him, he would ensure the appropriate sources in West Berlin would learn of Manfred's real identity.

17

The Order of Battle for Baku Military District, together with a potted biography of known formation commanders and principal staff officers, ran to a page and a half of A4 paper. Two names had been underlined by Harper – Colonel, now Major General Vasili Petrovich Yagoda, former commander of 11 Security Brigade, and Lieutenant General Nikolai Andreyev, erstwhile General Officer Commanding Baku Military District, whose promotion had appeared in the February '85 List. Radford noted in passing that *Red Banner*, the official newspaper of the army, had reported that Andreyev had been transferred to Far East Command at Vladivostok. The newspaper didn't say where Yagoda had gone after relinquishing command of the frontier troops.

"Those two are the only officers who've been promoted and moved on since the fire," said Harper. "All the others, the Chief of Staff and the commanders of 42nd Mountain, 93rd and 107th Mechanised, 8th Airborne and the 201st (Guards) Tank Division are still in post."

"Would I be right in thinking the Kirova Depression is within 11 Security Brigade's operational area?" Radford asked.

"You would." Harper gave him another sheet of A4 to read. "This is a record of the air traffic control net which you advised me to ask for. It's really quite illuminating."

The extract provided by Government Communications Headquarters at Cheltenham was a verbatim record of various transmissions involving a reconnaissance helicopter known as callsign Strella One and Hermitage, the appointment code name for air traffic control, which had taken place on the fourteenth of October, the day the first batch of aerial photographs had been taken. The pilot of Strella One had joined the net at 1000 hours and informed control that he was on a reconnaissance mission for Exercise 'Forward Spring'. At 1105, Strella One had notified a change of course; then, eight minutes later, the pilot had come up again to report what appeared to be a large fire in the south-east corner of the Kirova Depression. In acknowledging the message, Hermitage had reminded Strella One that the Kirova Depression was a prohibited area controlled by Watchdog, the standard codename for all frontier security units. Either Strella One had failed to appreciate the significance of control's advice or else he'd decided to ignore it. At 1207 hours, the monitoring station in Cyprus had heard Strella One say that he was going in to take a closer look at the fire. Responding to this latest development, Hermitage had immediately ordered the pilot to turn back; then, within a matter of seconds, there had been so much interference on the frequency that no further transmissions had been captured for the next four hours thirty-eight minutes. When at last Hermitage had become audible once more, the control station had been trying to re-establish contact with Strella One. In the opinion of the operator who'd monitored the exchange, the level of interference could not be attributed to freakish atmospheric conditions.

"Well?" Harper demanded when he looked up from the transcript.

"I go along with the operator," Radford told him. "The net was being deliberately jammed by the KGB frontier troops. Strella One had violated their airspace at a particularly sensitive time when they were burning the opium crop. They ensured the pilot couldn't report what he'd seen; then they either shot the helicopter out of the sky or else they blew it up after the pilot had landed near the scene of the fire."

"It was a recce mission," Harper said, "so there would have been several passengers on board. What do you suppose the KGB did with them?"

"Killed them along with the pilot," said Radford. "And the General Officer Commanding Baku Military District subsequently participated in the cover up."

"A little far-fetched wouldn't you say?"

"Is it though? According to this potted biography, Nikolai Andreyev is sixty-two which means he must have been the oldest serving Major General in the Red Army. Couldn't he have been promoted because he knew when to keep his mouth shut?"

"Mm." Harper considered the suggestion, then said, "Yagoda certainly did all right. He got himself promoted over the heads of thirty-seven more senior colonels which caused quite a bit of ill feeling. He's stationed in Budapest now, has some sort of roving commission."

"How did we come by that information?"

"From one of the passed-over colonels. People are apt to get a bit hot under the collar when they feel they've been done down. This particular colonel happens to be masquerading as one of the Second Secretaries at the Soviet Embassy in Belgrade. He sought out our SIS man at a diplomatic shindig hosted by the French and had a quiet word with him. It doesn't matter how good their cover is, these professionals can always sniff one another out."

Radford looked up at the pigeons roosting on the ledge outside the porthole window in Harper's office. One bird, who appeared to be more aggressive than the others, had already seized most of the available space and was now jockeying to grab the rest.

"Anyway, our Russian friend was only too eager to mark Yagoda's card for us."

"Why would he do that?" Radford asked.

"To get his own back by making Yagoda virtually unemployable outside the Soviet Union and the Warsaw Pact. By now, every Western Intelligence agency will know he's KGB."

211

"Yagoda is responsible for the deaths of eleven people that we know of and all we can do is make sure he stays at home. Is that what I'm supposed to tell Krystyna Zander when I return to Tetbury Gardens?"

"Yagoda isn't an entrepreneur," Harper said coolly, "he lacks the necessary imagination. He's the equivalent of the works manager, the man who's good at getting things done. Someone in Moscow Centre had this brainwave, sold the idea to the State Security Committee and then put the whole thing together."

It sounded like an excuse for doing nothing. There was no way they could get to Yagoda and anyway, despite being a Major General, he was still only a highly-placed mechanic. And yet Radford doubted if Harper would have summoned him to his office to hear what amounted to a capitulation.

"I mean to have Yagoda," Harper said quietly, as though reading his thoughts. "He doesn't know it yet but he's going to defect. What's more, Vasili Petrovich is going to stay here once he has defected. There's going to be none of that bloody nonsense of him running back to Mother Russia the first time he hears a balalaika on the radio."

"How are you going to manage that?"

"I'm not sure yet." Harper shrugged. "Maybe we can reach him through Kalin or Dollmann?"

Two names they couldn't put a face to; Radford couldn't see them making a lot of progress in that direction.

"We'll use Winkler to establish contact."

"I thought you gave him to the British Security Service Organisation?"

"We'll borrow him."

What Harper gave with one hand, he took back with the other. Adrian Carpenter wouldn't like it, but knowing something of the way the Director operated and the kind of support he was capable of drumming up, Radford was prepared to bet the MI5 man would be forced to swallow his objections.

"Of course you'll have to keep Miss Zander sweet," Harper said idly. "I don't want her rocking the boat."

It was another way of saying that Krysia was astute enough to realise the Bartowski affair had ceased to be a law enforcement matter the moment Winkler had been identified as an East German Intelligence agent. It was also apparent that Harper was anxious to ensure the US State Department didn't muscle in on the act, which they certainly would do if Krysia took it into her head to pass on all the information she had gathered.

"Depends on what you mean by keeping her sweet," Radford said. "Tell me exactly what you have in mind."

Harper spent the next twenty minutes doing just that.

The morning was better than the night before – a clear blue sky and a sun with some warmth in it replacing a bitterly cold wind interspersed with snow flurries. Dollmann saw the change in the weather as a kind of personal omen. Although he'd had to spend the night in a hotel after Heidi had refused to let him in to their apartment, he'd arrived at the office feeling he had the situation well under control. All he had to do now was sit back and let the tapes do the talking for him. As soon as Leber heard his conversation with Ilse, he would realise he had more to lose than Dollmann and would quietly back off. His complacency lasted until mid morning when it was shattered by a phone call from Dresden.

The man who spoke to Dollmann after the operator at Normannenstrasse had put him through, had a thin and very precise voice.

"Herr Dollmann?" he said. "My name is Noske. I'm the manager of the Volksbank here in Dresden . . ."

"I'm a busy man, Herr Noske," Dollmann said, interrupting him. "What is it you want?"

"You have an account with us."

"Account?" Dollmann frowned, then recalled he'd never got around to closing the checking account he'd had before he'd married Heidi and moved to Berlin on promotion. Once a year, his parents religiously forwarded the statement the bank had sent to their address in Dresden and once a year he'd vowed to do something about it and never had. What was the outstanding credit balance? A hundred and eighty something Marks? "I'm amazed you should phone me about such a trivial amount," he said, voicing his thoughts.

"I would hardly call 467,683 Marks a trivial sum," Noske said primly.

Dollmann swallowed. "How much?" he asked hoarsely.

The banker repeated the amount and then went on to explain that the bank had just received 467,500 from Zürich following the transfer of his account with the Neu Standard Gesellschaft. It seemed he would have had an even bigger windfall if he'd arranged for a nominee to purchase East German Marks on the free market before moving his money out of Switzerland, but Dollmann was too preoccupied to pay much attention to what Noske was telling him.

"There must be some mistake," he said. "The money doesn't belong to me."

"According to our records it does, Herr Dollmann, and we have a telex from the Neu Standard to prove it. Furthermore, your secretary phoned the bank half an hour ago to ask if we'd received the money. Naturally I refused to discuss the matter with her. After all, I'd only her word that she was your secretary."

"So she gave you this number and suggested you rang me?"

"Yes. Did I do wrong?"

"No, Herr Noske, you were absolutely right to call me."

Dollmann put the phone down. The switchboard operator would have heard every word of their conversation and it was probably on tape as well. Leber had gone to considerable lengths to frame him and it was unlikely that he would have overlooked such an obvious precaution. He wondered who was supposed to be his secretary – Ilse or some girl from another branch of State Security whom

214

he'd never met? He would know soon enough if he didn't beat Leber to the punch and to do that, he would need to get in touch with Horst Winkler, otherwise known as 'The Actor'.

It was impossible to guess what Krystyna Zander was thinking. Her face was the picture of studied concentration and she appeared to be hanging on to his every word. Watching her closely, Radford came to the conclusion that she would probably have the shirt off his back in a game of poker.

"Do you guys really think you can take Yagoda?" she asked as soon as he'd finished briefing her.

"Harper believes we can and he's not one for making extravagant claims."

"I like it." Krysia reached for another cigarette from the pack she'd left on the low table fronting the couch. "The only thing that bothers me is how much am I allowed to pass on to my boss in Chicago?"

"As little as possible," Radford told her. "The success of this operation is entirely dependent on secrecy."

"Are you implying you'd like me to stay here cooped up in Tetbury Gardens until it's all over?"

Radford shook his head. "That wouldn't be practicable. We're in for a long haul; persuading Yagoda it's in his interest to come across isn't something that can be done overnight. We've got to convince him his life is in danger."

"And if you should be successful, Mike, how will it benefit the FBI?"

"We'd expect Yagoda to give us the names of every pusher Stefan Bartowski recruited."

This was the sweetener Harper had dreamed up and it had sounded like a smooth con even when he'd put it across. Listening to himself as he regurgitated the offer, Radford felt the words stick in his throat.

"I think your Mr Harper is trying to do a snow job on me."

Krysia waited for him to deny it, her whole attention seemingly captured by the glowing ember of her cigarette.

"You're right," he agreed, "we are trying to pull a fast one. Forget what I said about the pushers. It's more than likely Yagoda had never heard of Bartowski before Moscow Centre put his name on the hit list. Before his promotion came through, Vasili Petrovich was strictly middle management. He was in charge of the farmers who grew the opium poppies and looked after the factory which produced the heroin. The operation was the brainchild of some genius in the First Chief Directorate and it may or may not have been sanctioned by Andropov when he was running the KGB. With Gorbachev about to assume Konstantin Chernenko's mantle, the big wheels panicked; the former Minister of Agriculture is known as Mr Clean and they decided to obliterate every trace of the operation. Yagoda had already done a good job wrapping things up on the home front and he was the obvious choice to perform the same task outside the borders of the Soviet Union."

How Bartowski had originally been recruited was ancient history and unimportant. He had probably started wheeling and dealing with heroin in Saigon and the Vietnamese had marked his card for the KGB. According to Krysia, before going to Berlin, he'd spent a year in Turkey on detached duty with the US Military Mission. The Russian Intelligence Service would have considered Ankara as good a place as any to establish contact.

"You understand what I'm saying?" Radford demanded.

"What do you think I am? A dumb Polack?" Her eyes glinted angrily. "I know when I'm being squeezed out. The Bartowski case has gone political and there's nothing you guys would like better than for me to pack my bags and go on home." Krysia leaned forward and stubbed out her cigarette in the ashtray with unnecessary force, then said, "Well, I'm not going to oblige you. And there's

216

another thing you should bear in mind, Radford, once I've dug my heels in, I don't give an inch."

"I can well believe it."

"This is a personal matter . . ."

"Your career isn't going to suffer," he said hastily. "No one could have done a better job than you and Harper will make sure your Bureau chiefs in Washington know it."

"Screw the chiefs; I don't give a goddamn about my career."

"You can't mean that," Radford told her.

But it soon became evident that she did. The personal involvement had nothing to do with her career, everything to do with an older brother who'd got hooked when a freshman at the University of Chicago. In 1978, some nine months after dropping out, he'd taken a fatal OD. He had been the only son and Krysia's father had never gotten over it.

"You know what really bugs me about the drug scene, Radford? The fact that we never manage to bust the suppliers. So okay, maybe Yagoda isn't the big fish, but he's no minnow, and I want to be there when you land him."

"It's going to be a long haul," he said.

"So you've already pointed out."

"Will your people give you leave of absence?"

"Who knows?" Krysia shrugged. "If necessary, I'll resign. I'm trained as an attorney, and can always find some law firm willing to take me on."

The telephone in the adjoining room began to ring, its tone shrill and insistent.

"There are no prizes for guessing who that is," said Radford.

"Yeah?" A lopsided smile appeared. "Well, if it's Harper," she said, "just be sure you tell him the score."

He wondered how he was going to get the message across without giving the impression that Krysia was holding a pistol to their heads, but, in the event, it turned out to be a lot simpler than he'd anticipated. Harper was in an

217

ebullient mood. With the help of a certain amount of judicious pressure from the Cabinet Office, he'd persuaded Adrian Carpenter to let him use Winkler as a runner, and his one concern now was to get the show on the road before anyone had time for second thoughts.

Radford was to leave for Berlin that afternoon to liaise with 'Electra' and Whattmore would be joining him the following day, armed with the print-out from the Neu Standard Gesellschaft. He had absolutely no objection to Krystyna Zander tagging along; in fact, Harper thought it was a good idea and because he was sure she would make herself useful in all sorts of ways, it was only right that all her expenses should be met from the contingency fund. To Radford, he seemed to be saying that it was a convenient and inexpensive means of keeping her in line.

From the centre point of Vladivostok, Lieutenant General Nikolai Andreyev's Far East Command extended north-eastwards to include the island of Sakhalin in the Sea of Japan and north-westwards to Birobidzhan some seven hundred and fifty kilometres from his headquarters. His first act on relieving his predecessor had been to instruct his Chief of Staff to arrange a comprehensive tour of his domain beginning with Sakhalin.

Andreyev had demanded and set a cracking pace as if determined to convince his subordinates that at sixty-two he was more resilient than a lot of men almost half his age. He had left Vladivostok late on Sunday the seventeenth of March; now, thirty-six hours later, he was on the way back in a Tupolev 144. In between time, Andreyev had visited every garrison on Sakhalin by helicopter, had conferred with his opposite number commanding the Soviet air and missile forces, had watched a simulated air strike against a hostile naval task force operating in the Sea of Japan and had been the guest of honour at four official receptions.

There had been no let up, and no one had suffered more than the Political Commissar for Vladivostok District.

Observing the General still busily quizzing his G3 Operations staff officer, he seriously considered the possibility of approaching his Political Directorate with a view to seeking an early move from his present appointment. On reflection, however, he decided such a request was unlikely to be received favourably and might even harm his career. The trouble with Andreyev was that he had too much spare time on his hands. His wife had died in 1979 and both daughters were married, one to a doctor who was a senior medical officer of health in Leningrad, the other to a diplomat currently posted to the Soviety Embassy in Damascus. A man with no interests other than the army was a menace; he tended to be a workaholic and expected everyone else to follow his example.

He eyed the General surreptitiously. Moscow had given Andreyev a five star rating for political reliability, an accolade that was not bestowed lightly. The Commissar had no idea why the Party thought so highly of him and his instincts told him it would not be wise to enquire too deeply into that. Promotion had come late for the General and he suspected this was directly connected with the political assessment, but that too was something he preferred to keep to himself.

Like it or not, he would have to learn to live with the General, though just how long that would be was a teasing question. Andreyev had the complexion of a man with high blood pressure, he had a quick temper and if the past two days were anything to go by, he was inclined to drink too much on social occasions. Unless he learned to pace himself better, the day might not be far off when the General would have a heart attack.

The prediction came true sooner than the Political Commissar had expected. One hour out from Tamari, the air quartermaster approached Andreyev, presented the Captain's compliments and asked if the General would like to inspect the flight deck. Andreyev nodded, got to his feet and then fell back. The dull ache in his left arm which he'd attributed to a mild touch of rheumatism, suddenly affected the whole of his left side and his chest felt as though someone had plunged a knife into it. He opened his mouth to call for a doctor but the only sound to come from his lips was a curious death rattle that sounded like so many dried peas being washed in a colander.

The news of Andreyev's death was broken by Radio Moscow in the early evening bulletin and was repeated in the TV newscast at nine o'clock together with a brief obituary. American and European political commentators hailed the announcement as an example of the more open form of government the West could expect now that Mikhail Gorbachev was firmly in power. Its effect on certain elements of the KGB and satellite Intelligence Services was however destined to be nothing short of catastrophic.

18

Dollmann disliked the Russian on sight. Although Kalin had simply been a name until Leber summoned him to his office, he'd known something of the KGB man's reputation and for once a preconceived image was not at odds with reality. Kalin was everything he'd imagined him to be – a shambling bear of a man whose unpredictable temper made him twice as dangerous. The animosity he aroused in Dollmann was to a large measure inspired by fear. Convinced the two men were going to confront him with evidence of his long-standing relationship with Ilse and the small fortune transferred to his account from the Neu Standard Gesellschaft in Zürich, Dollmann was still deeply suspicious when the Russian began to question him about the way he'd attempted to deal with Krystyna Bartowski.

"I don't understand why you steered her to Paris." Kalin shook his head as if to underline his incomprehension. "Why couldn't you have eliminated her while she was in West Berlin?"

"We thought it was too close to home." Dollmann looked to Leber for support and wasn't surprised when the older man avoided his gaze and remained silent.

"Too close to home?" Kalin repeated incredulously. "I think you'd better explain yourself, Comrade Dollmann."

"No one had said anything about Krystyna Bartowski and I didn't like the look of it when she suddenly appeared on the scene. It was too much of a coincidence and to my way of thinking, she was either a plant or someone had got to Bartowski's sister and turned her round."

Subsequent events had proved him right but at the time, Dollmann had thought nothing of the kind. Every operation he'd ever participated in had had a clearly defined objective and to begin with, this one had been no exception. But Moscow's reaction when Krystyna Bartowski had surfaced had provided evidence of panic in high places and with Leber's agreement, he'd sought to distance Normannenstrasse from a potential disaster.

"And your suspicions were correct?"

Kalin's voice lacked all expression. Only the lengthening silence that followed told Dollmann it was a question, not a statement of fact.

"We know the runner we used to contact Krystyna Bartowski in Berlin was under surveillance. After the incident at the Georges Pompidou Centre, three men collected her from the hotel where she was staying. One of them was masquerading as a gendarme."

"How do you know he was an impostor?"

Kalin had arrived on Tuesday evening and had spent most of yesterday conferring with Leber. Dollmann wondered what else they had found to talk about if it hadn't been the Paine–Bartowski case.

"I'm surprised Manfred didn't tell you," he snapped. "The car they were using had diplomatic plates."

Kalin digested the information slowly, as though reluctant to accept it. "This runner of yours," he said eventually, "have you been in touch with him in the last day or two?"

Dollmann felt his stomach lurch. Had he been wired up for a polygraph, the pen would have moved right off the graph paper.

"No." His voice was little more than a harsh whisper. Clearing his throat, Dollmann tried again. "No, I discussed the situation with Herr Leber and we both came to the conclusion that he should be left in limbo for the time being."

"I think you should find out if he's still functioning," Kalin said.

"That would not be a good idea, would it, Manfred?"

"We can't leave him in quarantine for ever," said Leber. "So long as we go about it carefully, I don't see why we shouldn't contact him."

Leber and Kalin were acting in concert. They knew about his fun evenings with Ilse, they'd tampered with his bank account and now they were trying to catch him out over Winkler. He wondered if Manfred knew he'd already taken the necessary steps to get in touch with him.

"You want me to approach 'The Actor'?" Dollmann asked.

"Yes." Leber smiled. "You don't have to go into West Berlin; make him come to you."

"Is that an order?"

"I prefer to call it a request."

"Perhaps you'd like to put that in writing?"

"Why don't you send me a minute expressing your objections, Erich?" Leber said blandly. "Then it would be a matter of public record, right?"

"Yes."

"Good. Now suppose you do as Major Kalin asks and get in touch with Winkler?"

There was, Radford thought, a lot of truth in the old adage about more haste meaning less speed. He and Krysia had arrived in Berlin yesterday afternoon to find that 'Electra' had been summoned to Bonn to attend some urgent conference on anti terrorist measures. The head of the BSSO had however left a message with the Deputy Controller inviting them to meet him at nine o'clock on Thursday morning at 28 Calvinstrasse, a pre World War Two apartment house across the River Spree from the Tiergarten. Arriving five minutes before the appointed time, they had then spent the next three quarters of an hour cooling their heels in the PA's office while 'Electra' chaired an emergency staff meeting in the conference room.

"Sorry about that," he said apologetically when they finally got to see him. "Some of the points I picked up in Bonn couldn't wait. You know how it is."

"These things happen," Radford said.

"I would have warned you off, but no one appeared to know where you were staying."

'Electra' was a tall, silver-haired man in his late fifties. On closer acquaintance, the codename seemed even more ridiculous. Just what point there was in concealing his identity when everything about him suggested he was an ex-cavalryman whose principal interests in life were hunting, shooting and fishing was hard to tell.

"Adrian tells me you want to borrow Winkler?"

"I thought he'd already agreed we could," said Radford.

"Yes indeed. Knowing Cedric, I'm surprised he ever parted with him in the first place."

Radford smiled dutifully. In two short sentences, 'Electra' had contrived to give the impression that he was on first name terms with both men. News of this friendship had evidently failed to reach Harper; while briefing him, the Director had consistently referred to the MI5 man in Berlin by his codename.

"Still, that's all water under the bridge. The point is, how else can we help you?"

"It all depends on how you're playing Winkler," Radford told him. "I assume he's being kept under surveillance?"

"His phone is tapped and we follow him to and from his place of work at the Commerz Bank in An der Keppe over in Spandau. Naturally, Winkler isn't aware of this; the poor slob thinks he's in the clear because we gave him a contact number after we'd finished debriefing him on Monday." 'Electra' flashed a brilliant smile in Krysia's direction. "When you're running a double agent like Winkler, it's not easy to tell which side he's really working for. You can bet he'll be on his best behaviour if he thinks he's being watched."

"But if Winkler believes you trust him, he may not be quite so careful?"

"Exactly, Miss Zander."

"So what's the score with Winkler?" Radford asked.

"It's too early to say yet but he's given us some helpful information."

'Electra' gazed at the window to Radford's left, seemingly contemplating the chestnut tree outside which was just beginning to bud. Like all the trees within the inner city, it was comparatively young. Of the ones planted at the turn of the century, those that had survived the Russian bombardment in the closing days of the war had been cut down to provide the Berliners with fuel during the bitterly cold winter of '46.

"Winkler must have been a pretty useful talent scout," 'Electra' continued. "It's his job to look after the accounts of all the British servicemen who bank with the Commerz, which means he knows all the black sheep who are perpetually in financial difficulties. He also knows which units they're serving in."

"I can see how a hostile Intelligence Service could exploit that kind of information," Radford said.

"Yes, we'd give a small fortune to have someone with the same kind of access. Anyway, Winkler has provided us with a list of names he passed to the East Germans over the years. Checking each one out to see whether he or she has strayed from the straight and narrow will take a lot of time. That's why I say it's too early to tell yet."

"But what do your instincts tell you?" Krysia asked.

"To be very sceptical. Winkler is much too eager to please us, his new masters. Earlier this morning he called his case officer to report that on his way to work he'd seen a marker from his former friends. They want him to get in touch with them."

"And has he?" Radford asked, cutting in.

"Not yet. Their standing operating procedures require Winkler to phone in at the first available opportunity, which in this instance will be sometime during his lunch hour."

"They knew Lance Corporal Garrold was tailing him the night he met Krystyna."

"Quite. I think it's much too early for the opposition to

arrange a meet in order to satisfy themselves that he's clean."

Radford could see what he was getting at. The East Germans were bound to have an informer amongst the Kripos and it was reasonable to assume they were aware that Winkler had been arrested on Saturday. They'd probably been told the precise time he'd been released the following afternoon and had been given a pretty accurate description of himself. The East German Intelligence Service would therefore have to be incredibly stupid to seek Winkler out barely four days later.

"The dead letter box where they left the marker," said Radford. "Were you aware of its existence before today?"

"It featured on the list he gave us when we were debriefing him. But that doesn't mean to say he didn't persuade some innocent third party to place the marker on his behalf."

"Why would he do that?" Krysia asked.

"To make himself look important."

"Well, even if it is a hoax," said Radford, "I'd still like your people to back off and leave me with a clear field."

"No surveillance, no cover, no back up." 'Electra' made a production out of consulting his wristwatch. "Winkler will be all yours on the dot of 1200 hours. Okay?"

"Couldn't be better."

Radford got to his feet and thanked him again, then waited for Krysia to say goodbye and was quietly amused by the brief tug of war which occurred when the MI5 chief tried to hold her hand longer than was strictly necessary.

"You obviously made a conquest there," Radford told her when they were out on the street.

Krysia shot him a strange look, halfway between puzzlement and irritation. "Why don't you just unlock the car?" she said tersely.

Radford dug the keys out of his pocket, unlocked the nearside door of the VW they'd rented from the Hertz agency, then walked round the front and got in behind the wheel. As soon as Krysia had fastened her seat belt, he passed her the street map from the glove compartment.

"You navigate," he said.

"Where to?"

"An der Keppe Weg in Spandau."

"You're going to call on Winkler at the Commerz Bank?"

"That's the general idea."

Krysia opened the map, refolded it to the section she wanted and traced the route with her forefinger. "We want to get on to the Siemensdamm," she said. "You'd better turn left at the junction ahead and we'll take it from there."

"I hope you know what you're doing," he joked as he pulled out from the kerb.

"I hope you know what you're doing too, Radford," she said in a voice that sounded concerned.

"You needn't have any worries on that score, Krysia. Our friend back there has got it wrong. He's got it wrong because the conclusion he's drawn is based on a number of logical assumptions. Of course the opposition wouldn't go near Winkler if this was a conventional Intelligence operation, but you and I know it isn't. We're dealing with a bunch of gangsters who are running scared and the normal rules of the game don't apply."

"You want to turn right at the next junction," Krysia said calmly.

Radford nodded, and tripped the indicator. "My guess is they'll instruct Winkler to meet them on their own ground."

"In which case, he may be reluctant to keep the appointment."

"He won't be on his ownsome; I'll be there to keep him company!"

"You're crazy, Mike," she said.

"You want to make yourself useful?"

"I thought I already was."

"Whattmore's flight is scheduled to arrive at 1355 hours and I don't think I'm going to make it. Could you meet him at the airport? I know you've never met Dennis but you could ask the British Airways desk to page him."

"Consider it done," Krysia told him.

"I hope he's bringing more than one copy of the print-out from the Neu Standard Gesellschaft. If he hasn't, you'd better get several photocopies made."

"Right."

"One last point," said Radford. "There's a Special Signals Unit here in Berlin like the one in Cyprus. Get Harper to have them monitor every teleprinter, radio telephone link and secure speech facility between East Berlin and Budapest from 1800 hours this evening."

"Why Budapest?" she asked.

"Because that's where Yagoda is."

The sky was a faded blue, there was a lot of fluffy cumulus on the horizon and the sun made it seem like a nice Spring day, but appearances were deceptive and there was a definite chill in the air. Krysia thought she could feel it in the car even though the heater was on and a shiver ran down her spine.

Dollmann left the safe house in Pankow, drove back to Normannenstrasse and parked the Wartburg in the protected compound behind the State Security building. Between the parking lot and the main entrance he rehearsed his story yet again, knowing that he would be subjected to the grilling of a lifetime by Kalin and Leber as soon as he walked into the latter's office. His decision to brief Winkler over an unguarded link was easy enough to justify. Winkler didn't have access to a secure speech facility and there was no way he could get through to the State Security building on an ordinary Bundespost line. Explaining why Winkler had been able to react so swiftly was much more difficult. In the space of rather less than seven hours since Leber had ordered him to get in touch with Winkler, 'The Actor' had phoned the cut-out in Neukölln, had been given the Pankow number to ring at a given time and had then been told which RV to use and when he was to be there. If Leber ever got around to doing a time and motion study, he might well conclude that someone had anticipated his instructions.

Dollmann checked in at the reception desk, took the lift up to the second floor and then stopped by his office to collect a large scale street plan of Prenzlauerberg before walking in on Leber. It was difficult to decide who was the more intimidating, the ex-Gestapo officer or Kalin. Both men looked grim and at first Dollmann thought the moment he'd been dreading had finally arrived.

"Well?" Leber demanded in a hectoring voice.

"Winkler sounded in good heart. When I asked him how he'd been keeping, he said that last Saturday and Sunday had been a bit of a nightmare. Apparently, some neurotic woman in the adjoining apartment accused him of indecently assaulting her and the Kripos carted him off to the Kluckstrasse precinct for questioning. For a time, Winkler thought he'd been picked up because the police had been watching Bartowski's sister and had seen them together but later on it became evident they hadn't."

"Do you believe his story?" Kalin asked.

"I'm not sure," Dollmann said cautiously.

"It's too glib," Leber growled. "You can almost hear the case officer rehearsing him sentence by sentence."

"You're saying he's been turned?" Kalin said.

"That's my opinion, for what it's worth."

Dollmann turned his back on the two men and walked over to the display board. Unless he acted quickly, Leber would persuade the Russian they should cancel the RV with Winkler and everything would be lost. Dollmann couldn't say just when he had abandoned his original plan in favour of defecting, but he knew tonight was the only opportunity he was ever likely to get. Telling himself to keep cool, he unfolded the street plan of Prenzlauerberg and pinned it up on the display board.

"With all due respect, Manfred, we want proof, not opinions. We'll know for sure if Winkler has changed sides when I meet him tonight." Dollmann swung round to face them, then pointed a forefinger at the map. "Right here," he added dramatically, "at 2305 hours."

Kalin came forward to take a closer look, his eyes narrowing suspiciously. "Why there?" he asked, glancing over his shoulder at Leber.

"Because it's isolated," Dollmann said, before the older man had a chance to reply. "The opposition won't bother to put a tail on Winkler if we tell him to come in through Check Point Charlie. Unless we find somewhere less public, they're not going to show their hand. It's as simple as that."

"I still don't like it," Kalin said.

"You won't find a better crossing place than the conduit south of the abandoned 'S' Bahn station at Bornholmerstrasse. The enemy may think it has possibilities but there's a lot of meadow land their side of the wall and we have the advantage of the higher ground."

Kalin had made his views known; he didn't like the site and now the final decision rested with Manfred. In a creditable attempt to convey the impression that he personally didn't give a damn which way it went, Dollmann took out a packet of cigarettes and calmly lit one.

It seemed a lifetime before Leber finally made up his mind and came down on his side.

19

Radford started the engine, then put the heater on full blast and waited for the warm air to clear the mist from the windscreen. Within a matter of seconds, two half moons appeared above the vents and rapidly expanded to reveal the railway embankment directly to their front. The wall, an ugly concrete structure crowned with a necklace of barbed wire, was some twenty yards beyond the tracks. Behind this obstacle there was an electrified fence and an anti-personnel minefield, both of which were covered by two observation towers, one on the high ground opposite the abandoned 'S' Bahn station at Bornholmerstrasse, the other due south at the U-bend of the suburban line to Schönhauser Allee in the Eastern Sector.

"You'd better cut the engine, Mike," Krysia told him quietly. "We don't want the Vopos taking an unhealthy interest in us."

"Why should they?"

The parkland to the south of Bornholmerstrasse where they were parked was a favourite spot for courting couples from the Wedding District of Berlin, and there were at least two other vehicles in the vicinity.

"Okay, so I'm jumpy."

You're not the only one, Radford thought, and switched off the engine.

"Do you think Winkler is going to show?" she asked presently.

"I honestly don't know," he said.

Winkler hadn't looked too happy when they'd parted

company after he'd phoned the Pankow number and received his instructions from his former case officer. It was always possible that some convenient last-minute illness would keep him at home, and there was nothing Radford could do about it. It was one thing to hold Winkler's hand when he rang the Pankow number because his erstwhile associates hadn't known beforehand where he would be calling from, but quite another to bear-lead him all the way to the RV. The former case officer had been very specific; he had told Winkler the precise time he was to leave his apartment house in Siemensstadt and exactly what route he was to take to the rendezvous. Radford thought no one would have gone into that kind of detail unless they proposed to run a check on the German before he arrived at the appointed meeting place.

"Are you still going to cross over if he doesn't show up, Mike?"

"Why not? I know the way."

"You're crazy," Krysia told him angrily.

"So you've said before."

A car started up somewhere over on their left, then the main beams swung towards them as the driver picked his way through the brush, looking for a track which would take him back to the road. Knowing the headlights were bound to illuminate their Volkswagen, Radford drew Krysia close and kissed her fiercely. He saw her eyes widen slightly as the glare lit up the interior, then her lips parted and he went on kissing her some time after the car had disappeared into the night. Finally, she placed a hand on his shoulder and gently pushed him away.

"You certainly believe in realism," she murmured.

"What makes you think I was faking it?" Radford said.

"I got the impression there was nothing doing in that direction . . ."

He touched her lips with his finger and traced the familiar smile.

"But I'm surely open to persuasion," she added.

This time her mouth found his with tenderness, warmth

and a darting tongue. He unbuttoned her coat, slipped one arm inside and hugged her round the waist.

"That's a novel approach," Krysia said.

"You know something? You've got a hell of a lot of backbone."

"And you've got a hell of an original line, Mike."

"I'm sneaking up on you," he told her.

An 'S' Bahn train passed them on the up line, its brakes squealing as it slowed for the tight bend outside Gesundbrunnen station.

"How much longer have we got?" she asked.

Radford glanced at the clock in the dashboard. "The down train should be along in four minutes."

"You be careful then; two medals are enough for any man and this isn't the Falklands."

"Who've you been talking to?"

"Dennis Whattmore," she said. "You asked me to meet him at the airport, remember?"

"Good old Dennis."

"Don't knock him, Mike; he's your biggest fan."

"He hardly knows me," Radford said, then recalled that amongst other things, Whattmore was the Department Security Officer and would therefore have access to his vetting file. "I suppose he also told you that before I went to the Falklands, I was co-habiting, as the Army so delicately puts it, with a girl in Hereford?"

"No, of course he didn't. It's none of my business."

"She was a legal executive in those days," he said, as though she hadn't spoken. "A very bright, very ambitious lady. She told me that before she was finished, she meant to have her own law firm. It wasn't until I returned from the South Atlantic and asked her to marry me that I discovered a husband and children were not included in her plans for the future. For a while, I thought the guys who indulged in 'slam, bam, goodnight and thankyou mam' might well have a point."

"You don't owe me any explanations about your private life, Mike."

"Better you should hear it from me than anyone else," Radford said.

Away in the distance, he could hear a faint but regular drumming noise. As the sound grew louder, it was possible to recognise the clickety-clack for what it was.

"The down train," Krysia said in a flat voice.

Radford reached up and tripped the switch above his head so that the courtesy light wouldn't come on when he opened the door. "The meeting is set for 2305 hours," he said. "If I'm not back by 0100 hours, make tracks for Headquarters Berlin and break the news to good old Dennis that he's got a major diplomatic incident on his hands."

"Then he blows the whistle?" Krysia said.

"No. He makes sure the Special Signals Unit continues to monitor the traffic to Budapest until this time tomorrow night. *Then* he can blow the whistle."

"Right."

"The keys are in the ignition," Radford said.

The clickety-clack noise was getting louder and the occasional bluish-white flash lit the night sky as the pick-up shoe hit a slightly uneven spot on the live rail.

"You take care," Krysia said. "You hear me?"

The train came on round the bend doing a steady thirty miles an hour. Opening the door, Radford got out of the car and moved off into the darkness, first heading deeper into the woodland, then circling back towards the narrow road near Gesundbrunnen station where he was due to meet Winkler.

The observation tower on the corner of Helmut Just Strasse was manned round the clock by two Vopos. The remainder of the guard, consisting of the guard commander, the junior NCO in charge of reliefs and the four off-duty sentries, occupied the end house in the street within a stone's throw of the observation tower. The sentries were relieved every two hours by the guard commander or his second-in-command, depending on who happened to be on duty at the time. Standing orders also laid down that, once posted, the sentries were to be visited every twenty minutes, a requirement to which Dollmann knew most noncoms only paid lip service during the hours of darkness. Tonight, however, things were different. Instead of scampering back to the guard room after posting the 2200 hour shift, the NCO in charge of reliefs had remained in the observation tower with Dollmann and Major Kalin. Back in the end house, Leber's presence meant the guard commander was unable to get his head down and had to remain properly vigilant.

Dollmann watched the down train to Heiligensee disappear into the far distance, the red warning lights on the rear car rapidly becoming tiny pinpoints before they finally vanished altogether. In a few minutes' time, the up train from Bernau would appear from roughly the same direction and would pass immediately below the observation tower before veering away to the next stop at Schönhauser Allee. It was the one area in Berlin where the suburban lines in both sectors came together to run side by side for a brief distance before going their separate ways again, a fact which Dollmann likened to the political climate that kept the city permanently divided.

"Shouldn't be long now," Kalin observed in his fluent German.

Dollmann noticed that the Russian was looking at the field telephone on the windowledge between the two sentries and knew he wasn't referring to the imminent arrival of the up train. Winkler had been kept under observation from the moment he'd left his apartment house until he'd alighted at Gesundbrunnen station to walk the rest of the way to the RV. Before much longer, one of the Guardians would phone in a report to the contact number in the Pankow District where the subscriber would then relay the message to him through Leber.

"Let's hope he's clean," Kalin said.

"It won't make a jot of difference if he isn't," Dollmann told him. "I'm still going to meet Winkler."

"I wonder if that's altogether wise?"

Somehow Dollmann managed to contain a heartfelt sigh. They'd been over that ground before and he'd thought Kalin had been convinced by his argument, but it seemed he'd been mistaken.

"Unless I talk to Winkler," he said patiently, "we won't ever know if he's been turned. If I think he has, we'll use him to run a disinformation exercise against his newly-acquired friends. Alternatively, should it transpire that the opposition is merely watching Winkler, I'll still feed him with false intelligence against the time they eventually decide to pick him up."

Kalin froze like a gun dog, his whole attention captured by the unmistakable sound of a train. Glancing to his right, he saw the headlights of the motorman's cab coming towards them and instinctively looked at his wristwatch.

"One thing you have to give us," Dollmann observed sardonically, "our trains are always on time."

But would the British be as punctual? Every night a reconnaissance patrol from the duty battalion turned off the main road above the abandoned station at Bornholmer-strasse and came down the narrow lane that ran parallel with the railway. When he emerged from the conduit the other side of the wall, he would present a fleeting target to the sentries in the observation tower and he was counting on those two Fox scout cars to act as a deterrent. The Fox scout car was armed with a 30mm Rarden cannon plus a coaxial machinegun and no one, least of all the sentries, could be sure just how the British would react if they believed they were being fired on from across the border.

The Bernau train was clearly visible now. Reacting to the warning signs well short of the curve, the motorman reduced speed and was doing less than thirty when he passed the observation tower. For a brief moment the headlight beam picked out the disused platelayers' hut in the killing zone, then it was hidden from view by the six car unit as it approached the bend in the track. In that same instant, the field telephone buzzed and Dollmann moved to answer it.

Leber said, "Winkler's clean, no one's on his tail."

"Would you mind repeating that for the benefit of our friend here?" Dollmann said and passed the phone to Kalin.

Leaving the Russian on the line to Leber, he climbed down from the observation tower, crossed the railroad tracks and picked his way through the anti personnel minefield to the platelayers' hut. The killing zone was illuminated by floodlights positioned at ground level between the wall and the electrified fence fronting it, so that any would-be escaper moving across the death lane presented a well-defined target for the marksmen in the tower.

Dollmann knew that, had they orders to do so, either one of the Vopos he'd just been talking to could drop him with a single aimed shot. At every step along the way, he expected to receive a tremendous punch in the back or to the head that would precede total oblivion, but nothing happened. His pulse still racing, Dollmann opened the door to the platelayers' hut and stepped inside.

2258 hours: another six minutes to go before he could make his move. Reaching into his trenchcoat pocket, Dollmann took out a 9mm Makarov automatic and drew the slide back, jacking a round into the breach. Then, from the other pocket, he produced a silencer and locked it into the retention grooves machined on the barrel. If either Kalin or Leber entered the hut before he went under the wall, it was his intention to kill them as quickly and as silently as possible.

Radford heard the sound of Winkler's footsteps shortly before he appeared round the bend in the lane. Although the German was walking on the right-hand side of the road, he failed to see him even though he passed within a few feet of his position. Despite doing his best to give the impression that he hadn't a care in the world, the tune he was whistling to himself was off-key and lacked any sort of melody. When Radford finally caught up with Winkler after having satisfied himself that no one was following him, the German gave a frightened yelp and almost jumped out of his skin.

"For Christ sake," Radford whispered fiercely, "what are you trying to do? Rouse the whole neighbourhood?"

"You should have warned me," Winkler complained. "You could give a man a heart attack sneaking up on him like that."

"Suppose you stop moaning and get a move on. We haven't got all night."

Radford grabbed the German by the arm and hustled him across the lane and into the ditch below the railway embankment. The conduit Winkler had been told to use lay on the other side of the embankment and was part of the old drainage system for the area which had never been repaired after it had been partially destroyed by the 3rd Shock Army of Marshal Zhukov's forces in April '45. Signalling Winkler to follow him, Radford crawled up the embankment and cautiously raised his head above the crest. The nearest observation tower was some thirty yards to the left but the disused conduit was much harder to spot. It lay somewhere midway between his position and the East German vantage point, its precise location screened by the undergrowth in front of the wall.

"You go first, Horst," Radford said quietly.

Winkler glanced left and right, then stared at the sentries in the observation tower. "They'll see me," he muttered.

"So what? They're expecting you."

"What are you going to do?"

"I'll crawl," Radford told him. "Now get up and cross the embankment and don't look back."

For a moment it looked as though Winkler would refuse to budge but then with a faint sigh he got to his feet, gingerly picked his way across the tracks and went down the other side. Radford followed the German, raising himself just high enough off the ground to clear each rail in turn before rolling down the embankment into the parallel ditch. When his eyes became accustomed to the shadow, he spotted Winkler cowering in the bushes a few yards away.

"What are you hiding for?" Radford whispered in his ear. "The sentries can't spot us; we're in dead ground."

"I wasn't hiding, I was looking for the entrance," Winkler said in a low voice and with as much dignity as he could muster.

The conduit was roughly six feet above the ditch and slightly to their right. The opening had been camouflaged with loose earth and rubble to make it blend in with the rest of the derelict landscape.

"I'm glad you were able to find it, Horst."

"It wasn't easy," said Winkler sulkily.

Radford unbuttoned his reefer jacket, took out one of the photocopies Whattmore had made of the computer print-outs from the Neu Standard and gave it to Winkler. "You know what you have to do with these?" he asked softly.

"I give them to my control and tell them there's plenty more where they came from. Then I make the necessary introductions and act as your interpreter."

"Good." Radford squeezed Winkler's shoulder. "Now let's get weaving."

Working in tandem, they cleared the obstruction blocking the mouth of the pipe with their bare hands, then crawled inside, Winkler leading. Roughly twenty feet long, the pipe led to a vertical shaft directly below the plate-layers' hut.

The field telephone on the shelf behind the door made a feeble buzzing noise as though the cable was earthing itself somewhere between the observation tower and the hut. Answering it, Dollmann grunted into the mouthpiece.

Kalin said, "The sentries spotted a man crossing the 'S' Bahn a few minutes ago. He's about your height and was heading towards the conduit."

"That'll be Winkler."

"So it would seem." The Russian paused, then said, "I've just been informed that two armoured reconnaissance vehicles are moving south on the narrow road from Bornholmerstrasse station."

"The border patrol," Dollmann told him and rang off.

The British were totally unreliable. The one night he wanted them to be on time and they were at least ten minutes early. Now there would be nothing to distract the sentries when he started to cross the embankment on the far side of the wall. Unless . . .? Unless he borrowed Winkler's top coat. They were about the same size and the sentries wouldn't know the difference from the rear when they picked him up in their starlight scopes. A slight change of plan then; instead of shooting Winkler in the tunnel, he would persuade him to change clothes and then use the poor fool as a decoy. Smiling to himself, Dollmann raised the trapdoor, looked down into the wide shaft and saw a faint beam of light in the feeder pipe.

"You needn't bother to come up, Winkler," he said brightly. "I'll join you in the shaft, there's room enough for two."

"But not for three." Winkler crawled out of the pipe and stood up, pausing to catch his breath before continuing. "I have a friend with me who wants to meet you."

"What?"

"An Englishman. He has something very important to say to you."

Dollmann backed away from the shaft, his mind grappling with the problem of how he was going to deal with the second man. If there was one. "Let's hear from you then, Mr Englishman," he said hoarsely. "I'd like to welcome you to East Berlin in your own language."

"You already have." Radford emerged from the conduit to find Winkler still clinging to the ladder which led to the hut above. "I'm sure you're very friendly," he said, "but we'll hit it off much better if you allow Horst to join you up there."

240

"I'm not stopping him."

"That's good, because he's got a couple of very interesting bank statements I'd like you to see. The originals were supplied by Wolfgang Thierack, the finance director of the Neu Standard Gesellschaft in Zürich. Until they were both murdered, the numbered accounts belonged to Master Sergeant Stefan Bartowski and Staff Sergeant Harry Paine." Radford watched the East German take the printouts from Winkler, then said, "If you look at the final entry on both statements, you'll see that their respective accounts were subsequently transferred to the Volksbank in Dresden. One of the principal beneficiaries is a Herr Erich Dollmann."

"Who are you, Englishman?"

Radford thought he recognised a note of personal involvement in the other's voice as well as an underlying air of hypertension. "My name's Radford," he said. "You wouldn't be the mysterious Erich Dollmann by any chance?"

"Perhaps. What do you do for a living, Mr Radford?"

"I'm a captain in the British Army."

"Good. Then you can escort me to your military headquarters in West Berlin."

The unexpected was supposed to be the norm according to the army but to be suddenly confronted with a would-be defector was outside even that all-embracing dictum. At any other time, Radford would have regarded the acquisition of a top ranking Intelligence officer as a definite coup but right now, Dollmann was merely a pain in the backside.

"Forget it," he said. "I'm not taking you back."

"I have a Makarov automatic that says you will, Captain."

"Don't be stupid. My superiors aren't interested in you, they'll shove you back through Check Point Charlie so fast your head'll spin."

"I'm running out of time and patience, Captain."

Dollmann was hovering on the brink. If Radford pushed

241

him too hard, the East German might well crack up and shoot Winkler just to show he wasn't bluffing.

"Take it easy," Radford said in a soothing voice. "I'm sure we can come to an arrangement. We're interested in a certain Major General Vasili Petrovich Yagoda; use these computer print-outs to force him into early retirement and we'll greet you with a golden handshake. Better still, deliver him into our hands and you can have yourself weighed in diamonds like the Aga Khan."

"You're asking for the moon," Dollmann told him.

"It's not impossible if you go about it the right way."

"And I suppose you're going to tell me just how it can be done?"

"I wouldn't be that presumptuous," Radford said. "But I can give you a few useful cards if you'll let me."

It took Dollmann only a few seconds to consider the offer and reach a decision. "You've got three minutes," he said tersely. "Any longer and the others will become suspicious."

It was a tall order. Yagoda was unlikely to defect unless he believed his accusers had all the facts at their fingertips and Radford had no idea how much Dollmann already knew. There wasn't time to find out either; all he could do was list the salient points at machinegun speed and hope the East German would absorb the information he needed. Amongst other things, he told Dollmann about the destruction of the opium poppies in the Kirova Depression on the nineteenth of October and the various exchanges between Strella One and Hermitage which had been monitored by the British before the air traffic control net had been deliberately jammed by the KGB border troops. He also told him how an air photo interpreter had subsequently identified the wreckage of a Mi-1 recce helicopter at the scene of the fire.

"We can prove Yagoda is a racketeer," he said, winding up. "And we guarantee that Mikhail Gorbachev will find it interesting reading. Be sure you tell him that."

"Have you finished?" Dollmann asked.

"Yes."

"Do you have a contact address in West Berlin?"

Radford hesitated, then said, "I'm staying at the Lichtburg Hotel."

"No doubt Herr Winkler can find it should the necessity arise. Meantime, he will stay here as my guest."

"Oh no." Winkler started towards the ladder and was stopped dead in his tracks before he could take another pace. Still keeping his eyes on Radford at the bottom of the shaft, Dollmann smashed a backhand into Winkler's nose and sent him reeling into a corner of the hut.

"You bastard," Radford said in a low voice.

Above him, Dollmann took careful aim and squeezed the trigger. Long before Radford heard the hollow cough from the silenced automatic, the round had passed close enough to his head for him to feel the displacement of the air in its path.

"Don't push your luck, Captain," Dollmann said. "Go on back while you've still got a chance. You won't help Winkler by staying here."

Radford didn't like it but there was a certain logic in what Dollmann said. Ducking low, he crawled into the pipe and made his way to the far end. The trapdoor slamming behind him sounded like a pistol shot.

Surfacing the other side of the wall, he replaced the earth and rubble they had previously removed from the entrance. Then, keeping to the shadows as much as possible, he crawled up the embankment, crossed the railroad tracks and ran down the other side.

When he got back to the car, Krysia greeted him as though he had just returned from another planet, which in a sense he had.

20

Dollmann stole a glance at his wristwatch and wondered how much longer they'd be cooped up in Leber's office. In the world outside the drawn blinds, the first light of day would be showing by now, but time had evidently ceased to have any meaning for Kalin. The Russian had withdrawn into his shell as though in a trance and for the past hour or so had been content to leave the interrogation to Leber. What Kalin made of the situation was impossible to guess seeing he wasn't sharing his thoughts with anyone, but Leber's hostile attitude suggested he was determined to prove that, at the very least, Dollmann was being manipulated by the British.

"Why should we believe these computer print-outs are genuine?" Leber asked, resurrecting in a slightly different guise a question he'd raised before. "Forgery is one of the few things the British Secret Intelligence Service is really good at."

Dollmann looked up and did his best to out-stare the ex-Gestapo officer. "If it's a forgery," he said calmly, "how did they know that the equivalent of 467,500 had been transferred to my account from the Neu Standard in Zürich?"

"Perhaps they're trying to frame you, Erich."

Unintentional or not, it was the drollest thing Leber had said in years. "Someone is," Dollmann said with heavy emphasis.

"As a high-ranking Intelligence officer you'd be worth half a million to the British," Leber continued, developing his point. "They probably used Thierack to transfer a large sum of money to your account with the Volksbank, hoping it would spook you. And their clever little ruse nearly succeeded, didn't it, Erich?"

They had come full circle. Dollmann had had a hard time rebutting Winkler's accusation that he had tried to defect and now it looked as though he would have to fight the same battle all over again.

"So Winkler wants you to believe, Manfred."

"I thought he was very convincing," Leber said.

"We didn't call him 'The Actor' for nothing. Nor should we forget that he's now working for the British. You heard him admit it himself."

"Only after you'd knocked him around, Erich."

Kalin shifted in his chair, the first sign of activity he'd shown for quite some time. "A question?" he growled. "You discharged one round from your pistol. Why?"

"That's easy," Dollmann said. "I fired a shot at Radford, hoping to wound him in the leg. Winkler was making a nuisance of himself and there was no other way I could stop him."

"Are you saying that Winkler helped the Englishman to escape?"

It would have been a very convenient explanation except that Dollmann couldn't think of one good reason why the Russian should want to help him out of a tight corner. To the contrary, he could think of several reasons why Kalin would lay a trap for him.

"Winkler isn't the stuff heroes are made of; he had the same idea as the Englishman and wanted to get out himself."

"My congratulations, Erich," Leber observed sourly, "you seem to have an explanation for everything."

Dollmann sighed theatrically. "You're just reluctant to face the facts," he said with exaggerated patience. "I'd never heard of the Kirova Depression before I met Radford, and I certainly didn't know the KGB were producing heroin."

"The British are running a disinformation exercise," Kalin told him.

"Maybe they are, but if they flood the market with this phoney computer print-out backed up with a lot of aerial photographs, it's going to embarrass Chairman Mikhail Gorbachev to say the least. In his shoes, I'd want some very convincing answers to a lot of awkward questions. For instance, I'd want to know why an undistinguished officer like Vasili Petrovich Yagoda was promoted to Major General over the heads of thirty-seven more senior colonels."

"Are you saying the British are trying to set the Party and the KGB at each other's throats?"

Dollmann masked his feelings behind an impassive exterior. Suddenly, the whole thrust of the enquiry had turned in his favour, but he would still need to keep his head and play it cool.

"Your guess is as good as mine. You've got a new man in power and it could be they're out to undermine his authority. Instead of looking for a scapegoat, we should be thinking of a way to hit back at them."

"On the lines that if we can embarrass the British Government sufficiently, they will drop this absurd project?" Leber suggested.

"Precisely," Dollman said.

"Perhaps we should manufacture another incident like Gleiwitz?"

The place name sounded familiar to Dollmann but he couldn't remember where he'd heard it mentioned before. The allusion meant nothing at all to Kalin who said so loud and clear. Then, as Leber went into a lengthy explanation, he recalled a lecture at training school, something about an incident on the old Polish/German frontier in August 1939. Hitler had wanted an excuse to justify his forthcoming invasion of Poland and the Gestapo had staged a bogus cross border raid on the local radio station at Gleiwitz. They'd collected a number of prisoners from the concentration camps, dressed them in Polish army uniforms and a detachment from the Brandenburg Regiment had then shot them down in cold blood to make it look authentic.

"What you're suggesting is sheer lunacy," Kalin said, as soon as Leber had finished. "Moscow won't thank us for starting World War Three."

"I really had something less exotic in mind." Leber stared at Dollmann, a faint smile hovering on his lips. "You were a very attentive student in your younger days, Erich. I'm sure you recall a lecture on the abduction of Captain Sigismund Best and Major Richard Stevens of the British Secret Intelligence Service?"

Dollmann nodded. "They were running an espionage network from the British Passport Control office at The Hague and were in touch with various anti-Nazi groups in Germany. One day in early November 1939, they were lured to a café midway between the Dutch and German customs posts at Venlo. They thought they were going to meet General von Wietersheim, one of the conspirators in the German High Command who were planning to arrest Adolf Hitler. Instead, they kept a rendezvous with an SS snatch squad led by Alfred Naujocks who bundled both men into a car which whisked them across the frontier."

At first, the anecdote seemed to make little impact on Kalin. The KGB man just sat there, a vacant expression on his face; then just when it seemed they would have to spell it out for him in words of one syllable, he finally made the connection.

"We could do the same," he said. "Only this time we make the bait so attractive that they can't wait to cross the frontier."

"According to Erich, the British have expressed an interest in Major General V. P. Yagoda," Leber said casually.

Kalin picked up one of the bank statements and weighed it in his hand as if by doing so he was somehow able to assess the validity of the document.

"You can ask Winkler if you don't believe me," Dollmann said quietly.

"I may just do that," Kalin told him.

"I think we should adopt a more positive approach." Leber solemnly regarded each man in turn. "Let us assume for the sake of argument that the information is correct. Two questions then arise. Will Major General Yagoda agree to participate, and is Moscow likely to sanction such an operation?"

Kalin said, "We won't know the answer to either question unless we produce an outline plan – at the very least."

"Quite. As I see it, our first task is to choose a suitable location."

Dollmann wondered if his ears had deceived him but as Leber continued to hold forth, he knew there was nothing wrong with his hearing. All of a sudden, they were of the same accord; he didn't know what had caused them to come together nor was he the slightest bit interested. Individual motives were unimportant when people were united in a common purpose.

Between them they rapidly agreed that Berlin was not a suitable location. The city was too much of a flashpoint and Radford's superiors would be reluctant to take any chances. Furthermore, if they were to seriously embarrass the British Government, it was necessary to involve Bonn and that meant the incident would have to be staged somewhere in the Federal Republic. They left the precise location open but they were able to select four possible sites off the map. And while the scenario also needed a certain amount of polishing, they considered the outline plan was sufficiently advanced to be submitted to Yagoda.

"You will get in touch with the Comrade Major General then," Leber said, pressing Kalin.

"After I've spoken to Winkler in private."

Dollmann lit a cigarette. The honeymoon was over before it had really begun. The KGB man was his old self again; hostile, suspicious and dangerous.

"Why so depressed?" Kalin asked him. "I'm only availing myself of the offer you made a few minutes ago."

What passed for a smile stretched his lips. It had all the warmth of a Siberian winter.

Winkler touched his swollen nose and winced. It was almost twice its normal size, both nostrils were blocked with congealed blood and he was convinced the bone had been broken. Breathing was also a painful business which could hardly be considered surprising in view of the hammering Dollmann had given him about the body. If the ribs weren't actually broken on the left side, they were certainly cracked. It was all Radford's fault; the Englishman had forced him to go into East Berlin against his better judgment and had then deserted him the moment Dollmann had turned nasty. If it hadn't been for Radford, he wouldn't be here now, incarcerated in a tiny, pitch-dark cell somewhere in the basement of the State Security building on Normannenstrasse.

The sound of heavy footsteps echoed in the corridor, then stopped outside his cell. A key rattled in the lock, the door opened and the overhead light suddenly came on, bathing the cell in a harsh glare. Respect was a favourite word with the guards and a prisoner was expected to show it at all times. Mindful of this, Winkler pushed himself up from the wooden platform on the floor where he'd been sitting and painfully got to his feet. As his eyes became accustomed to the harsh glare, he recognised the visitor and was thankful he had stood to attention as a mark of respect. If there was one man he was terrified of, it was Kalin. Although the Russian hadn't so much as laid a finger on him during the interrogation, Winkler had a presentiment that he knew more ways of hurting a man than either Leber or Dollmann could imagine.

Kalin said, "You're a very accomplished actor, are you not, mein Herr?"

"I wouldn't say that." Winkler tried to summon an ingratiating smile but felt it slide away under the cold, implacable gaze of the Russian. "As a matter of fact," he added feebly, "the president of our local amateur dramatic society thinks I'm rather mediocre."

"Then he's mistaken; that was a very convincing performance you gave upstairs a short while ago. You had me almost believing that Herr Dollmann would have defected if the Englishman hadn't stopped him."

"It happens to be the truth."

"I don't believe you," Kalin said in a dangerously quiet voice.

"I swear to you I'm not lying."

The Russian grabbed a fistful of Winkler's hair, rapidly twisted a few strands around one finger and yanked them out of his scalp. The pain was excruciating and he cried out, his voice a high keening wail until it was transformed into a muffled sob as Kalin clapped a hand over his mouth.

"You're a lying little shit."

Winkler shook his head. Speech was difficult when the Russian was squeezing his cheeks between forefinger and thumb, but he did his best. "The bank statements are genuine," he mumbled. "So is everything I told you about the Englishman wanting Major General Yagoda."

"Oh, I believe that part of your story," Kalin murmured. "It's the bit about Herr Dollmann which I find hard to swallow. I think you made it up to get even with him after he'd smacked you across the nose."

Winkler hesitated. It was impossible to tell what the Russian wanted from him; his eyes were cold and gave nothing away. If Kalin would only give him a little smile or a nod of encouragement, he'd know what to say.

"Didn't you?" Kalin said, prompting him.

"No, it never occurred to me."

The Russian spun him round, pressed him up against the wall and sank a fist into his left kidney. The shock wave exploded in his brain and Winkler thought the top of his head would detach itself from the rest of his body.

"You will not repeat your malicious story to anyone," Kalin said. "Herr Dollmann had no intention of defecting and never has had. Do I make myself clear?"

"Yes." Winkler knew it was the one word the Russian wanted to hear from him and he said it fervently.

"The rest of course is true. At first we didn't believe your story but subsequently we changed our minds when you stuck to it under extreme duress." Kalin turned him round again and looked into his eyes. "Isn't that so?"

"Yes."

"Good. I do believe we're beginning to understand one another."

Winkler couldn't think why the Russian should now want to shake hands with him, but that was his prerogative. Then Kalin said something about demonstrating just what he meant by extreme duress and the last thing Winkler recalled hearing before he blacked out was a loud crack as the KGB man snapped the bone of his little finger.

Two things woke Radford, the onset of cramp in his left arm and the persistent trill of the telephone. Still half asleep he tried to remove his arm from under Krysia's neck while simultaneously rolling over on to his right side to answer the phone. It was not the kind of manoeuvre which could be executed with any hope of success in a single divan, and he ended up on the floor entangled in the duvet while leaving Krysia half in, half out of the bed.

"My God, Radford," she said in a strangled voice, "what are you trying to do, break my neck?"

"Not intentionally," he told her. "I thought I was reaching for the phone."

"Allow me." Still half out of bed, Krysia placed a hand on his back to support herself while she lifted the receiver from the cradle and passed it down to him.

Whattmore said, "I thought you'd like to know that our friends across the way have just called their area supervisor in Budapest."

"That's sooner than I expected," Radford said.

"Well, don't get too excited, Michael; it may be quite some time before we hear anything more definite."

251

"I'll try to be patient." Radford peered at the luminous face of his Omega and saw that it was a few minutes after six. "If you've nothing else for me," he said, "I'll come into the office around eight thirty. Okay?"

"Fine. Say good morning to Krysia for me."

"I will when I see her," Radford said and hung up on him.

"Would I be right in thinking that was Dennis?" Krysia asked.

"You would."

"Well, you are a sweet old-fashioned guy, trying to protect my reputation."

Krysia got back into bed and re-arranged the duvet. She had come to him in the night and he was glad that she evidently had no intention of returning to her own room just yet.

"Your reputation was never in danger," he said. "Whattmore didn't know you were here; he was just fishing for information, something which comes naturally to an ex-cop."

"Do I have to fish for it too?"

"Of course you don't, you're entitled to know what's going on." Radford lay down beside her and she raised her head so that he could slip his left arm under her neck, then snuggled up to him.

"So okay, I'm listening," she said.

"A few minutes ago, Dollmann or one of his associates at Normannenstrasse called Budapest on the secure radio telephone link. Hopefully, the man at the other end was Yagoda but we shan't know that for sure until our people succeed in unscrambling the gobbledegook."

"How long will that take?"

"Don't hold it against me if I'm wrong," said Radford, "but with any luck we should have a clear text by late afternoon."

A lot would depend on the quality of the recording. The clearer the tonal sound, the more chance there was that the computer would be able to categorise the interrupted

252

voice pattern and select the correct key variable to restore normal speech.

"How do you see Yagoda reacting?" Krysia asked him.

"Your guess is as good as mine," he said.

"I think I'd cut and run in his shoes. He's not big enough to ride out the storm that's on the way and he knows what happens to people who become a major source of embarrassment."

Krysia was right, he thought. Yagoda had never been anything but middle management; he'd taken his orders from some big wheel in Moscow Centre and had run the production end of the business down in the Kirova Depression. Last October he'd received instructions to terminate the operation and everyone connected with it and had made such a good job of the assignment that he'd also been the number one choice to wind up the foreign market. There must have been a time when Yagoda had thought he was indispensable but it could well be that that euphoria had evaporated with the announcement on Tuesday evening by Moscow Radio that Lieutenant General Nikolai Andreyev had died of a heart attack.

"Yagoda knows too much," said Radford. "Chances are he's astute enough to realise his superiors in Moscow already regard him as a major threat. Now Dollmann is telling him the British are going to make sure Mikhail Gorbachev learns what the First Chief Directorate has been up to and overnight he's a prime candidate for the hit list."

"I'm glad we see eye to eye," Krysia said dryly.

"Except if I was Yagoda, I'd make tracks for the Austrian border. It's quicker and safer than coming to Berlin where he might think he was walking into a trap."

"Berlin or Vienna; what does it matter which route Yagoda takes so long as he comes across?"

"It matters to Winkler," Radford said.

All hell would break loose when Moscow learned Yagoda had defected. Every frontier would be closed and anyone who'd had anything to do with the KGB General would have a lot of explaining to do. Winkler's chances of getting out were therefore about zero.

"I should never have left him behind," Radford said ruefully. "Instead of taking a hard line with Dollmann, I should have escorted the bastard to Headquarters Berlin like he wanted me to. But no, I had to go for the jackpot."

"Because those were the orders you'd been given," Krysia said firmly. "If Harper had wanted Dollmann, he would have said so. Isn't that so?"

"Yes."

"Then let's not have any more of this crap about you leaving Winkler in the lurch. You did the best you could for him, Mike."

"Maybe."

"There's no maybe about it. You didn't have too many options; Dollmann was armed and you weren't."

Everything Krysia had said was true but with hindsight Radford thought he could have handled it better. He should have pretended to go along with Dollmann and then jumped him when he came down into the shaft.

"You've gone awful quiet," Krysia observed. "You're not still brooding about Winkler, are you?"

"No," he lied. "I was just trying to figure out what we can do to move things along."

Krysia pressed herself even closer, her body warm, soft and infinitely exciting. "I've got one practical suggestion," she said and proceeded to show him.

The map store was on the second floor of the State Security building, roughly midway between Dollmann's office and Leber's. For security reasons, the windows overlooking the rear parking lot had been bricked up and the only means of ventilation was a small grille high up on the wall which was about the size of an extractor fan. The thermometer on the back of the door had been stuck at 70 degrees Fahrenheit for as long as anyone could remember but the stuffy atmosphere was not the reason why Dollmann was perspiring. Yagoda had arrived from

254

Budapest shortly after eleven fifteen and for the past two hours he and Kalin had been conferring with Leber.

He could understand Yagoda wanting to question Winkler personally but this should have been a mere formality. Kalin, who'd met the KGB General at the airport, had undertaken to give him a full background briefing on the way to Normannenstrasse. The protracted meeting in Leber's office suggested to Dollmann that someone had been bad-mouthing him again.

The discordant noise of the buzzer resolved the uncertainty. Moving to the door, Dollmann peered through the Judas peephole to identify his visitors before he admitted them. Yagoda was not at all like he'd imagined him to be. Instead of the lean, hawk-face bird of prey his reputation had implied, Dollmann found himself confronting a dumpy man with sallow, round features and protruding fishlike eyes.

"I've heard a great deal about you," Yagoda announced in passable German.

"All of it good, I hope," Dollmann said weakly, then quickly got out of the way as the General moved purposefully towards the four maps arranged side by side on display boards.

Kalin said, "These are the four possible locations I mentioned, Comrade General."

Yagoda produced a pair of reading glasses and studied the nearest map. "Which site would you say was the best, Herr Dollmann?" he asked.

"There's not much to choose between them. The British might think twice about the unauthorised crossing point in the vicinity of Lübeck because the Danes are very sensitive about that area, even though it's scarcely on their doorstep. Bad Harzburg and Duderstadt are all right, but if you really pressed me, I'd go for Eisenach." Dollmann made straight for the map farthest away from where he was standing and pinpointed the town. "Fifty-eight miles from Weimar, forty-two from Kassel in the Federal Republic where the Headquarters of the Bundesgrenschutz responsible for the frontier section as far south as Rotenburg is located. The unauthorised crossing point north of Eisenach appears to be a blind spot in our defences which the British would find attractive."

"The map doesn't seem to support your contention," Yagoda said tartly.

"I'm talking from personal knowledge of the area," Dollmann said. "I was in charge of the State Security section at Eisenach in 1971."

According to the map, Route E63 to the Federal Republic passed through the middle of Eisenach. In reality, the crossroads in the town centre had been converted into a T-junction and the traffic diverted left and right by a series of misleading road signs which turned the driver back into the German Democratic Republic. The authorised border crossing point lay north of the town in a secluded valley which could not be seen from the main road. Access to the Customs post was via an unmarked country lane which eventually became a dual carriageway. The unauthorised crossing point was situated in another re-entrant some three miles farther north.

"Who is allowed to use this unauthorised crossing point?" Yagoda asked.

"Just one farmer."

"The land has been in his family for several generations and extends across the border," Leber added, chipping in. "The original farmhouse lies within the German Democratic Republic, a mere thirty yards from the minefield. We built him a new house farther back so that we could use the old one as a guard post. The location of this post is marked with a black pin, the observation towers on either flank are denoted by red pins."

Yagoda peered at the map, a stubby finger tracing the contour lines in the immediate vicinity of the positions Leber had described. "Somebody deserves to be shot," he said angrily. "Those damned observation towers and the guard post are not mutually supporting."

"Because they were never intended to be part of a

defensive position," said Dollmann. "That's why the British will find the area irresistible."

"I see." The scowl on Yagoda's face hadn't entirely disappeared but it was noticeably less malevolent. "And exactly how do we propose to lure the British across the frontier?"

"You're the bait, Comrade General," Kalin said. "Winkler will tell them that we intend to secure your unwitting co-operation by persuading you to take part in an operation designed to cause the maximum political embarrassment to the British government."

"Why should they take his story on trust?"

"Every successful deception plan contains an element of truth and this one is no exception. Indeed, an outsider will find it impossible to distinguish between fact and fiction."

"You'd better be right," Yagoda growled.

"There is one other factor," Kalin continued remorselessly. "Winkler's case officer is a man called Radford and he's convinced there's a traitor in our midst."

"And who might he be?"

"Dollmann," Leber said before the Russian had a chance to answer.

Yagoda removed his reading glasses and carefully tucked them into the top pocket of his jacket. A faint smile appeared, his jowls began to quiver and he exploded with laughter. "Brilliant," he roared and thumped Dollmann on the shoulder.

On Saturday evening shortly after eight o'clock, Winkler returned to West Berlin the way he'd departed via the conduit from the platelayers' hut. After forty-three hours in Communist hands, he looked definitely the worse for wear. His nose was still swollen, the little finger on the right hand had been set in a splint and his ribs were bound up with a wide adhesive strapping. He also had extensive bruising in the area of the left kidney and was passing blood in his urine.

The message from Dollmann which he gave to Radford from his hospital sick bed was succinct and unambiguous even though it was couched in veiled speech. The VIP, Winkler repeated faithfully, would be available for collection eight miles north of Eisenach at grid reference 813504 on Monday 25 March at 1930 hours.

21

Transmit and Receive were loud and clear; adjusting the
boom mike on his flying helmet to bring it closer to his
mouth, Radford gave the pilot a thumbs up. The sergeant
nodded, checked the instrument panel one more time,
then built up the revs and lifted off from the grass field
behind the Bundesgrenschutz eight-storey headquarters
building in Kassel. They were, Radford thought, a micro-
cosm of NATO. Sitting in a row behind him were an
Unteroffizier from the Bundesgrenschutz, a liaison officer
from 1 Belgian Corps and Krysia Zander. To complete the
picture, the Lynx helicopter and pilot had been supplied
by 4 Regiment, Army Air Corps.

The International Staff at SHAPE could spend months
drafting a paper outlining the pros and cons of an anti-
missile missile system for consideration by the Council of
Foreign Ministers who would then agree to refer the draft
back to the International Staff for further detailed study.
Harper, on the other hand, had managed to secure the
co-operation of the Belgians and West Germans, plus a
not insignificant amount of logistical support from Rhine
Army in rather less than thirty-six hours and over a Sunday
at that. He had obviously gone through his list of influential
friends and acquaintances, foreclosing on past favours and
twisting a few arms. It was also evident to Radford that,
with the exception of Krysia, none of the others had been
told what it was all about. The sergeant pilot thought they
were on a recce for some future exercise involving the
Belgian Corps, the Unteroffizier was under the impression

they were on a routine border patrol and the Belgian liaison officer assumed he was there in case his services were required as an interpreter.

Maintaining an altitude of four hundred feet, the pilot turned due south over Eschwege and without violating the air space of the German Democratic Republic, took them on a sightseeing tour of the border. Conditions were perfect; it was a clear, bright morning and they had unlimited visibility. The countryside below was an undulating patchwork of green and brown, the kind of landscape a tank commander would regard as paradise, especially since the wooded areas on the high ground were neither big enough nor sufficiently dense to canalise movement.

The man-made fence was an ugly scar on the face of the countryside. In places, the barrier was a steel-mesh fence crowned and fronted with coils of razor-sharp barbed wire; in others, it was a crudely finished wall of concrete breeze blocks. The killing zone was farther back and resembled an autobahn under construction. Every tree, every hedgerow which had stood in its path had been uprooted. To make the rape complete, the topsoil had been removed and a crop of anti personnel mines sown in its place. The observation towers were sited within the no-go area between the barrier and the minefield.

"Those track marks you can see in the no-go area close to the fence," said Radford. "What caused them?"

"Dobermans," the Unteroffizier said casually, then added, "In certain areas, dogs are used to patrol the wire at night. The animals are tethered to a guide wire which allows them freedom of movement between two fixed points up to half a mile apart. The Dobermans are savage and are trained to kill; they are, however, kept on a short leash so that they cannot pursue their quarry into the minefield. The dogs are expensive, you understand, and naturally the Vopos do not wish to lose any of them accidentally."

"What other unpleasant surprises have the Vopos got?"

"Old-fashioned mantraps, trip flares and a variety of

weapons on fixed lines. The small arms can be anything from a shotgun to a fully automatic rifle and they are activated by trip wires attached to their trigger mechanisms."

The wall had turned the whole country into one vast prison camp for seventeen million people. Maybe most of the inhabitants had no desire whatever to leave the German Democratic Republic but the artificial barrier was there and they were caged in. And for the ordinary man or woman, there was absolutely no chance of holidaying anywhere but within the Communist Bloc.

"That's Eisenach ahead," the pilot said, pointing to a black smudge on the horizon.

With the air speed indicator registering seventy-five knots, the black smudge rapidly took shape; a matchstick pointing skywards became the factory chimney of a brick-yard, an interrupted black line was a clutch of houses on the outskirts of town. Eight miles north of Eisenach, Radford spotted the farmhouse at grid reference 813504. It lay at the head of a re-entrant and was practically in dead ground from the observation towers on either flank which were sited on the reverse slope of the crestline. A narrow tarmac road looped down the forward slope, ran past the original farmhouse and continued on through a gap in the minefield. There was a barrier across the road where it passed through the steel-mesh fence marking the east–west border. Glancing back as they overflew the road, Radford could see that before reaching the checkpoint, a driver would have to make an S-turn to avoid the concrete road blocks which had been positioned diagonally opposite one another.

"Do you want to take another peep at it?" the pilot asked.

"After I've had a look at Rotenburg."

Rotenburg was the next town of any consequence in the Federal Republic. It was also the southernmost boundary of the Bundesgrenschutz unit based on Kassel and it was important to keep up appearances for the benefit of the

Unteroffizier. As they swept past the authorised crossing point in the next valley, Radford could see that the slip road leading to the Customs post was double-banked with juggernauts waiting to be inspected. Then they were over Eisenach and veering to the right to conform with the border. Twelve minutes later, they reached Rotenburg and turned back on a reciprocal course.

"We've got company," the pilot announced.

"Where?" Radford asked.

"Coming up behind us." The pilot jerked a thumb in the rough direction. "An East German Hind. I had a feeling their curiosity would get the better of them before very long. Just give the word and I'll lose him."

"I'm not worried about the Hind. Ease off and let them catch up with us."

The helicopter rapidly overhauled them and then throttled back to keep station approximately a hundred and fifty feet away on their right. Side by side they flew on past Eisenach, the Customs post and the former farmhouse. At Eschwege, Radford told the pilot to break away and head due west. When he was satisfied the Vopos had lost interest in them and were returning to base, he ordered him to double back to a large wood half a mile from the border directly opposite the farmhouse guard post.

"I haven't seen anything of 1 Belgian Corps," said Radford. "Are there no units this far forward?"

"Not in peacetime," the liaison officer said emphatically. "In war of course it would be different."

"Naturally."

There was a snort of suppressed laughter from Krysia which quickly became a diplomatic sneeze. So far as the forthcoming operation was concerned, however, the absence of Belgian forces in the area meant there was one less thing to worry about.

Acting on Radford's previous instructions, the pilot approached the drop point at contour height and utilised every scrap of cover to ensure they weren't observed by the sentries in the observation towers across the border.

"This is where we leave you," Radford told the pilot. "Soon as we're clear of the helicopter, take the Unteroffizier and the Belgian liaison officer back to Kessel. Go out the way you came in – low and sneaky."

Unclipping his seat belt, Radford grabbed the holdall between his feet, opened the side door and jumped out. Once clear of the rotor, he moved forward into the pilot's line of sight and waited for Krysia to join him. Hovering a few feet off the ground, the pilot then rotated the Lynx through ninety degrees and took off, skimming the hedgerow bordering the road west of their position. Observing the helicopter slip beneath the power lines in the far distance, Krysia gave a low whistle.

"Don't tell me we did that," she said.

"We did."

"I'm glad I kept my eyes closed."

"So did I half the time."

Radford helped her across the ditch at the top of the field, then moved into the wood and picked up a track which took a meandering route to the hillcrest. Keeping well down, he crept up to the skyline and checked out the cover on the forward slope before crossing the ridge. Much of the forward slope lay in shadow and the wood was still dense enough to screen him from the watch towers across the border. Moving to his left, Radford found a small hollow on the forward edge of the copse which offered a commanding view of the minor road leading to the unauthorised crossing point and made an ideal observation post. Unfastening the holdall, he took out a sniper's telescope complete with bipod and set it up.

"What are you looking at?" Krysia asked.

"The barrier across the road." Radford adjusted the wormwheel to bring the landscape into sharper focus. "A driver could never get up enough speed to break that steel pole in two. He'd have to drop down into first gear to negotiate those concrete blocks in front of it."

"Is there no way of avoiding them?"

"Only if you're prepared to drive through an anti personnel minefield which is all of a hundred yards deep. Given the usual density of one mine per yard of front, you've got a ninety per cent chance of coming through unscathed. Unfortunately, if you happen to run over one of those little brutes, it'll blow the wheel off."

"They wouldn't have anything bigger in there, would they?"

"An anti tank mine?" The Bundesgrenschutz at Kassel had been adamant the Vopos hadn't sown any of those but even so, they'd refrained from giving Harper a copper-bottomed guarantee. "I suppose anything's possible," Radford continued. "One of those could reduce a car to scrap metal. It wouldn't do the occupants much good either."

"Terrific," Krysia murmured.

"Not to worry, we could get lucky." Radford pushed himself up into a kneeling position and took a small battery-powered audio beacon from the holdall. "Would you mind keeping an eye on the opposition while I set up this homing device?" he asked.

"Sure. Anything special I'm supposed to look out for?"

"The old farmhouse guard post; I want to know just how many Vopos are on duty there."

"Right."

"Whattmore and Drew will be joining us late this afternoon," he said awkwardly.

"So you told me before we left Kassel. I don't know Drew, but if he's half as nice as Dennis, we'll get along just fine."

Radford looked away and swore under his breath. Harper should have put her wise before they'd boarded the helicopter but the Director had left it to him. "This is your operation, Michael," he'd said airily, "and it's your job to make the team pull together."

"I've got a confession to make."

"Yeah? What sort of confession, Mike?"

"You've already met Drew. He was the guy who drove us out to Ecouen when the French were supposedly going

264

to deport you. The whole thing was a put-up job, I should have told you long ago."

"You know something, Radford?" she said lightly. "There are times when you try my patience. What do you take me for, a dumbo? I knew he was a fake before we'd even cleared the outskirts of Paris. No French driver could be that mute in traffic. I just played along with you guys because the good old Bureau had left me dangling."

"I'm sorry," he said humbly.

"That's okay," she said. "You're forgiven. Now let's get on with the job."

The phone rang, breaking the oppressive silence in Leber's office. Like a rabbit mesmerised by the headlights of a vehicle, Dollmann watched the ex-Gestapo officer lift the receiver and answer the incoming call. His face remained totally impassive throughout the short exchange and his occasional monosyllabic grunt gave nothing away either. When he put the phone down, he addressed himself to Major General V. P. Yagoda as though Dollmann and Kalin were not present.

"That was sector control at Muhlhausen. The English have been taking a look at us; one of their Lynx helicopters was sighted over Eschwege at 1045 hours." Leber left his desk, walked over to the map that had been pinned up on the wall and pointed out the border town to Yagoda. "The helicopter then flew south to Rotenburg before doubling back to Eschwege where the pilot subsequently headed due west to give the impression he was returning to base."

"Are you sure it wasn't a routine border patrol?" Yagoda asked.

"Quite sure. The English don't usually patrol that far south because it's out of their area and the Belgians stay well away from the border."

"So where are the English now?"

"I expect Herr Radford is watching the guard post from one of the woods on the forward slope of the opposing ridge. He's probably hoping we'll arrive in daylight."

Dollmann lit a cigarette to calm his nerves. They would leave Berlin on the E6 autobahn and head for the Hermsdorf interchange where they would join the Dresden Karl Marx Stadt and Eisenach autobahn. It was a five hour drive and their start time was crucial, but if he pressed too hard for an early departure it would only make the others suspicious. As it happened, help came from an unexpected quarter.

"We must do our best to oblige the English," Yagoda said. "We should arrive at 1830 hours while it is still light enough for this man Radford to recognise Herr Dollmann. I presume the Volga limousine we're using will indicate that one of the occupants is a Major General?"

Leber nodded. "There'll be a two star plate on the front and rear fenders."

"No pennant?"

"It wouldn't be appropriate to fly one – you're not a formation commander. Besides, we don't want to alarm Herr Radford. The English probably know the formation signs of every Soviet division forward of the Oder-Neisse Line thanks to their military mission in the German Democratic Republic, and he might jump to the wrong conclusion."

"A valid point." The Russian nodded approvingly as though his original question had been part of an oral test which Leber had now passed with flying colours. "You and I will ride in the back of the staff car; Major Kalin will be in uniform and will sit next to the driver."

Yagoda fell silent. Dollmann wondered why he had become the centre of attention, then the reason slowly dawned on him.

"You want me to drive?" he asked incredulously.

"Who else?" Yagoda demanded. "There's only room for four in the limousine."

The guard post was just a hundred and fifty yards from the border and he would have the keys to the car. With great difficulty, Dollmann managed to hide his feelings.

22

Whattmore and Drew arrived together but in separate cars, identical Wartburg saloons which Harper had acquired from a specialist dealer in Kassel. Guided to the final rendezvous by the audio beacon, they were met by Radford and directed to a lying-up area on the reverse slope within easy access of the minor road which skirted the wood and led to the unauthorised crossing point. When satisfied that neither vehicle could be seen from the road, Radford led both men forward to the observation post where Krysia was still keeping watch on the opposition.

"All right," he said, "let's hear what you've brought us."

"Four Clansman radios, an assortment of Soviet small arms, two shovels and a large quantity of sandbags." Whattmore grinned. "Incidentally, what are you planning to do with the sandbags, Mike? Build yourself a wall?"

"There's a minefield over there and we're going to sandbag the floor of each vehicle in case we're forced to drive through it. One layer under the seats might just save us from a very unpleasant experience."

"No one ever said this was going to be a picnic." Drew moved a few feet to his left to get a better view of the foreground. "Do we know how many Vopos are occupying that farmhouse?" he asked.

"I've seen four including a woman," Krysia told him without looking up from the telescope.

"I'll need to go forward then, somewhere in the vicinity of that small fold in the ground, twelve o'clock from here and approximately three hundred yards from the farmhouse. I can cover the front and both sides of the building from that position."

Radford had spent several hours studying the ground to their front and knew there was precious little cover forward of the wood. Although his arc of fire would be restricted by any vehicle moving downhill from the farmhouse towards the roadblock, Drew had clearly picked the best available site.

Drew said, "I've got a Dragunov sniper rifle."

"Image intensifier?"

"That and a silencer."

Three hundred yards was about the maximum range for an image intensifier but even so, the target would only show up as a yellow blob in the ambient starlight captured and magnified by the 'scope. The silencer would reduce the stopping power of the Dragunov rifle but Harper had been adamant that in the event of a shoot out, he didn't want the Bundesgrenschutz to hear anyone returning the fire from the Federal Republic. And if anyone should get hurt on the other side, he had taken steps to ensure the wound would be inflicted by a Soviet bullet from a Soviet weapon.

"I figure two magazines should be enough," said Drew.

"So do I. You can move out at 1915 hours when it's dark. That'll give you fifteen minutes to get into position."

"Whatever you say, General; you're in charge round here."

"You'd better believe it," Radford told him. "If I don't like the way things are shaping up, we're not going anywhere near the farmhouse."

The message Winkler had passed on had told him where and when they could collect Yagoda; Dollmann had also outlined how he was going to deliver the KGB General. But the odds against him being able to pull it off were so astronomical that if he did appear at the guard post with Yagoda in tow, there was a strong possibility that it would all be part of an elaborate double-cross. Radford put the disturbing thought out of his mind; only positive thinking coupled with positive action would see them through.

"The second Wartburg is a back-up in case we have a last minute power failure," he continued. "Soon as I give the word, Dennis, you're to come forward, pick me up from the roadside and go on down to the roadblock. Assuming the barrier's down, I'll get out and raise it; then you drive past the concrete obstacles, make a U-turn the far side of the minefield and reverse towards the guard post. If we're fired upon during this stage of the operation, don't wait for me to join you – just get the hell out of it. Okay?"

"You won't have to tell me twice," Whattmore said fervently. "I've got a healthy instinct for self-preservation."

"Good. Drew will give us what covering fire he can."

"And what am I supposed to be doing while all this is going on?" Krysia asked.

"You go back to the command vehicle and brief Harper."

The radio relay truck, which 19 Signal Regiment had agreed to provide, was scheduled to arrive at 1800 hours and under Drew's direction, it would park in the vicinity of the two Wartburgs. Equipped with a secure speech facility, it would provide a one-to-one link with Harper at the Bundesgrenschutz headquarters in Kassel. If there was a foul-up, it was Harper's job to make sure there were no political repercussions.

"Are there any other questions?" Radford waited long enough to satisfy himself no one had any, then said, "Okay, we'll take a time check. When I say 'now', it will be exactly 1650 hours."

Drew possessed a watch which did practically everything except reproduce the Greenwich Time signal. His pained expression suggested that Radford's Omega was definitely fast but he refrained from making a meal of it. Leaving Krysia to watch the farmhouse, they then returned to the vehicles and checked out the Clansman radios.

"Wonders will never cease," Drew said when they found all four in good working order.

Lying next to the sandbags in the trunk of the car Whattmore had been driving were two Makarov 9mm automatics complete with silencers and a Stechkin machine pistol. The only pistol capable of fully automatic fire, the Stechkin was equipped with a shoulder stock which increased the overall length of the weapon from under nine inches to twenty-one and a quarter when engaged with the pistol grip. Capable of consistently hitting a man-size target at a hundred yards on repetition, the effective killing range of the Stechkin was dramatically reduced when the 20-round magazine was expended in a series of rapid fire bursts. Moreover, the machine pistol was not the kind of weapon which was easy to conceal.

"I'll take one Makarov, you take the other," Radford told Whattmore. "Better tuck the Stechkin between the front seats where either one of us can grab it in a hurry."

"Let's hope we don't need it."

"Amen to that."

Radford broke open a carton of 9mm, loaded the magazine with eight rounds and pushed it home into the hollow pistol grip. Then he slipped the automatic into the shoulder holster he was wearing under his combat jacket and picked up two of the Clansman radios. Telling Drew to let him know when the truck from 19 Signal Regiment arrived, he made his way back to the hollow on the forward slope.

Nothing much had happened in his absence; the same lone sentry was still manning the roadblock and there had been no signs of activity in the vicinity of the guard post. Taking Krysia's place behind the telescope, he zeroed in on the steel-mesh fence either side of the barrier. Between the fence and the forward edge of the minefield, there was a no-go lane some twenty yards wide. There were no man traps, shotguns on fixed lines or trip flares in the grass strip; instead, pug marks showed it was regularly patrolled by guard dogs.

"I wonder where they kennel the Dobermans?" he said, thinking aloud.

"Is there a Vopos barracks in Eisenach?" Krysia asked.

"Bound to be."

The dogs and their handlers would probably arrive with the night guard. It was pure supposition of course but Radford couldn't see the Vopos leaving just one sentry on the roadblock during the hours of darkness. That meant the twenty-four hour guard of an NCO and three men would have to be doubled in order to meet the commitment.

"When's that sentry due to be relieved?" he asked.

"1845 hours," Krysia told him. "They appear to be doing two hours on, four off, and that guy came on duty before you left with Drew and Whattmore."

The afternoon wore on, the shadows gradually lengthening in the valley. The radio relay truck from 19 Signal Regiment arrived promptly at 1800 hours; then half an hour later, a black Volga saloon appeared on the opposing skyline and came down the lane to stop outside the farmhouse. Of the four occupants who alighted, Radford instantly recognised Dollmann and was able to place two others from the descriptions Winkler had given him.

"The burly guy in army uniform is Kalin," he told Krysia. "The ageing blond Aryan is Manfred Leber."

"And you figure the squat civilian who's inspecting the guard is Yagoda?"

"I hope so," Radford said and watched the four men troop inside the farmhouse, the guard commander and off-duty sentries tacking on behind Dollmann.

Dollmann thought the guard commander was understandably apprehensive. Instead of the night guard of one and three he'd been expecting, the duty officer at Sector Headquarters in Eisenach had phoned him a bare fifteen minutes before they were due to arrive to warn him that several VIPs, including a high-ranking Soviet officer, were about to visit his guard post. The kitchen was the only room that had been furnished and he was willing to bet that up till fifteen minutes ago, it had been a bit of a pigsty. Now everything had been squared off; the table wiped down, the cooking utensils cleaned and put away, the sleeping bags neatly folded and laid out for inspection on the double tier bunks. Only this wasn't the usual snap inspection as the guard commander was beginning to discover from Leber.

"You mean you actually want the British to attack this post, Herr Direktor?" he said incredulously.

"Yes, for reasons which do not concern you." Leber smiled fleetingly, then added, "They will of course be walking into a trap. The night guard which should have reported to you at 1830 are presently lying up in the vicinity of watchtower 84 immediately to the north of here. At 1915 hours, they will arrange a diversion which will lead the British to believe that one of our patrols has intercepted a defector. You and the other two members of the guard will then leave this post and pretend to go to their assistance. Is that clear?"

"Perfectly, Herr Direktor."

The guard commander understood what was required of him all right but his obvious lack of enthusiasm made it very evident that he wasn't too happy with the orders he'd been given. He looked even more disquieted when Leber told him the barrier across the road was to be raised at 1925 hours.

"Herr Dollmann will come forward and engage the sentry in conversation; then for the benefit of the English who will be watching us, he will be seen to club him unconscious and raise the barrier." Leber smiled again. "There's no need to look so worried," he said. "By the time this happens, the night guard will have made their way forward into the no-go area via a lane in the minefield and will be in a position to cover the roadblock."

And that was the whole trouble, Dollmann thought bitterly. Dealing with the sentry wouldn't be a problem; the dummkopf would obligingly look the other way believing no one was actually going to chop him down. The ambush party in the no-go area wouldn't be alarmed when they saw the sentry collapse at his feet because it was part of the script, but they would open fire the moment they realised he was about to cross over into the Federal Republic. If he was going to arrive in one piece on the other side, he would have to walk back to the guard post and use the goddamn Volga saloon.

Radford concentrated on the small fold in the ground which Drew was making for. The blond man couldn't be all that far from it now; he had passed through their position some ten minutes ago and had been moving swiftly.

"He's good," Radford murmured, "bloody good. I lost him before he'd gone a hundred yards."

"Me too," Krysia whispered.

Away to their left, a flare soared up into the night sky, its brilliant white light suddenly illuminating the immediate area below. A split second later, a Kalashnikov started chattering.

Radford picked up the Clansman radio, called Whattmore and told him to bring the car forward and halt on the road in line with his position.

"No lights," he said emphatically. "I don't even want to see a glimmer from the instrument panel. We've got a real firework display going on up here."

Two more flares soared into the air and there was another short burst from the Kalashnikov. Moments later, the guard tumbled out of the farmhouse and ran towards the observation tower on the north flank.

"What do you make of that?" Krysia asked.

"I'm not sure. If it's a deception plan, some influential character has gone to a lot of trouble to lend Dollmann a helping hand."

Through the starlight scope, Radford saw a slight figure leave the farmhouse and walk down the road towards the barrier. Although the face was just a blur, there was no mistaking the East German Intelligence officer. While still some distance from the sentry, he started waving his arms in the direction of the dying flares as though demanding to know what the hell was going on. The Kalashnikov ceased firing as the last flare went out, then the momentary silence was disturbed by a muffled crump.

"My God," Krysia murmured, "some poor devil must have stepped on a mine."

The sentry appeared to think so too and instinctively turned his back on Dollmann to gaze in the direction of the northernmost observation tower. As he did so, he toppled forward, cannoned into the barrier and went down hard, the victim of a ferocious chopping blow across his neck.

"Shit," Radford said. "I guess this is when I earn my pay."

Rolling away from the telescope, he scrambled to his feet and ran towards the road and the waiting car. Scarcely breaking step, he snatched the door open and got in beside Whattmore.

"Move it," he shouted. "Move it."

Whattmore didn't need any urging. The engine had been quietly ticking over the whole time he'd been waiting and shifting into first, he released the handbrake, let the clutch out and put his foot hard down on the accelerator. Changing up through the gear box, he was in top before they'd covered a hundred yards. The barrier was in the vertical position and everything was looking good: too good. "Come into my parlour said the spider to the fly." Radford found himself repeating the doggerel learned in childhood.

Dollmann started back towards the farmhouse. The Volga saloon was a hundred and fifty yards from the barrier, a distance which someone who was only moderately fit could cover in under twenty seconds, except that he couldn't afford to make a run for it when Leber and the other two were probably watching him. But if they were a latent threat, at least he had nothing to fear from the sentry behind him. One single blow expertly delivered; that was all it had taken to break his neck.

Dollmann walked on, the ignition key in his left hand ready to crank the engine. He was less than twenty feet from the car when he heard the sound of a pistol shot inside the farmhouse; then Kalin and Yagoda came running.

At the very last minute, Whattmore saw the sentry lying in the road and instinctively stood on the brakes. He knew, without Radford telling him, that the man was dead, but at first he couldn't bring himself to run over the corpse and the delay proved fatal. Some kind of altercation was going on up ahead and as he weaved between the concrete roadblocks, he saw Dollmann jump into the air and go over backwards. In the same instant, the guard commander and two men appeared round the left side of the farmhouse.

The NCO immediately halted, brought the Kalashnikov up into his shoulder and loosed off a couple of rounds while the two Vopos under his command were still adopting a kneeling position. Aiming too low at first, all three rapidly corrected the error and began to hit the vehicle. Wounded in the left hip, elbow and shoulder, Whattmore lost control of the Wartburg, swerved off the road and ploughed into the minefield. A voice from a long way off told him to keep his foot on the accelerator but he was incapable of complying with the instruction.

Radford grabbed hold of the steering wheel, yanked it hard over to the left in order to bring them back on to the road and, at the same time, pulled the choke out to keep the engine running. For a brief moment it looked as though they really did stand a ninety per cent chance of coming through the minefield unscathed; then, just as the front wheels mounted the road, there was a loud crump and the whole of the rear axle was displaced. The blast effect was sufficient to lift the car and slew it round into the path of the oncoming Volga saloon.

Drew watched the two vehicles collide, saw Radford

emerge from the wreckage and took aim. Apart from the three guards near the farmhouse, the Vopos had managed to infiltrate several marksmen into the no-go lane by the fence where they were ideally placed to cover the roadblock. It was, Drew thought, essential to deal with them first before engaging the more attractive target. Taking up the slack on the trigger, he held his breath and squeezed off a shot, then swinging right, he took out the guard commander and forced the other two men to retreat behind the farmhouse. Harper had made it very clear that in the event of a firefight, every effort should be made to avoid a bloodbath and he did just that.

Radford kept the Makarov automatic trained on the two Russians, then leaning sideways, he groped for the Stechkin machine pistol with his left hand. Before Whattmore had swerved off the road, he'd seen Kalin swoop on something which Dollmann had evidently dropped. Thereafter, he'd no idea what had happened until he'd found himself on a collision course with the Volga saloon. Clearly, Dollmann had not been the only one who'd intended to defect, but now it was beginning to look as though Kalin was having second thoughts. He could understand that; they were out in the open halfway between the farmhouse and the roadblock and life was about to become distinctly unhealthy. The guards who had been shooting at them from the left side of the building had been forced to withdraw, but there was a back door and once they were on the inside, they'd be in an even better position to bring fire to bear. There was an even more compelling reason for Kalin to change sides yet again; before very long reinforcements were bound to arrive from both observation towers.

The Stechkin was wedged between the front seats and just out of reach. It was also underneath Whattmore who had toppled over and was lying on his right side, his head pointing towards the nearside door. To get at the machine pistol, Radford knew that he would have to take his eyes off Kalin and duck under the sill, a move that was fraught

276

with danger. He braced himself like a sprinter waiting for the starting pistol, then signalled his intention with a slight bobbing motion. Seizing what he mistakenly thought was a golden opportunity, Kalin made his move and paid for it. As he attempted to squeeze the trigger of his automatic, Radford shot him in the chest a millisecond before Yagoda completed the execution by putting a bullet into the Major's right ear which blew his skull apart. Then smiling nervously, Yagoda dropped his pistol and rapidly clasped both hands together and put them on top of his head. Still pointing the automatic in the General's direction, Radford ducked under the sill and grabbed the Stechkin.

Krysia ran as she had never run before, legs pumping, arms thrashing as she drove herself to reach the spare Wartburg before it was too late. Reaching the crest, she plunged down the reverse slope, lengthening her stride with every step. A signaller called to her from the radio relay truck to ask what was happening; ignoring him, she wrenched open the car door and scrambled into the driver's seat.

The key was in the ignition and the engine caught first time. Shifting into first gear, she put her foot down and took off like a bullet from a rifle. Once on the road, she turned right and headed down into the valley, the three cylinder two stroke engine screeching like a chisel being sharpened on a revolving grindstone. Approaching the barrier at speed, Krysia dipped the clutch, applied the handbrake and executed a hundred and eighty degree skid turn that left pieces of burning rubber on the tarmac. Before the vehicle stopped moving forward, she rammed the gear shift into reverse, twisted round to look over her shoulder and put her foot down on the accelerator. At a speed close on forty miles an hour, Krysia shot through the barrier, weaved past the concrete road blocks and backed up towards the farmhouse.

It was the finest and most inspired piece of driving Radford had ever seen. Taking what cover he could behind the wrecked Wartburg, he ripped off two quick bursts at the Vopos firing at them from the upper windows of the farmhouse and signalled Yagoda to make a run for it. Moving sideways like a crab, the KGB General scuttled towards the car Krysia was driving and scrambled in beside her.

Radford shoved the Makarov automatic into his shoulder holster, transferred the Stechkin to his right hand and reaching into the car, grabbed Whattmore's jacket by the collar. There was no gentle way of doing it; despite accurate suppressive fire from Drew, the Vopos from the observation towers were closing in on them and speed was vital. Ignoring his screams, Radford hauled Whattmore out of the vehicle and dragged him along the ground to the other Wartburg. The car was only a few yards away but it seemed to take for ever and he ran out of ammunition just as he reached it. Tossing the empty machine pistol into the back, he grabbed Whattmore by the seat of his pants and still retaining a firm grip on his collar, heaved him on to the seat like a sack of potatoes. Diving in after him, Radford just had time to close the door before Krysia moved off. Between the start point and the barrier, the Wartburg collected several bullet holes in the rear mud-wing near the petrol tank. Then the Vopos ceased firing and it slowly dawned on them that they were safe.

At exactly 1942 hours, the Foreman of Signals in charge of the radio relay truck spoke to Harper on the secure speech facility to report that the merchandise he'd been expecting had arrived intact. The whole operation had lasted precisely twelve minutes; it took just over twice as long as that to get a medevac helicopter on the scene to pick up Whattmore.

23

For the tourist, Trafalgar Square was the National Gallery, St Martin-in-the-Fields and Nelson's Column; it most certainly was not Carfax House. A completely anonymous building on the south side resembling a book with its spine pointing towards the Square, it didn't rate a mention in any of the guide books, and was even beyond the ken of the proverbial cab driver who was supposed to know London like the back of his hand. It was the first time Krysia had been inside the place and she couldn't understand why the uniformed commissionaire in the lobby had acted as though she'd been granted a rare privilege. The sixth floor was nothing to write home about and that especially applied to the end turret room which belonged to Harper.

Quaint was a word that readily sprang to mind except that there was nothing quaintly charming or olde worlde about a porthole window that was regarded as a public convenience by just about every pigeon in the neighbourhood. The furniture was positively Dickensian and clashed horribly with the fitted carpet, as did the aerial photograph which hung between two military prints depicting The Charge of the Light Brigade at Balaclava and the Imperial Guard recoiling before the British Squares at Waterloo.

"So that's the Kirova Depression," she said, gazing at the aerial photograph that Drew had sarcastically labelled 'Picture of the Year'.

Harper nodded. "Not very impressive, is it?" he added. "How about Major General V. P. Yagoda?"

"Oh, he's very impressive. By the time we've finished debriefing him, I fancy we won't be getting quite so much sanctimonious claptrap from young Mr Gorbachev, which will come as a blessed relief for the Foreign Office."

"Is that what Dennis Whattmore lost an arm for? So that the Foreign Office can rack up a few debating points?"

"Of course it wasn't," Harper said, quite unruffled. "As a result of everything that happened at Eisenach, we think Gorbachev may well get down to some serious negotiations on arms reductions. We've also acquired a great deal of hard information on many of the leading lights in the First Chief Directorate and the Politburo."

Krysia waited expectantly, hoping Harper would quote a few examples, but it rapidly became evident that he had no intention of taking her into his confidence. He had reverted to the old 'need to know' principle and she was now an outsider.

"Am I allowed to know what happened to Leber?" she asked.

"Why not? We've got nothing to hide. Kalin shot him, or at least according to Yagoda he did. Leber was the odd man out, the only one of the quartet who had no intention of defecting. But he was a former Gestapo officer with a long list of war crimes in France and Poland who owed his freedom to the protection afforded him by successive Chairmen of the KGB, from Beria to the present incumbent. Yagoda believed that no matter how co-operative he might seem, he would never forget where his loyalty lay. That's why they decided to kill him when the opportunity arose. They weren't quite so sure about Dollmann; he gave every indication of wanting to defect but equally, there were grounds for thinking he could be an 'agent provocateur'. In the end, Kalin decided they couldn't afford to take any chances with him either."

"Real nice people," Krysia said dryly.

"They were becoming deeply suspicious and paranoiac, like the Mafia, only twice as dangerous." Harper opened a thin folder which lay on his desk and took out a TWA airline ticket. "Compliments of the Department," he said, passing it to her.

Depart Heathrow 1225 hours, Thursday 28 March, arrive Kennedy 1630, then American Airlines to Chicago: Krysia scanned the various columns, then looked up. "First Class?" she queried.

"A small token of our appreciation."

"It's a return ticket."

"We're hoping you'll come back," Harper said.

"I already have a job, or at least I did when I left Paris."

"You still do. As a matter of fact, the Foreign Office wrote a glowing commendation to your State Department which should stand you in good stead." Harper moved a letter opener from one side of the blotting pad to the other. "However, I must confess I hoped Radford would persuade you to come and work for us."

"Well, you know Mike," she said. "He doesn't believe in pressurising people; he just gives you the facts and leaves you to make up your own mind."

"I'm sure you'd find the work very interesting, and rewarding too. And it isn't as though the Paine investigation has been completed yet."

"I'm a law enforcement officer, Mr Harper, not an Intelligence agent," Krysia told him.

"Dollmann was an executioner," Harper said, brushing her point aside. "He was successful because he was told exactly where and when to strike by the surveillance team who'd kept the Paines under observation. I'd like to see you run those people to ground."

"I'm an American," Krysia reminded him. "Maybe the assignment you've just mentioned wouldn't cause any problems but one day there could be a clash of national interests. Then what happens?"

"We'd never put you in that position, Krysia."

Radford had said the same thing to her when they'd discussed Harper's offer. Where national interests were involved, the relevant papers would be stamped 'UK EYES ONLY' and she would never get to see them. He had also told her that British officers on secondment to the US Department of Defence were subject to a similar exclusion order, but that wasn't quite the same thing. They were simply filling an exchange appointment for two years while she was being offered a full career. She had no idea how many 'UK EYES ONLY' papers were in circulation but no matter how Harper might dress it up, she would always be an outsider and that in turn was bound to govern just how far she could go.

"You don't have to make up your mind here and now," Harper said.

"I'm not so sure . . ."

"We want you to think about it; that's why we gave you a return ticket."

"Well, okay, I'll think about it." Still smiling, Krysia stood up. "And now I really must be going," she said, "otherwise one of your traffic wardens will be giving Mike a parking ticket."

"We certainly can't have that." Harper escorted her to the lift at the far end of the corridor and pressed the call button. "I'm an incurable optimist," he told her as they shook hands. "That's why I'm not going to say goodbye."

Radford leaned across the seat and opened the nearside door for Krysia as she emerged from the building. One look at the composed expression on her face told him all he needed to know and the sinking feeling which had begun the moment he'd woken up now became an even deeper depression. In the corridors of Whitehall, it was said of Harper that he could sell a deep freeze to an Eskimo but in Krysia he had clearly met someone who was sales resistant.

"Hi," she said, getting in beside him. "I didn't keep you waiting long, did I, Mike?"

"No time at all." He smiled mechanically. "Said all your goodbyes?"

"Harper refused to, but then to quote his own words,

he's an incurable optimist. In return, I promised to think about his offer."

Probably as far as the outskirts of London, Radford thought as he started the engine. Pulling away from the kerb, he turned left, went through Admiralty Arch and carried on down The Mall towards Buckingham Palace.

"How long will it take you to drive out to Heathrow?" Krysia asked.

"Forty, perhaps fifty minutes depending on the traffic."

They were making small talk like casual acquaintances without a lot in common. The warmth and intimacy they'd shared in Berlin had cooled on their return to London as though Krysia had already made up her mind that she was unlikely to see him again and it was best not to get too emotionally involved.

"Do you have to go back?" he asked.

"My job, my home and my family are all in Chicago."

And no one had given her a good enough reason to stay on. "I'm going to miss you," he said in what had to be the understatement of the year. In truth, there was going to be a big hole in his life after Krysia had gone.

"I'm not likely to forget you in a hurry either, Mike."

Her voice was very low and he could barely hear her above the noise of the traffic. It was also hard to tell what she was thinking when all he could see was her face in profile as she sat there gazing steadfastly to her front.

"We're in Constitution Hill now," he said, attempting to forestall an awkward silence. "Hyde Park Corner is up ahead; we turn left there into Knightsbridge and follow the A4 trunk route out to Heathrow."

"Are we going past Harrods?"

"Yes."

"That'll be nice," she said vaguely.

They'd gone there yesterday and Krysia had bought presents for her father and brother-in-law. There had been other souvenirs; a vanity case for her sister from John Lewis's and at Hamleys in Regent Street she'd bought her nephew a radio-controlled model plane.

"I guess Customs are going to welcome me with open arms," Krysia said.

And maybe someone else would too unless he did something about it. Ignoring the left turn into Knightsbridge, Radford went on round Hyde Park.

"I don't want you to catch that TWA flight," he said bluntly. "I want you to stay here with me. So okay, we only met a fortnight ago and a lot of people would say we hardly know one another, but I can't imagine what life is going to be like without you and I'm not anxious to find out."

No one could predict what the future might hold for them but he would do everything he could to make her happy. There was a lot more in the same vein, arguments which, if not always wholly logical, were not found wanting for lack of conviction. When he finally ran out of inspiration, there was a momentary silence, then Krysia opened the glove compartment and took out a copy of Nicholson's *London Street Finder*.

"You're about to go past Park Lane for the third time," she informed him.

"So what?"

"Well, I think you should take the next left into Piccadilly." The impish smile he'd come to know so well appeared on her mouth. "It's the quickest way back to Tetbury Gardens."

NICHOLAS GUILD

THE LINZ TATTOO

He was big. A Nordic giant of a man with broad shoulders and golden hair. Like a Viking god – the stuff of a thousand heroic sagas.

And he played the cello beautifully. Sensitivity, control and that something else that is the mark of genius – he had it all. Sent off to New York and the Juillard School, his future as a virtuoso performer had been assured. Except that war and tragedy had changed all that. Now he had a new and overwhelming ambition in life.

And he killed people. The Nazis had slaughtered his parents, left his native village a burning ruin: that was a score he had to settle. And in particular, Colonel Hagemann of the SS had to be tracked down across the wasteland of post-war Europe and destroyed.

He was big, coldly obsessive – and blood didn't bother him a bit.

A Royal Mail service in association with the Book Marketing Council & The Booksellers Association.

Post-A-Book is a Post Office trademark

JAMES PATTERSON

BLACK MARKET

The threat was absolute:

At 5.05 Wall Street will be destroyed.

No demands, no ransom, no negotiations. A multiple firebombing would wipe out the financial heart of America. Stop the world's financial system dead.

There was just one extra point: a demonstration – just in case the threat wasn't taken seriously.

At 9.20 am Pier 33–34, once the docking point for the great trans-Atlantic liners, was destroyed. A sudden fire storm; flames rising four hundred feet over the Hudson River. Within minutes nothing left but a glowing red hot metal skeleton, cranes toppled, transit sheds gutted . . .

The threat was real. All emergency systems blared into life. The countdown to catastrophe had begun . . .

'Fast and furious'
The Wall Street Journal

NEW ENGLISH LIBRARY

KEN ROYCE

NO WAY BACK

The Intelligence agencies of a dozen countries knew
him as The Arab. Sometimes it seemed that he had
spent a lifetime killing for the cause, under orders. But
this time it was personal.

As soon as he saw that the girl was dead he knew with a
cold certainty that she would be avenged. Not just the
man who had given the orders and the man behind
him . . . Stage by stage he would move up the chain of
command and at every stage he would kill.

Detective Superintendent George Bulman was the first
to realise what was happening – and to know that he
was caught in a conflict of loyalties.

CORONET BOOKS